MERCY

LINDSAY MARIE
MILLER

DON'T MISS THESE OTHER BOOKS BY
LINDSAY MARIE MILLER

The Girl in the Woods

Emerald Green

Honey Gold

Me & Mr. Jones

Mr. Jones & Me

Jungle Eyes

Island Smile

Coastal Spirit

Single

An Arrangement

An Accident

AND LOOK FOR HER NEW NOVEL

Available in January 2018

Preface

Life never turns out the way you think it will, the way you expect it to, the way you wish it would. I look back on days in my youth often, when I should have been happy, should have felt less entitled, should have been anything but a spoiled little brat. What happened to me is something that I never asked for, never knew I needed, never knew I would want back some day.

I made so many mistakes that night. Mistakes that could have been easily avoided. Decisions that were obviously not the best ones, not the right ones at least. But none of that matters now.

Death has forced me to appreciate life. His life. My life.

It all comes back to me in flashes. The way he looked that night. The way he made me feel.

The fear. The desire. The lust. Everything.

I was lonely. I was angry. I was a woman acting like a child.

But it happened. I was there. He was real.

And I remember it all.

Chapter 1

C old wind rushed in like a surging force to remind us that winter was here to stay. As Bridgette opened the door to the taxi cab and pulled me out behind her, I yanked at the hem of my skin tight dress. The red satin fabric clung to my body like a second skin, fitting much tighter than a glove.

"Oh, yes!" Bridgette lifted her head and eyed the neon sign of the club overhead. Then she clamped her hand around my wrist and tugged me alongside her, finagling our way inside.

"Bridgette! Wait!" I staggered back in a pair of six inch stilettos, shoes she swore would help me embrace my independence as a woman in a male-dominated society.

"Oh, come on!" She dug her nails into my skin until I made it through the corridor past the entrance and could actually glimpse what was inside. "Cool," she muttered under her breath.

My eyes raced about the night club, an eclectic fusion of dance music and flickering lights glittering through the smoke. I had that eerie feeling in the pit of my stomach that I was going to get spotted, that someone would recognize me, and then we would both get caught. At the time, her empowering words about the freedom of college, distance from my parents, and having my own space to do whatever I wanted had felt so refreshing to hear. I deserved a night out without rules or regulations.

But now my goody two shoes persona had resurfaced, and I just wanted to go home.

"Bridgette," I whined, turning my head to the side when she flipped her long red hair. "I don't know about this."

"Come on, Anna." She spun me around to face her and pointed at the club scene surrounding us. "Look at this. Gorgeous men. Music. Dancing. Alcohol. Fun. Isn't that what you wanted?"

"I don't know, I—"

"I've been babysitting you all semester," she reminded me. "It's time to have some fun for a change."

"But Bridgette." I struggled to keep up as she headed for the bar. "I'm not twenty-one yet. I can't drink."

"Well, you'll be twenty soon, and that's close enough." She spotted a pair of empty stools and took a seat, inching the skirt of her super short black dress just past her rear. "Come on, Anna. Live a little."

When she leaned over the counter to order a drink, I plopped down on the stool beside her. Every nerve ending was begging me to run for the door, because I had never felt so vulnerable. Even though I had longed for freedom, it hardly felt comforting to be willingly unprotected.

"But what if someone recognizes me?" I grabbed Bridgette's arm and searched her golden brown eyes. "What if someone figures out that I'm..." Dropping off, I looked around and sighed.

"The President's daughter?" she finished, not talking as softly as I would have liked.

"Not so loud," I hissed, narrowing my eyes at her.

"Anna, that was almost ten years ago. You're an *Ex*-President's daughter. Remember?"

"I know, but Daddy said—"

"Forget what your Daddy said. We can finally have some fun without those secret service men around."

Rolling her eyes, she leaned forward to bear enough cleavage to make most men stop and stare. With a sly smile, she tapped the bartender's shoulder and waited for him to reveal himself. When he turned around, my eyes dropped to the tattoos around his forearms. Images of snakes and barbed wire permanently inked into his skin. I never understood the guys Bridgette went for, but we had never shared the same taste in men. She was actually a few months younger than me, but acted like she had landed on this earth at the age of thirty-five. When it came to the opposite sex, I had lived the sheltered life of a politician's daughter and only child for so long that I hardly had the opportunity to notice. Bridgette, on the other hand, was always on the look-out, searching with her eyes wide open.

"Listen Bridgette, I finally got him down to one guard. I don't think tonight is the best idea."

The bartender set two tequila shots on the frosted glass counter. "Ladies, on the house."

"Thank you," Bridgette swooned, batting her black lashes at the tall, muscular blond. He must have been ten years older than us, with enough veins in his neck to make me question steroid use.

"I want to go back to the dorm," I begged. "Please."

Cocking her head to the side, Bridgette raised a violet fingernail at me and glared. "You were the one who needed a night out. You were the one who said in high school you never got to have any fun. You were the one who said you've been trapped in a box your whole life. Isn't that why you chose Princeton in the first place? To get away from Mommy and Daddy in DC?"

"All right," I snapped back at her. "I'm sorry. I know what I said, but I've changed my mind."

"No." She downed the tequila shot and then slammed it against the counter. "One night, Anna. That's all I ask. And then we'll go back to boring club meetings at the library and studying all the time. But you give me one night to have a good time. After a year and a half of being your roommate, it's the least you could do."

"Fine," I consented. After all, Bridgette rarely dragged me off to her sorority parties. And I had been the one to initiate all this. Only now, I couldn't understand why. I just wanted to get back to our dorm room and go to bed. I didn't feel safe here, but maybe eight years of police escorts will do that to you.

"YAY!" She clapped her hands together and pulled me in for a hug. "There's the girl I know."

"Just tonight," I reinforced. "After that, you can leave all the barhopping to yourself."

"Bartender?" Bridgette pursed her pouty pink lips at him. "Another?"

With a wicked grin, he filled another shot glass with tequila and slid it across the counter. Glancing straight ahead, I peered into the reflective panel behind the bar, shelves of liquor bottles over a mirror. My long golden hair glowed beneath the strobe lights, as Bridgette had taken the time to style the smooth strands into soft, natural-looking waves. I was wearing a dark shade of red lipstick and enough eyeshadow to make my green eyes look gray. I wasn't entirely sure what had possessed me to want to look like this. At nineteen, perhaps I was a late bloomer where teenage rebellion was concerned.

Before I knew it, nearly an hour had passed of

Bridgette making eyes at the bartender. In time, he took notice and began touching her in quick, subtle gestures. Flicking his wrist to stroke her arm. Hunching over the counter to swipe away a red lock of hair. Brushing a stray eyelash away with his thumb.

When I began to grow uneasy, my eyes shifted around the club. For some reason, I had been lucky enough to go unnoticed so far. With so many guys drunk on the dancefloor, I had escaped the threat of loose, sloppy playboys with their grabby hands. The room was dimly lit, and with the amount of makeup plastered on my face, you could make the argument that I might have been hard to recognize.

But then I saw him. One man standing in a sea of jostling bodies. He wore a full suit with everything but the tie, and his eyes were unsteadily fixed on me. Swallowing, I squirmed in my seat and reached out for Bridgette. But when I turned around, she was gone. "Bridgette?"

My heart felt lodged in the middle of my throat, incapable of a steady beat. When I noticed that the bartender was gone as well, my vision flicked to the sight of them both heading to the dancefloor arm in arm. Sweat broke out along the surface of my skin, and I felt painfully thirsty all of a sudden.

"Hello."

Freezing in place, I dared to turn my head and glance up at the man who had been watching me.

"Is this seat taken?" He motioned to the empty bar stool, while I glanced over at Bridgette, her body clinging to the bartender like she was fire and he was air.

"No," I uttered, clenching my jaw as he sat down. His arm brushed against my elbow in the process.

Deciding that now was the time for some liquid courage, I brought the tequila to my lips and downed the shot in one swallow. Then I pushed the empty drink aside and wiped the back of my hand against my mouth. The taste was bitter and foul, not at all what I had expected.

When I lifted my gaze back up at him, his soft blue eyes glazed over my figure like a feather. Warm blush rose to my cheeks, but I hoped that he couldn't see. In that moment, I studied his thin upper lip and the full bottom one beneath it. The early stages of a beard were taking shape on his face, dark hairs that looked more like scruff than whiskers. For a second, I wondered what it would feel like to run my fingers through them.

"Would you like to dance?" he asked, gazing deeply into my eyes. It was almost hypnotic.

"Okay," I agreed. Something inside left me feeling like I had no choice.

With his eyes on me, the tall stranger took my hand and led me onto the dancefloor. To be honest, I could hardly walk in these shoes, and the skin tight dress only worsened the situation. But he wrapped his arm around my body and pulled me into him the moment we emerged into the crowd.

Unaccustomed to dancing with the opposite sex, I hesitated when his hand flattened against the base of my spine. My breath hitched at the back of my throat as I gazed into his glittering blue eyes. They looked honest.

Regarding me with a vacant stare, he grabbed my wrist and set my hand on his shoulder. I leaned away from him in an attempt to create some space between us. But that only made him shorten the distance. Before I knew it, his breath was rushing against my face, and there was nowhere to run.

I let him twirl me around in a circle at the end of the third song, laughing and out of breath from the sudden burst of energy. Happiness blossomed around my heart like a flower when I caught him smiling. Perhaps Bridgette was right. Sometimes you have to step outside your comfort zone. Sometimes you have to do what you are afraid of, because then it won't scare you anymore.

Curling my arm around the nape of his neck, I felt my body relaxing from the first shot of tequila. His hands raced across my back as I inhaled the scent of his cologne. I had been deprived of male interaction for far too long, and I resented my parents for never letting me experience this in my prime.

As I leaned my back against him, his arms encircled me in a warm embrace. I felt light, giddy, euphoric. And when the stubble of his beard brushed against my neck, I grew weak in the knees.

But something dreadful caught the corner of my eye. Across the dancefloor, I saw the bartender squeezing Bridgette's arm as she bucked against him. Panic flitted across my features when he dug in and began dragging her away, until she disappeared into a sea of people and flashing lights.

I looked back at the beautiful stranger behind me and cried, "That's my friend!"

"Let's go," he demanded, folding his fingers through mine.

My heart beat faster, but I reveled in his touch. With his help, it was no trouble weaving through the obnoxious swarm of club goers. By the time we reached the hallway leading to the restrooms, I squeezed his hand tighter, my nails sinking into his flesh. When we rounded the corner, I broke away from him and burst into the women's bathroom.

Bridgette was on the floor with her hands tied behind her back and a gag in her mouth. I gasped and backed into the protection of the beautiful stranger behind me when the bartender took the gun he had aimed at her and turned it on me. My hands flew in the air as the world went topsy-turvy around me.

"What are you doing?" the man who had danced with me asked. Perhaps I should have known his name by now. "We've already got this one."

Alarm rippled through my veins as Bridgette let out a muffled scream. The beautiful stranger placed his hand over my mouth as the blond bartender locked the entrance to the bathroom. I bucked and fought against the two of them, but they tossed me on the ground alongside Bridgette. Before I could think of a way to defend myself, my wrists were bound and they slipped a black bag over my head.

Chapter 2

I woke to the sound of Bridgette's piercing scream through the wall. My arms were tied to the back of my chair, and the black bag remained over my head. As I took each breath, the noise rattled in my eardrums as if I were firing a gun inside of a conch shell and then holding it to my ear.

Fear had no feeling but the bitter taste it left in my mouth. I was shaking and shivering from the cold, though the temperature was blazing hot. Maybe it was pure shock that had my teeth clacking together.

When the noise stopped, I worried that Bridgette might be dead, that maybe they got sick of hearing her wailing cries and killed her. But then I heard the sound of someone opening a door, and a pair of boots marched across the short distance to me. Bristling with fear, I lacked the time or sight to brace myself before he swung his fist against the side of my face. Even with the bag over my head, it hurt like hell.

Not a word came from his mouth as he loaded the gun. I could hear the distinct clink of each bullet sliding into the next barrel. Desperate to escape, I toyed with the rope around my wrists, but it was no use.

"You know who I am," I boldly declared. Despite my terror, I wanted him to speak. I couldn't be sure which man was in the room: the blond bartender or the beautiful stranger. If I was going to die, I wanted to at least know who killed me.

"Yes," a surly voice hissed. The distinction was unmistakably clear. It was the bartender.

"You're going to kill me," I assumed.

"Why yes, sweet thing." He placed his hand on my thigh and then touched the cool metal of the gun to it. "You and your red-headed friend should have been more careful."

My chest rose and fell as I gasped for air, sudden tears streaming down my face.

"Wait," a newly familiar voice called. I listened as the beautiful stranger entered the room, taking more careful steps than his predecessor. "Let me do it. I'm the one who found her."

A loud ringing pierced my ears, though it was caused by nothing more than my own fear.

The bartender scowled and waited a beat. "Fine."

I felt him lingering nearby, as he squeezed my thigh for the last time. Disliking his touch, I slapped my knees together and tried my best to keep still. When he let go, my entire body relaxed.

"You can have her," he growled, tossing the gun at the beautiful stranger.

I heard the sound of it gliding through the air until he caught it. More pounding footsteps and then the door slammed shut. Uneasiness settled at the pit of my stomach. I was alone with my captor.

Even now, I can remember how strange it felt to swallow. Like the act of resting my tongue against the roof of my mouth might create too much noise. Though what was I afraid of him hearing? He already knew where I was.

I felt the warmth of his body enveloping me as he stalked closer. Slick sweat ran like condensation between my palms, further heightening my degree of panic. Ever since the bartender touched my legs, I had been unable to stop them from shaking.

Without a moment to waste, he ripped the black bag off the top of my head, and I was blinded by an overwhelming florescent light. Dust rained down from the ceiling as I coughed and gagged, rapidly blinking my eyes to grab ahold of my surroundings. Try as I might, jerking and tugging at the rope around my wrists only seemed to make the binding texture sting worse.

When he took a step closer, my eyes connected with his, and I knew my life was over.

Looking back now, I should have begged and pleaded with him to stop. At nineteen, there was so much of my life that I had yet to live. I didn't want to leave now. I wanted to stay. I wanted to survive.

But he squared his jaw and raised the pistol at me. Despite the weapon aimed at my face, I could not tear my eyes away from him. His glittering blue eyes were so much like an angel's that it made me cry.

As tears streamed down my cheeks like forking channels, he closed his mouth and clenched his teeth. Out of the corner of my eye, I watched his thumb cock the pistol. Then there was nothing left to do but wait.

Perhaps I should have asked why. After all, didn't I deserve to know the reason for my murder? But his lingering gaze had me transfixed, mesmerized. Despite my fear, I didn't want to look away.

The beautiful stranger inhaled and moistened his lips, then took another step closer.

Accepting my fate, I shut my eyes and let every teardrop skirt down my skin without delay. But then several seconds passed and then a few more, then a hundred more. All I kept thinking was, *Why hasn't he killed me yet?*

Confused by his lagging pace, I fluttered my lashes and gazed up at him. The moment he looked into my eyes, the man lowered his gun and sighed. His chest rose and fell with every breath.

"Scream," he hissed, barking the word at me like an order.

I gasped for air and swallowed. "What?"

"I said scream!" He pointed the gun at my face, but his hand was shaking.

So I did what he said and let out a rip roaring wail of terror. When my ears started to ring, he fired the gun at a burlap sack and white powder spewed across the floor. For the first time, I spotted the bags at the back of the room and wondered at their significance. Weapons? Money? Drugs?

I stopped screaming the moment he fired that gun, and the beautiful stranger came towards me. Too terrified to move, I kept still as he removed a knife and cut the ropes binding my wrists and feet.

"What are you—"

"Shut up," he commanded, lifting a trap door in the ground.

Fear had yet to stop pulsing through my veins when he grabbed my arm and jerked me out of the chair. The bartender burst into the room with a loaded gun aimed directly at my head. Quick and fearless, the beautiful stranger pushed me to the floor and shot the blond three times in the chest.

As he collapsed to the ground, the beautiful stranger grasped my shoulder and shoved me through the trapdoor. I heard the sound of boots stomping as he climbed in after me and closed the secret passage overhead. Not sure who or what to fear, I drew in a staggering breath when footsteps pounded up above. The beautiful stranger pulled my back into his chest and clamped his hand over my mouth.

"Don't say a word," he whispered in my ear, the stubble of his beard sending shivers down my neck.

Too terrified to speak, I offered a few silent nods and stayed still. As voices shouted back and forth overhead, the beautiful stranger circled his arms around my waist. Quiet and submissive, I sat between his legs as he reloaded the gun right in front of me, his head leaning over my shoulder to see.

When the voices grew louder, I lifted my eyes to the ceiling to listen. But then a gunshot pierced through the floor overhead and the beautiful stranger grabbed my hips and forced me onto all fours. "Go!"

My elbows dug into the metal beneath me as I crawled through the tunnel. He pushed against the back of my thigh when gunfire erupted behind us, compelling me to pick up the pace, despite every scrape and bruise along the way. I reached a fork in the tunnel and then another, until the sound of bullets piercing through the surface overhead was no more.

"Move, Anna!" he barked behind me. "Go!"

My heart hammered loudly in my chest as I followed the path before me. Eventually, the tunnel expanded in width and height enough for us to stand up and walk. A pool of water appeared before us in the dark passageway, stretching onward and leading to a soft white light at the end.

The beautiful stranger grabbed my elbow and jerked me to my feet. As he hauled me towards the light, water rose up to our knees, while we waded through the indoor river. Five gunshots sounded one after another and I screamed, turning back to see three men dressed in black running towards us.

But he dug his nails into my forearm and pushed me forward until we reached the end of the tunnel. Up close, the light was nearly blinding as I glanced down at the steep drop below. Water flew down from the tunnel and into a wide river, violently rushing up against the rocks. Surely, the fall alone would kill us.

"You're going to have to jump," he prompted, grasping my chin.

I heard them coming towards us, their boots dipping in and out of the water as they stormed forward.

"What?" I shook with fear at the thought. "No, I can't!"

But the men were drawing near, and we were running out of time.

"Take my hand," he softly crooned. "Come on, Anna. Take it!"

I didn't even know his name, but what choice did I have?

When he lifted his open hand, I took it. And

together, we jumped.

Chapter 3

When my body submerged beneath the river, it felt like ice. Pin pricks over my arms, my legs, my chest. A sharp, stinging sensation that was so cold it nearly burned with heat. Frozen fire if you will.

I held on to his hand as the current tugged us forward, until we were well out of sight. But then I slammed into a boulder, and it snagged the hem of my dress. Panicking, my hand slipped from his grip and I sank beneath the rapids. Despite much kicking and screaming, the fabric would not rip.

My arms flailed about as I clung to the rock. I tried to lift myself out of the water and climb over the other side of it. But it was no use.

In my youth, I had never been able to keep from inhaling through my nose in a swimming pool. I could hold my breath underwater, only where shutting my mouth was concerned. But now, I wished it was a skill that I had mastered or at least learned. How useful such a talent would have been at a time like this.

When I felt the water enter my lungs, I had never experienced anything like it. Soon, I gave in completely and succumbed. The scorching fire was too much, and all I wanted was peace, a world without pain.

The next thing I can remember are two hands pounding against my chest. I lurched forward and coughed the burning liquid from my lungs, pressing my palm into the ground for support.

As my eyes adjusted to the rushing water ahead, I found myself sprawled out on the riverbank in the light of day. It must have been early morning, because the sun had yet to reach that high place in the sky.

I was shivering and shaking, my body bruised and shocked. Someone touched my head and stroked my wet hair as I caught my breath. When enough oxygen had returned, I looked up. And there he was.

The beautiful stranger. Thoroughly soaked from our journey in the river. Dripping from head to toe.

In that moment, I was struck by how attractive he was. Long dark hair hanging past his forehead. The weight of the water had smoothed out his curls. His piercing blue eyes glittered with every bit of darkness, while at the same time exuding light. I lifted my hand to touch the dimple in his chin and then stroked my fingertip along the firm structure of his jawline. His stubble felt prickly and rough.

He touched my hand and uttered, "We must go."

I held on to his arm as he pulled me to my feet. My shoes were missing, and I wondered how long my feet had been bare. But after surviving death, that hardly seemed to matter now.

The beautiful stranger led me into the forest and we spent the day walking through the trees. In the eerie quiet, I was terrified to make a sound, worried that someone was nearby watching, just waiting for the opportune moment to take me. I did not know this man, but I trusted him.

When night came, I sat down and watched him build a fire. For the past eight hours, he had said nothing to me. Should I have asked? Anything? Everything? I kept seeing flashes of us dancing together in the club, a distant memory that never felt real. Had that only been one night ago? Last night?

"Who are you?" I asked once I had gathered up the courage.

The beautiful stranger looked at me, his hands warming over the fire. For dinner, he had caught two squirrels and a rabbit. While a city girl like me should have been repulsed, the meat had never tasted better. I was famished, ravenous, and he knew how to cook game properly. Like it wasn't his first time. Like he had lived off the land and slept in front of a fire many nights before.

After staring silently ahead, he lowered his gaze and pursed his lips at me.

"Well. Who are you?" I repeated, more deliberate this time.

He exhaled aloud and glanced at me, tucking his hands beneath his arms. "I am no one."

Disliking his tone, I sat up and softened my eyes. "Just give me a name. Please."

He leaned back against a piece of firewood and replied, "Julian."

Warmth flooded my veins. I had a name. Even if it wasn't a real one. Even if it wasn't his.

"Julian," I repeated. "What happened last night? Who was that man? Where is Bridgette?"

He dodged the first two questions and lowered his eyes. "Your friend is dead."

My heart sank into my stomach, and my throat felt like a knife had just ripped through it. As if someone had torn the organ out of my breast, and I had swallowed it whole.

Feeling weak, I stood up and ran behind a tree where I could get sick. I fell onto my knees as bile rose up at the back of my throat and vomited onto the forest floor. After wiping my mouth, I pressed my palm to my forehead and attempted to get ahold of myself. *Bridgette.*

She had been my roommate from day one in college and perhaps the only girl I had ever been able to call a true friend. My years at the White House had not been conducive for budding companionships, for fear of danger or threat. But

Bridgette had been fun, and at Princeton she had always had my back.

For what felt like an eternity, I wept alone behind the tree. The only sensation my body recognized was pain, which made me feel even more selfish. Bridgette was dead, and I was complaining about something as insignificant as *pain*? I bet she would take the pain over death any day.

"Anna," Julian said, kneeling down beside me. "You're cold. Come by the fire where it's warm."

When he reached out his hand, I nodded and took it. Julian led me back to the flames, but we kept our distance from each other. Despite the warm heat, I clung to myself and shivered.

"I never told you my name," I noted, catching his eye across the fire.

He pinned his brows together, confused by my obvious statement.

"Do you know who I am?" I pressed, boring my green eyes into his surly gaze.

"Anna James, former first daughter, student of Princeton University. Your father served two terms as Commander-in-Chief for the United States and was nearly impeached after leaking government secrets."

I clenched my jaw at his words. My father had done nothing of the kind.

"You're five eight. You weigh a hundred and eighteen pounds. You'll turn twenty in January."

"How long have you been watching me?" I

should have felt more afraid of him, but I didn't.

"Eight weeks," he muttered dryly.

Cutting to the chase, I put the puzzle pieces together. "You were hired to kill me."

"Yes," he hissed. Julian stared into my eyes, waiting for me to ask why.

"So why didn't you?" I wondered, rubbing my elbows to keep warm.

"What?" He looked over at me, clearly caught off guard.

"Why didn't you kill me?" I held his gaze and glowered, refusing to look away.

Smoldering, he chewed at his lower lip and said, "Because I couldn't."

"What?" I nearly snapped, oddly offended by his words. He was an assassin of all people.

"Because I couldn't, Anna!" he snarled, raising his voice. "I just couldn't," he whispered.

I watched him set his sights on the flames and tried to keep from feeling so cold.

"But why?" I wanted to know, pushing him further.

He rose to his feet and stormed towards me, balling his hand into a fist. Then he lowered his gaze and looked deep into my eyes, his voice soft and morose. "Because I didn't want to."

Taking in shallow breaths, I looked up at him and shivered.

"Are you afraid of me?" he asked.

"No," I boldly replied. "But maybe I should be."

Julian placed his hands on his hips and sat down beside me. Perhaps he wanted me to prove that I truly wasn't afraid of him. His shoulder brushed against mine, and I had never craved body heat so badly.

"Come here." He wrapped his arm around me. "You'll freeze to death if you don't."

Too cold to resist, I put my head on his chest and reveled in his warmth. He placed his dry jacket over my shoulders and held me close, the way a lover would. Tired of fighting sleep, I shut my eyes and imagined myself back in that club with him dancing by my side.

Why couldn't he have been a typical guy? Why couldn't he have taken me home and led me into his bedroom? Why couldn't I have been nothing more to him than a one night stand?

But such fantasies were child's play compared to my situation. I was sleeping in the arms of a trained assassin. The one who had been hired to kill me.

* * *

"Anna," he hissed. "Wake up, Anna."

I stirred awake lying on the ground with his jacket beneath my head. Leaning back on my elbow, I found him standing before me as though he had been there for a very long time, just staring at me.

"How long have you been watching me sleep?" I wondered, threading my fingers through my hair.

"About an hour." He knelt down and grabbed my shoulders, helping me to my feet. "We have to go."

I leaned in to his side and brushed the dirt from my red dress. "Go where?"

Julian put his jacket back on and took my hand. Then he bit his lower lip with a glower.

"What makes you think I would go anywhere with you?" I snapped.

He lifted his lips into a playful smile and came closer. "You don't have a choice."

I withdrew my hand from his grasp and backed away. "What do you mean I don't have a choice?" Distancing myself from him further, I took a shallow breath and swallowed. "I don't even know who you are, other than the fact that you're the man who was hired to kill me. I don't trust you."

"You don't have to." He stalked towards me and grasped my wrist. "You're coming with me."

When he dragged me alongside him, I had to hurry my footsteps to keep up. "Let me go!"

But Julian was too strong, his height and muscular build dominating me with ease.

"Stop!" I bucked and kicked against him, twisting my arm out of his hold. Then I took off running on my bare feet, emboldened by a moment of freedom.

Trees raced by as I sprinted onward, the forest around me a gray-green blur. My thighs began to burn like my lungs had when I was in the river the day before, but that only made me run faster. For a minute there, I truly thought I would be able to get away. But then his breaths sounded sharp and ragged behind me.

I screamed the moment he grabbed my arm, mercilessly tackling me to the ground. When I rolled onto my back, he held my hands over my head and pushed the full weight of his body into me. "Get off me!" I shouted, struggling beneath his strong hard frame. "Let go!" I demanded, gritting my teeth.

Julian lowered his face and silenced my screams with a rough kiss. Despite the shock of pleasure flooding through me, I resisted his attempt at seduction and kneed him in the groin. He groaned in pain and tilted his torso to the side, but his hands remained around my wrists.

A round of gunshots echoed in the distance, as I lay perfectly still and froze at the danger. Julian leaned back and looked over his shoulder, struggling to catch his breath. Then he eyed the forest behind me and turned his frosty blue gaze back on mine.

"You have to come with me," he demanded. "If you don't, they'll find you."

I furrowed my brow and peered up at him. "And why should I trust you?"

"Because you have to," he urged, echoing his earlier commands. "The only way you'll be safe is with me. No one else can protect you, Anna. Not like I can. I know these men. I can keep you safe."

Contemplating the situation, I glanced over his

beautiful face and wondered why he wanted me to trust him so much. Perhaps he knew that I already did.

"Do you want to live?" he breathed, staring down at me. "Or do you want to die?"

One gun shot and then another.

Following my instincts, I took his hand and let him help me up. Julian looked over me with relief and braided his fingers through mine. There was something so warm and human in his touch. I still felt his mouth on my lips and knew that nothing had ever made me feel so alive. I relished the sensation.

"Come on," he hissed, tugging me alongside him.

I hardly had time to think as he set the pace. My heart was throbbing and my veins were singing with adrenaline. But I did feel safe with him.

So I cast my troubles aside and ran away with the beautiful stranger into the forest.

Chapter 4

We must have walked for days, trekking through the wilderness by day, sleeping before a campfire by night. In these silent moments with Julian, I learned of his quiet, reserved nature. Sometimes, we just sat under the stars staring at the moon, warming our hands before the fire.

When three days passed and I had yet to hear gunshots, a mild calm settled my spirits. I tried not to think about Bridgette. I tried not to think about my family. I tried not to think about Princeton. But it was there, lurking in the deepest corners of my mind. It was always there.

One afternoon, the woods broke into a clearing of land, and I could hardly believe it. There was an abandoned house up ahead with peeling paint and rusted doors. We had found shelter at last.

Sighing with relief, I sprinted for the home and left Julian behind. The soles of my feet were dirty and rough from walking around with no shoes on. But I ran as far as my legs would carry me until I reached the front porch steps. There was a flimsy screen door, but when I opened it, the wooden door on the other side was locked. Desperate and struggling, I twisted the handle and banged my fist against the facing, but it was no use.

So I placed my hands on my hips and caught my breath, waiting for Julian to arrive. When he climbed up the steps and regarded me, I felt a delicious shiver travel down my spine. Julian spotted a garden shovel on the porch and bent down to grab it. Leaning against the side of the house, I crossed my arms over my chest and watched him with intrigue as he leapt down from the porch and landed on the ground.

"Julian," I called, but he had already disappeared.

Curious as ever, I jumped off the porch and followed him to the back of the house. He was on his knees digging up a patch of grass in front of one of the large trees. The shovel dug into the earth as he tossed clumps of dirt aside, eventually plunging his long fingers deep enough to retrieve a metal key.

Julian turned back and dangled the key in his hand. Then he threw it at me, and I caught it.

"What is this place?" I rubbed the excess bits of dirt from the key.

Julian filled the hole with dirt and replaced the patch of grass. Then he dropped the shovel and stood up, brushing the earth from his hands. "No one will find you here," he promised.

Our eyes met, and I could have sworn that I saw compassion in his glittering blue irises. He took the key from me and walked away, heading for the front of the house. Perplexed, I looked into the tangled thickets of the forest and felt goosebumps break out across the surface of my skin.

Running after Julian, I caught up to him at the front porch where he opened the door. "Let me go in first," he said, turning back to look at me. "To make sure it's safe."

"All right." I paced in a circle while he went inside.

Patience had never been a strength of mine, so I stood there looking out at the sunlight and waited for him to come back. It seemed like he was taking a long time just to aggravate me. But then he returned and called my name, holding the door open for me to come inside.

Chewing on my lower lip, I inched forward and searched him from head to toe. Then I glanced through the open doorway and took my first steps into the house. There was a long hallway with doors on either side that extended from the foyer, shades of dust and light all around.

"Come on." Julian pulled the screen door shut and then closed the front door behind it. "I'l show you around." He turned the key in the door until it locked, while I wondered at his swiftness.

Was the lock intended to keep me inside? Or to keep our enemies out?

"I'm hungry," I mumbled, placing a hand over my growling stomach.

"All right." Julian took my hand and led me down the corridor. There was something so intimate, yet protective in his touch. For a moment, I played with the idea that he wasn't holding my hand to keep me close or out of harm's way. I imagined that he was holding my hand because he wanted to.

When we reached the third door on the left, he opened it and motioned for me to go inside. I peeked into the entryway before taking another step, cautious of my unfamiliar surroundings. There was an open kitchen and bedroom with a table in front of the window. Apart from a cracked door nearby, the design was exactly like a studio apartment—all of the rooms in a living space merging into one.

"Shower." Julian pointed to the partially opened door, and I found it odd that someone would put a bathroom by the kitchen. "I'll find you some clothes if you'd like to change."

Feeling like a mouse in a trap, I let go of his hand and took a step back. My eyes fluttered about the room, one room, the only room I may ever see again. I wanted to get out of here. I wanted to go home.

"Is there a phone?" I wondered, draping my arm across my midsection. Nausea was rooted at the pit of my stomach and churning violently. "I'd like to call my parents. Let them know I'm okay."

"No." He gritted his teeth with a glower. "You can't call your parents. Or anyone else for that matter."

I walked around him so he stood between me and the main door. "And why not?"

"Because someone will trace the call," he replied. "And they'll find you."

Scoffing at his remark, I leaned into the counter and glared. "So what am I supposed to do?"

Julian clenched his jaw and stalked towards me. "You are going to stay here. Just as I have asked you to."

"But I don't want to be here!" I shouted. "I want to go home. I want to see my family."

He tilted his chin and looked down his nose at me. "Well, you can't."

Tears stung my eyes as I inhaled, drawing fresh breath deep into my lungs. Julian placed his hands over my shoulders, but I withdrew and shoved him away. "I guess I'll take a shower," I grumbled.

"All right." His voice was hardly more than a whisper. "I'll get you some clothes."

Sniffling, I faced the bathroom door and sulked. Perhaps he had spared me when the bartender wanted to take my life, but I hated him. He wouldn't let me leave, wouldn't let me see my family. Wasn't that the definition of a kidnapper? Was that what he was? Had he *taken* me?

"Here." Julian nudged my back with folded clothes. "I'm not sure how everything will fit."

I spun around and snatched the clothes out of his hands, biting my lip to keep from breaking down. Then I stormed into the bathroom and slammed the door behind me, feeling the shudder of the frame. Thankfully, there was a lock on the door, and I twisted it the moment it became my next discovery.

Trembling with fury, I dropped the clothes onto the toilet lid and sank down to the floor. He had given me a flannel button down shirt and a pair of blue jeans to wear. As water blurred my vision, I glanced down at the soiled red dress I had been wearing for days. I could hardly stand looking at the satin fabric, because then I remembered everything that had happened that night at the club. It felt like a dream, a horrible nightmare. My friend was dead. My *only* friend. But it must have been real, because I couldn't wake up.

When I tossed my head back, a pane of glass caught my eye. Curious, I stood up and walked over to the small square window—wide enough for someone to crawl through with my slender size. Too hungry to put up a fight, I marked the window with a Post It note in my mind. Something I would come back to at a later time, when the probability of a successful breakout was more likely.

A chance at escaping did leave me with some hope as I slipped out of the red dress. While I had no desire to stay here, perhaps I could make the best of it for a night or two. Long enough to find the right moment to flee. But then I was struck by the brutal nature of the cold, hard truth.

If I did escape, where would I go?

There was an unopened bar of soap as well as two brand new bottles of shampoo and conditioner in the shower. As the freezing cold water washed over me, I wondered if that should frighten me. Had the bath products been there long? Or had they been prepared ahead of time, waiting for me to arrive?

Kicking those thoughts aside, I threaded my fingers through my hair and rinsed the shampoo and conditioner out as swiftly as possible. The matter of washing my body was just as much of a race. Before the frostbite set in.

After the quickest shower of my life, I pulled the curtain back and covered my body with a towel. The soft cloth had never felt so warm against my skin. But I quickly stripped the layer of comfortability away and changed into my new clothes.

The long sleeve shirt was heavily red and covered in plaid. As I glanced into the mirror over the sink, it occurred to me that I must have looked like a lumber jack. Exhaling at my appearance, I rolled the sleeves back and wondered if these were

Julian's clothes. Had he once lived here?

I dried my hair with a towel and hung it across the shower rod. Then I glanced down at my bare feet and couldn't deny that they were freezing against the tile. One final look in the mirror, and I turned on my heel to leave the room.

Something smelled delicious in the kitchen, as I peered around the bathroom door. Julian stood in front of the stove stirring a packet of powdered cheese into a boiling pot of elbow macaroni. With his back to me, I cast an evil glower in his direction. I felt like a mouse in a cage. I wanted out of here.

When Julian looked over his shoulder at me, I ignored him and ambled over to the open pantry. Shelves were filled with canned goods, packaged products, items that took a long time to expire. The wheels were turning in my head, as I struggled to grasp the absurdity of it all.

"So what is this?" I asked. "A safe house? Some haven of rest?"

Julian lifted his head but kept his eyes on the task at hand. I turned back to him and loathed his silence. Surely, now was not the time to plead the fifth.

"I want my family, Julian. I want to go home. I don't want to stay here." I figured that I should try begging and pleading with him first. The *escape through the window* route was a last resort.

Julian flung the spoon into the pot, and I flinched at the sound of clanking metal. Steam rose up from the boiling macaroni as anger filled him, his chest rising and falling with each breath. My mouth felt very dry all of a sudden, my tongue the consistency of sandpaper. When Julian pressed his palm into the counter, I saw powerful blue veins emerging on the back of his hand.

"You're such a child," he hissed, obviously infuriated with me.

My heart hammered against my chest as I swallowed. "What?"

He turned around and cornered me until my back was against the wall. His blue eyes scorched like fire, despite the way they gleamed icy cold. "Do you know who I am?" he muttered.

No matter how I tried, I could not look away. He had me pinned to the spot. Caged. Trapped.

Julian knotted his fingers in my hair and leaned my head back. My lips parted as I took each shallow breath, afraid of what he might do. But no matter how I reacted, he just stood there and stared. I wanted to crawl into a hole and hide. But I couldn't.

"I could kill you with my bare hands," he said. "It's what I've been trained to do. My specialty."

I moistened my lips and shivered. The warmth of his body covered me, like radiating heat from the sun. Despite the freezing cold shower, I already felt my skin beginning to glisten with sweat.

"I spared you," he declared. "No one else would have."

"Why did you?" It took a great deal of effort to

keep from stumbling over the words.

I felt the heel of his hand against my cheek as his breath rained down on my face. But then Julian recognized the gravity of my question, and the anger slowly seeped out of him. I watched his chest return to a regular rhythm of inhaling and exhaling. He furrowed his brow and sighed.

"I couldn't do it," he confessed. "It's the way you were looking at me. The innocence in your eyes." Julian loosened his fingers from my hair and cupped my cheek in his hand. "You were too beautiful, too pure, too good. I followed you for months, and you never did a thing to warrant death."

My lower lip trembled as tears broke free. "What about Bridgette? What about my friend?"

"I didn't kill your friend," he assured me. "But there was no saving you both."

I opened my mouth to speak, and he smoothed the pad of his thumb across my cheek to wipe the tears away. There was something so gentle and cool in his touch. How could I find comfort in the arms of a killer?

"I have given up everything to spare you. My career is over, and every one of those men I have grown to trust are now my enemies." Julian curled his fingertips beneath my chin and scanned my face. "When I saved you—when I let you live and helped you escape—it was like signing my own death certificate."

I blinked up at him and felt the blood drain

from my face.

"Both of us, you and I, are in more danger than you can imagine." Julian skimmed his thumb along the edge of my lower lip, just close enough to my mouth to miss it. Then he withdrew his hand and leaned back, gazing at me from the newly established distance. "But I'm not going to hurt you," he promised.

"Why not?" I breathed, struggling for air among the throes of heated tension.

His eyes darkened, as every ounce of emotion left his face. "Because I don't want to."

Chapter 5

I sat down before the bare wooden table at the foot of the bed and played with my hands in my lap. Julian waltzed over from the kitchen and set a bowl of Kraft macaroni and cheese in front of me. When he handed me a fork, I kept my head down and took it.

Steam billowed up and wafted across my face as I inhaled the scent of creamy pasta. The meal had always been my go-to comfort food when I was growing up. Now, the irony had never been more on point.

I listened to the sound of his footsteps as he returned to the table and sat down across from me. There was an identical bowl of glistening orange noodles in front of him. He picked up his fork and started to eat, while I failed to acclimate to the awkwardness of it all. When I stared at the table and kept still, Julian noticed. My stomach was growling, but I felt too nervous to do anything. Especially eat.

"Aren't you hungry?" Julian lifted his head and watched me. "Eat, Anna."

I sat up straighter in my chair and looked down, lacking the desire for nourishment. I sank my teeth into my lower lip and wiped the back of my hand across my mouth. When I set my fork down on the table, Julian tilted his head at me and smoldered. The heat in his eyes was almost unbearable.

"I need to ask you some questions," I explained. "Before I can..." Words left me quicker than they had come.

Julian chewed at the inside of his cheek and exhaled through his nostrils. "Okay."

"What's your name?" I began, wasting no time.

He narrowed his eyes at me with a look of confusion. "I already told you. Julian."

"No." I shook my head as his eyes returned to mine. "Your real name."

Julian blinked several times and dug his elbows into the table. "That is my real name."

"All right," I accepted. Apparently, Julian was the only name I was going to get.

He stuffed forkful after forkful of macaroni and cheese into his mouth, chewing noisily.

"How old are you?" I gripped either edge of my seat with my hands as they began to sweat.

Julian cleared his throat and answered, "Twenty-nine."

Surprise must have flitted across my face, because he looked discouraged.

"You don't look twenty-nine," I observed. And it was the truth. Julian looked twenty-five at the oldest, and he could have passed for younger than that if he had wanted to.

"And your point is?" he returned. Perhaps it was that baby face and the dimple in his chin.

"Nothing." I lowered my eyes with the shake of my head. "So you kill people?"

"Yes." He batted his dark lashes and pinned me to the spot with the gleam in his eyes.

"You've killed people?" I changed the tense, because that somehow made it different.

"Isn't that the same question?" he countered, a bite of sarcasm to his voice.

"I guess." My cheeks burned red as I kept my face over the steam rising from my bowl.

"Luke is the last person I killed," he volunteered, making my insides flame with heat.

Daring to look up at him, I furrowed my brow and regarded him sternly. Surely, judgement was written all over my face.

"The bartender," he clarified. "But you should thank me for that. He really wanted you."

I mashed my lips together and shut my eyes tight. What sort of world had I stumbled into?

As a tear slipped down through my lashes, I continued with my questions. Julian seemed somewhat altered by the fact that I was crying. But maybe I was making more out of it than there was.

"How many?" I wanted to know.

"What?" he hissed, aggravated that the words were so vague.

I lowered my voice and whispered, "How many people have you killed?"

Julian stretched his neck and sat back in his chair, crossing his arms over his chest. He must have rolled his sleeves up while cooking, because I could see the bulging veins in his forearms. They were intimidating.

"A lot," he muttered with every bit of nonchalance.

I let out a painful laugh that sounded much more like a muffled cry.

"I don't really keep track of things like that."

"Really?" I declared. "Well then, what do you keep track of?"

Julian stared at me and ground his teeth together.

"I'm not afraid of you," I boldly announced.

Julian leaned across the table and said, "You should be."

Anger swirled hot and heavy through my soul. I hated his cockiness, his vanity, his contempt. He must have thought that he had played God in choosing to let me live. How wrong he was.

I rose to my feet and pushed my chair out. "I don't want to be here. Take me home."

Julian folded his arms and gazed up at me. "No."

"You're a coward," I snapped. "What makes

you think you can keep me here? I'm not your pet! I want to see my family! I want to go home! You can't keep me here! I won't let you!"

Julian remained calm as I gasped for air. Then he looked over me complacently. "Watch me."

Fuming with a vengeance, I picked up my steaming bowl of mac and cheese and threw it across the kitchen floor. The bowl shattered into pieces as slimy orange noodles scattered all over the ground. Julian gritted his teeth and glowered, balling his hands into fists at his sides.

When he stood up and towered over me, I stuck to my guns and snarled, "I hate you."

Julian shoved past me and grabbed a towel from the kitchen. Then he knelt down to clean up the mess I had made, refusing to say a word. Somehow, that infuriated me more than if he had yelled at me.

"Why did you do that?" he asked, tossing the dirty food into the trash.

When I kept quiet, Julian watched me with curious concern in his eyes. It was utterly perplexing.

Julian clenched his jaw and got rid of the broken bowl. When he began washing his hands in the sink, I realized how futile my attempt at riling him up had been. What a waste.

"Fine then," Julian grumbled. He wiped his hands off and returned to his bowl of macaroni and cheese at the table. "You can starve."

Furious, I ripped my fingers through my hair

and screamed. Then I let my wrath envelop me and lunged for Julian. But he grabbed my arms and stood up, defending his body from my impending violence.

"I hate you! I hate you!" I cried, beating my fists against his chest.

Julian grabbed my wrists and tried to turn my body away from him. But I managed to slam him up against the wall before I tripped over his chair and collapsed on the ground. Lying against him, I hung my head and wept. These were heavy, wet, embarrassing tears that I had rather not shed in front of a man like him.

My body shook with the force of emotion as I let everything I had been feeling come pouring out of me. Julian cradled my body in his arms and rubbed his hand over my back. Perhaps I should have been repulsed by his touch, but I wasn't. Instead, I clung to the fabric of his shirt and burrowed my head in his chest. He may not have been a good man. But right now, he was the only one I had.

Exhaustion seeped in as I closed my eyes and let him hold me. When my body grew limp, he stood up and carried me to the bed on the other side of the room. I lay back with a tiring breath and dozed off.

* * *

After wrestling with a nightmare, I jerked awake in the darkness. It took a moment to realize where I was, as I glanced about the room full of shadows. I must have fallen asleep hours ago, because it was now night time outside. No lights were turned on inside the house, and Julian was gone.

Slipping out of the covers, I walked through the kitchen and opened the door leading to the main hallway. But when I stepped into the long corridor, moonlight poured through the window at the end of the hall. My feet felt cold and bare against the hardwood floor, while I longed for a pair of socks.

"Julian?" I called. A board creaked beneath my feet, and it sent a bolt of fear straight to my bones.

I licked my lips and hurried to the end of the hall. The last door on the right was the only one that had been left open, so I peeked inside and found a wooden staircase. I was terrified, but I was also intrigued.

"Julian?" I crept up the staircase, and my heart hammered with every step. After climbing the flight, I reached an attic with carpet flooring and one wide window looking out over the land. There was a desk along the right wall with a computer and telephone. Just like that, hope swelled alive in my chest.

Without a moment to waste, I leapt for the phone and snatched the receiver out of its cradle. I shut my eyes in an attempt to catch my breath as my hands turned moist and shaky. My mouth felt uncomfortably dry while I struggled to recall the phone number at my parents' house in DC.

"Two-Oh-Two," I breathed, failing to calm myself. That was the area code in Washington.

After dialing the first three digits, a sense of confidence burst through my trembling fingers. The numbers came back to me one at a time. Like the way children recite the alphabet in elementary school. I pressed one button and then another, feeling closer and closer to my life line and a chance at freedom.

Before I touched the last number, Julian raced up the staircase and ripped the phone out of my hands. I heard the dial tone—my best shot at reaching the outside world—just before he threw the phone across the room and it crashed into the wall. As if that were not enough, Julian collected the remains and opened the window, tossing them into the cold black night.

Angered by his ruthless behavior, I bolted across the attic and shoved him aside. Then I ducked my head through the window and stuck my arms through. But he grabbed me before I could jump.

"NO!" I wailed, watching every chance of escaping my nightmare drifting away like burnt ashes.

Julian shut the window and locked it. Then he grabbed ahold of my wrists, no matter how I bucked against his strength and kicked his shins. Before we could make it to the staircase, he let go and I fell down at his feet.

When he tried to pick me up again, I screamed and scratched his cheek with my nails. I loathed the way he had control over my freedom. Julian had harnessed it, and I was like a tiger pacing in a cage.

As I succumbed to my choking sobs, Julian jerked me up in his arms and hurried down the staircase. His shoes pounded against the hardwood floors once we reached the main hallway. Then he walked into the apartment-styled space where he had kept me and locked the door behind us.

The tears gliding down my cheeks had arisen from anger, not sadness or fear. I hated how upset he had made me and even more so, the fact that he could see me crying now. Julian passed through the kitchen and dropped me onto the bed, while I reared up and balled my fists to attack him.

But Julian anticipated my every move, and he had my arms pinned by my sides before I could blink.

"Calm down and get ahold of yourself, or I'm going to have to tie you to the bed," he warned.

I gritted my teeth and clamped down, smoldering at him with a molten heat behind my eyes that burned like fire. When my body turned limp and I relaxed, his hold on my arms loosened. As he stood up and put some distance between us, I leaned back against the headboard and stuck my feet beneath the sheets.

Julian turned a light on in the kitchen and pulled out a bottle of Jack Daniels. I watched the amber liquid jostle inside the glass, reminding me of the drunken nights my father spent with politicians and lobbyists. He was a politician himself, and he had spent more evenings than not with that bottle in his hand.

After downing a tumbler full of whiskey, Julian smeared the back of his hand across his mouth. Then he took a deep breath and gazed at me, his piercing blue eyes frosty and aquamarine. I forced myself to look away, but heard his footsteps once he started pacing along my side of the bed.

"If you don't stop being so stupid, you're going to get us both killed," he barked.

I crossed my arms over my chest and held my head high, looking any way but his.

"What number did you dial, Anna?" he rasped. "Who were you calling?"

I breathed through my nose and circled my index finger over the fitted sheet.

"Anna!" Julian came closer and grasped my arm with force, but it wasn't painful.

"My mother and father!" I shouted back at him. "Who do you think I called?"

Julian lowered his dark lashes and let me go. "Did the call go through? Did it ring?"

"No," I grumbled. "You snatched it out of my hand before I could talk to them."

"Good." He rocked back on his heels and placed his hands on his hips. "I'm glad."

"Why?" I snapped. "You're happy that I have no connection to my family? That they don't know where I am? They don't know if I'm safe or not. They don't know if they'll ever see me again."

"Well, if you pull a stunt like that again." He pointed to the right. "I can assure you they won't."

"How?" I challenged. "What are you going to do to me?"

Julian scowled and stroked his beard. "It's not what *I'm* going to do to you."

As reality drifted through me, I recalled the look on that blond bartender's face. The evil gleam in his eye. Surely, Bridgette never saw him coming. I felt sure that he must have been the one to kill her.

"Who are these men?" I wondered. "The ones coming after me? The men that you work for?"

Julian clenched his jaw and shook his head. "I can't tell you."

"I don't know why I'm even trusting you in the first place," I sneered.

Julian sat down on the bed and touched my hand. "Because you have to."

Burning heat brushed over my skin as his eyes connected with mine. But then he moved his hand and stood, and it was like the moment never happened at all.

"We'll talk more about this later." Julian opened a dresser drawer and tossed me a long men's shirt. "Right now, you should get some sleep."

"What is this?" I held the white cotton shirt in my open hand and looked over at him.

"I thought that might be more comfortable for you to sleep in," he explained.

"Oh, okay." I pulled the sheet up to my chest and set the shirt aside. I was waiting for Julian to leave so I could change in privacy. Even though I had dozed off earlier, the baggy jeans and scratchy polyester shirt were not the most comfortable clothes to sleep in. In a way, I was grateful for this small kindness. Even if it was only a plain white t-shirt.

Julian turned the kitchen light off and pulled a chair out by the foot of the bed, where I had attempted to eat earlier. He sat down facing me and then poured another tumbler of whiskey. Moonlight filtered in through the blinds, while I pulled my knees into my chest and set my sights on him with a vacant stare.

"What?" he asked, lounging back in the chair to get more comfortable.

"I would like to change." I held his gaze and jerked my chin at him, my best attempt at persuasion.

"Well, I'm not going anywhere." He lifted the tumbler at me and then knocked the whiskey back.

Irritated by his demeanor, I stood up and held the white t-shirt to my chest. "Fine then." I kept my eyes down in an attempt to avoid his skeptic stare. "I'll change in the bathroom."

Before I could enter the kitchen, his hand clamped down around my arm. "No, you won't."

"Julian," I hissed, glaring up at him. Something in his touch warmed my spirit. I resented that.

He held my gaze in the dark and took a step closer. "You think I don't know there's a window in there?"

My eyes dropped to the floor as I mashed my lips together. There *was* a window in the bathroom. And I hadn't forgotten about it.

"Now I can't risk you trying to escape again." Julian inhaled and scanned my figure from head to toe. "If you want to change, you'll do it in here."

I swayed inward and jerked my arm from his grasp. "Fine," I bitterly remarked.

Julian smirked like the devil and stepped backwards until he landed in his chair. When he poured another tumbler full of whiskey and draped his left calf across his right thigh, I shivered. He straightened his pant leg out and then extended his hand just to mock me. "Proceed, Miss James."

I turned my back to him and stood by the bed. Then I pressed my palm into the mattress and tried to get a grip. My heart might as well have exploded in my chest, because I knew he was watching me.

"You've put me through a great deal, Miss James," he drawled. "Don't I deserve some kind of reward?"

I thought that must have been the whiskey

talking, but then the image of him in the club settled in my mind. The first time I saw him, he had been utterly striking. I had wanted to be his, but not like this.

Feeling brazen, I accepted his challenge and turned around. So he had dared me, and I had fallen for it. But surely a man ten years my senior knew how to exercise the powers of persuasion better than I could defend myself against them. He looked into my eyes across the room, and I knew what was going to happen before he did. I understood what was bound to transpire between us. He had me.

I unsnapped the button on the jeans and slid the zipper down, shimmying out of them as calmly as I could. Even though I had taken the bait, I didn't want him to see a weaker side of me. I wanted him to know that I could handle it and would not back down from any test he happened to spring on me.

After laying the jeans out on the bed, I met his gaze across the room and felt so wholly vulnerable and exposed. I was standing in my underwear with nothing but a flannel shirt over me. Thankfully, the garment fell to my thighs, but that would not help me when I had to take it off.

As I began unfastening the buttons, my skin ignited in flames. Rosy blush burned against my cheeks while I shuddered at the abrupt command to remove my clothes in front of him. When my eyes slid shut, the last button came undone and I felt the fabric rising and falling with the rate of my unsteady chest.

"I've had too much to drink tonight," Julian spoke. "Why don't you turn around for the rest?"

I fluttered my lashes and looked up to find him standing in front of me. "Julian?"

"Turn around," he whispered, the corner of his mouth lifting slightly.

Breathless, I opened my mouth to breathe and then did as he said. Julian placed his hands on the bare skin of my shoulders and slid the flannel shirt down my arms. When it fell to the floor, my heart stopped and I could not push away flashes of him dancing with me in the club the night we met.

"Arms up," he instructed, his warm breath ghosting across the back of my neck.

I lifted my arms in the air, and he slid the soft cotton shirt over my head. The hem of the garment ran along my mid-thigh as I let my body adjust to the cool fabric. Julian stood quietly behind me, while I wondered if he might stand there all night. Deep down, I burned for him to touch me again.

"Get in bed." Julian turned the covers down as I slipped beneath the sheet and blankets.

By the time I got comfortable, he had already returned to his chair by the window. He sat there and turned his head to the side, observing me, studying my figure like I was a work of art, like I might disappear.

Grasping the covers, I rolled onto my stomach

and tried to sleep.

Chapter 6

I opened my eyes the next morning and had trouble placing where I was. My right leg dug into my left, causing tingles of pain to shoot through my calf. Pushing the covers back, I dropped my feet to the floor and stood on my left leg, jumping around to lessen the discomfort of it falling asleep.

Last night came rushing back to me in a hazy blur. Like looking through the lens of a shaky camera. I snatched the pair of loose jeans up off the floor and pushed my feet through either opening.

At the sound of running water, I ambled into the kitchen and noticed the cracked door to the bathroom. Julian was in there taking a shower, and my heart leapt at the opportune moment laid out before me. Hurrying over to the window, I wedged my fingers through the blinds and gazed out at the open land.

I looked back over my shoulder and wondered if Julian would come after me. While I had been plotting to escape through the window in the bathroom, that was hardly necessary when he thought I was sleeping. The shower turned off and I froze. Now was my only chance left to run.

Quick on my feet, I scurried through the door and softly shut it behind me. For some reason, Julian had left it unlocked, perhaps thinking any protests from me to be improbable in the morning. I ran down the hall and reached the front door, remembering how swiftly he had locked it when we first arrived.

To my utter shock, this door was open as well. So I twisted the knob and let myself out, pushing against the screen door with ease. But then I stepped onto the cool cement and realized my feet were bare.

My shoulders sagged as I reached out and clung to one of the wooden posts by the front porch steps. Even if I were free, where would I go? What would I do?

My green eyes skittered across the clear cut land, acres in every direction that backed up to the woods. How would I survive in the wilderness? I had no money, no car, no food. I didn't have a jacket or a pair of shoes. Even if I left this place and got away from Julian, wouldn't I wind up dead in the end?

Recognizing my mistake, I sat down on the

porch and pulled my legs into my chest.
Goosebumps popped up like flowers in the spring
across either of my arms. With a regretful sigh, I
put my chin on my knee and stared out at the
dusty blue sky, just a shade lighter than gray.

The truth was, escaping Julian would only be
hurting myself. There were men out there who
wanted to hurt me, find me, kill me. And they
were lurking. They were lurking for me in the
shadows of the night.

The screen door creaked, but I felt no need to
glance back. Of course Julian was there. Watching
me.

"Are you all right?" he asked.

Despite the urgency of his voice, he hadn't run
through the house screaming my name. If we
could establish a level of trust between us, maybe I
wouldn't feel so out of control. After all, it wasn't
like I had relinquished my freedom to him. Was
it?

I looked over my shoulder to find him with a
towel wrapped around his waist. My eyes widened
at his degree of nakedness as I snapped my head
back around. I wanted to cry out in frustration on
the inside.

"Anna," Julian softly crooned, his bare feet
padding against the ground behind me.

"I thought I would make a break for it while
you were in the shower." Frowning, I stared down
at my toenails and noticed that most of the polish
had flecked off. What a different world I was living

in now. There would be no time for spas and pedicures. "But then I came out here and realized I have nowhere to go."

Julian sighed, and I swear it made the hairs stand up on the back of my neck.

"There is nowhere to run, nowhere to hide." I looked up at him and pursed my lips, dropping my eyes to the floor. "I've never felt so trapped." Then I set my emerald gaze on him and said, "And I still don't know why you saved me."

"Why can't you just think of this place as a safe house?" he suggested.

"Because it's not one," I replied. "It's a prison."

Julian clenched his jaw and put his hands on his hips. "You're such a brat," he hissed. "You could be dead! Did you ever stop to think about that?"

Fuming all over again, I rose to my feet and got in his face. "So what? I'm supposed to just like staying here with you all of a sudden? You wouldn't even let me call my parents," I reminded him.

"That's because I'm protecting you!" Julian grabbed my arm when I tried to shove past him. "Dammit, Anna. Don't you get it? The longer you stay here, the better your chances are of making it out alive!"

"And why are you protecting me?" I snapped back. "Is it ransom money you're after? Steal the President's daughter and bring her back safely?

Collect your prize when you're done?"

Julian narrowed his eyes and growled, "*Ex*-President's daughter."

Staring up at him with a hateful glower, I beat his chest and yelled, "Let go of me!"

The moment Julian released his grip on my arm, I stumbled back and fell off the edge.

"Anna!"

I wish I had thought to put my arms out to brace myself before the fall. But the heavy stone felt cool against my skin, even as it dug into my body deep enough to draw blood. I winced and lay still, comprehending that something must have struck my head as well. Or vice versa.

"Anna." Julian appeared before me and tugged at my waist, rolling my body over until I lay on the flat of my back. "Anna, are you all right?" He brushed his thumb against my temple and inspected my injuries.

"I'm fine," I barked with acid in my voice. "Get off me."

Julian rose to a standing position while I struggled to follow suit. My head was pounding and my knees felt weak, yet I forced myself onto my feet. Even at the expense of colliding with Julian.

When my head dropped to his chest, Julian picked me up in his arms and carried me back to the kitchen. Once I regained my bearings, it occurred to me how devastatingly hungry I was. Julian set me down on the counter and swiftly returned with a first aid kit. All I could do was try to keep my balance and squint through my eyes, even though the light wasn't unusually bright.

Julian lifted my chin and cleaned the bloody gash across my forehead. When he swiped the area with hydrogen peroxide, I grabbed his arm and flinched. His lean torso and six pack abs were on full display, as he stood there in nothing more than a towel. Why hadn't he changed already?

"Aren't you going to put some clothes on?" I grumbled, achy and in pain.

"Not until you're all taken care of." Julian grinned, and I shot him a hateful glare.

Lowering his gaze, Julian placed a bandage on my forehead and took the hint. My eyes were like piercing green daggers as I glowered at him with all of my might. I had never loathed someone so much. It was his fault for bringing me here, for choosing the life of an assassin, for agreeing to kill me.

Julian lifted the hem of my shirt to inspect my other injury, but I batted his hand away.

"Anna," he hissed, on the verge of losing his patience with me.

Even though I had put on a good show of holding my own, I was six seconds from spiraling out of control. I didn't want this anymore. I wanted my old life back with my overprotective mother and father. I wanted boring weekends in my pajamas studying college textbooks. I wanted my roommate and best friend. But Bridgette was gone. They were all gone. And for that matter, so was I.

A lonely teardrop skirted down my cheek as I regarded him with cold malice.

Julian set his hands along either side of my hips on the countertop and whispered close enough for me to feel his breath against my face. "I don't want you to hate me," he confessed.

As he gazed into my eyes, I gritted my teeth and scowled. "Well I *do* hate you, Julian. I hate you so much it—"

He crashed into me with a bruising kiss and stole my breath away. Warmth rippled beneath my skin like a searing tidal wave, and it felt so strange. How could a man like him have soft lips?

Despite my struggle for air, he claimed my mouth again, already coming back for more. I was floored and emotional, entirely out of my element, out of my comfort zone. So I reared back and smacked him across the side of his face. The sound of that slap echoed for miles.

Julian stood with his face to the side as anger boiled within him. For an instant, I was truly afraid of what I had done, knowing that he might hurt me. But Julian merely clenched his jaw and stared. His chest rose and fell with every intake of breath as mine did the same. The tension was almost frightening.

Julian lifted his long finger in the air and pointed at me. "I didn't deserve that."

A shudder rippled through me from the cold

gleam in his eye. Julian looked hurt.

"I..., I..., I—I" My lashes blinked so fast that I could hardly help the stutter.

Julian dropped the towel around his waist, and I looked away so fast that it made my head spin. My pulse thumped loud and hard as he got dressed in front of me. I shut my eyes to make sure that I wouldn't see anything. Then I heard a door slam and opened them again. Julian was gone.

* * *

After taking inventory of the kitchen, I discovered that the only food we had was either boxed or canned. So I settled on a package of cheese crackers and a can of tuna fish. Since I had skipped meals for so long, it was hard to keep myself from scarfing the food down without choking out of sheer urgency.

I slapped a bandage over my abdominal wound without looking at it. As far as I was concerned, there were more pressing matters at present. Every now and then, I heard the ceiling crack overhead and knew that Julian was pacing the floorboards upstairs. What was he doing in there?

In my need for understanding, I went through every drawer imaginable. But nothing of note showed up. I couldn't manage to find his driver's license, or any other relevant documents for that matter. I had no idea whose house we were staying at or where we were in the first place. Other than the middle of nowhere.

Once I tired of searching, my skin felt warm and flushed. So I lay down on the bed and dozed off, dreaming of my parents and home. I had wanted a break from my life so much that night at the club, but look what had happened as a result. It reminded me of the words my father would always say: *Be careful what you wish for.*

When I startled awake, Julian was stirring soup in a pot over the stove. I sat up in bed and pulled the covers back, remembering our heated altercation earlier. "How are you feeling?" he asked.

"Fine," I lied. I felt like hell, and before too long, I might start wishing that I was there instead.

"Come here." Julian motioned me forward with his hand. "Let's have a look at that."

Feeling like a child, I ambled over to him as he turned the burner down and led me into the bathroom. An awkward tension developed between us, but I followed his orders and kept quiet. Even when he slipped his hand beneath my shirt and slowly peeled the Band Aid off my skin.

"Did you even clean it?" he scolded, taking an accusatory tone with me.

"No," I confessed. My skin bristled when he moved in closer for inspection.

"You should have." His thumb glided against my hip, but his eyes were on the unsightly gash resting on the left side of my lower stomach.

"Something like this could get infected. Don't you know any better?"

Our eyes met, though only for an instant. I bit my tongue and looked away, especially when he cleaned the area with rubbing alcohol. Nothing had ever burned so bad in my life, but he wouldn't let up.

When the pain subsided, Julian covered the wound with gauze and a bandage. Then he turned to wash his hands in the sink, as I stared at his reflection in the mirror. He really was beautiful.

"Julian," I began, hearing the way my voice sounded so small. "I'm sorry. About today."

He turned the faucet off and dried his hands, spinning around to face me.

"I shouldn't have hit you." I opened my mouth to speak again, but I couldn't.

Julian took a step towards me as his eyes danced across my face. "Don't worry."

I furrowed my brow up at him, especially when he pinned me to the spot with that sultry gaze.

"I'll never touch you again," he promised. "Unless you want me to."

I parted my lips to reply, but he was out the door before I could make a coherent thought out of it.

Instead, we ate dinner at the table, though I failed to re-enact the tantrum I had thrown the night before. "This is good," I mentioned, savoring the salty vegetable taste. Who cared if it was canned? I was hungry.

"I'm glad you like it."

And those were the only words Julian and I said to each other for the rest of the night.

When the moon hung heavy in the sky, he turned all of the lights out and I climbed into bed. Turning away from him, I stared at the wall and pulled the covers up to my collarbone. While he sat in his chair by the window and watched me, I tried and failed to close my eyes. Even though I was exhausted.

Insomnia came to visit me tonight, because of the worrisome thoughts swirling around my mind. Would it always be like this? Was this my new life? Hiding away from assassins with an assassin?

I wondered how many lectures I had missed at school. Finals were approaching when I was taken. Finals that Bridgette no longer had the privilege of attending. I wondered what her family thought when they heard the news that she had been murdered. Maybe the cops just told them that she was missing. After all, how much did they know at this point?

But what had the police told my family? Surely, my face was plastered all over the news, a reoccurring headline. Who could think of a better story than a President's daughter gone missing?

I missed Daddy. Even if he had never been around when I was growing up. I missed him badly. But I missed my mother most of all. She was like my best friend. What must she be going through?

When sleep continued to evade me, I hung my head and cried. My fingernails dug into the bed sheet as I pushed my face into the pillow, letting out strangled, embarrassing moans. I was helpless and vulnerable. Suddenly, I didn't care if he saw me anymore.

My throat burned with the lump bulging at the bottom of it, stabbing sharp like a knife. But I couldn't help the tears coming down, even as their salt landed on my tongue. My sadness. My pain.

I wanted to taste it.

"Anna." The bed dipped as Julian sat down on the end of it. "What's wrong? Why are you crying?"

I unleashed another round of choking sobs, feeling my body tire with emotion.

"Anna," Julian whispered, the mattress squeaking as he inched closer.

Sitting up to face him, I dragged the back of my hand against my eyes and sniffled. When I met his gaze, Julian had never looked so concerned. It boggled me, because I couldn't understand why he cared.

"Hold me," I whimpered, knowing the reason why he hadn't touched me already.

As if I had breathed life back into him, Julian lurched forward and wrapped his arms around me. His hands were like palm prints on my back as he squeezed achingly tight. I held on to the collar of his shirt and rested my head in the crook of his neck. Despite my anger towards him, he felt so *warm.*

When Julian eased one hand off my back and held me at arm's length, I lifted my head from his chest. He gazed into my eyes, and I swear I saw his soul staring back at me. He was mesmerizing.

"I know you don't have any reason to believe this, but I'm going to protect you, Anna. I'm going to keep you safe." He rubbed my chin with his thumb and vowed, "I will never hurt you."

I blinked several times, scanning his features with confusion.

"Okay?"

"Okay." I nodded, surprised when he gave me a sweet smile.

Then I put my head back on his chest and curled my arms around his neck. Julian held my body close, like he thought I might break, as my breathing gradually slowed. My eyelids grew heavy, but I felt it when he planted a kiss on my forehead, a kiss on my temple, a kiss on my cheek.

The urge to sleep was overwhelming, but I fought to have the memory. So I stayed awake long enough to feel his lips ghosting against my cheekbone. Deep down, I had the eerie feeling that Julian was so much more than the man hired to kill me.

Chapter 7

As Julian cooked oatmeal for breakfast, I wondered at the uncanny situation I had found myself in. What if the man who had been hired to kill me wasn't my enemy anymore? What if he was my friend?

"Julian?" I sat across from him at the table, while he handed me a silver spoon.

"Yeah." He sipped at his coffee and failed to make eye contact. In recent days, I had learned to not ask questions. Like how there could be perishable items in the fridge. Items that must have been purchased in a grocery store. Items that had an expiration date which hadn't been met yet.

"Well... I was wondering..." I twirled the edge of my spoon into the crusty cinnamon exterior. Sometimes I put myself in his shoes and wondered if he enjoyed taking care of me. Did he like the fatherly duty?

"What, Anna?" he grew short with me, forcing his food down. "Spit it out."

I knew the answer he was going to give me, which was why I couldn't help dragging my feet with the question. Until he actually said no, there was still hope. Maybe he would give me some freedom.

"Well, the other day, when I went looking for you upstairs and—"

His piercing blue eyes were like a razor cutting through my soul.

"I saw a computer, and—"

Julian clenched his jaw and blinked every so often, but at least he let me speak.

"Well, I was just wondering if maybe I could look some things up online."

"What things?" He dropped a spoon in his nearly empty bowl, and it clattered against the ceramic.

I leaned across the table and lowered my voice in reassurance. "I need to know what's going on in the world: news, current events. I don't even know what day it is."

"It's Wednesday."

"No." I shook my head. "I mean the month, the day, the year."

Julian looked out the window and then crossed his arms over his chest, leaning into the back of his chair. "After what happened last time, I don't know if I can trust you."

I bit my lower lip and nodded. "Okay. But

what if you go in there with me?"

Julian narrowed his eyes and smoothed his palm over the tight fabric squeezing his arms.

"Please." I reached out and grabbed his hand across the table, banking on the minimal affection he must have for me. After the way he wrapped his arms around me last night, he must have cared.

At least a little.

But Julian stiffened and peeled his hand from mine. "I'll think about it."

He watched me eat breakfast and then cleared our bowls and silverware away. While I had regularly complained about the course load at Princeton, I would give anything to be in a lecture hall right now. Whether I was Julian's prisoner or not, one thing was for certain. I was miserably *bored.*

It felt like the whole world must have moved on without me, while I remained stuck in the past. Haunted by a night that I could never understand. And poor Bridgette. That was her last night ever.

After taking a quick shower, I found fresh clothes tailored to fit my figure and frame spread out on the bed. With a warm towel around my body, I looked over my shoulder and searched for Julian in the room. But the space was bare, so I slipped into the slim jeans and green long-sleeve t-shirt.

Eternally restless, I dried my hair and then headed outside. There was a pair of navy blue sneakers waiting for me on the front porch, along with two white socks. Surprised, yet grateful, I sat down on the steps and slid my new pieces of footwear on. Somehow, it felt like Christmas all of a sudden.

Rising up, I slipped my hands in my pockets and walked across the lawn. The grass was dry but green, and as I studied the gray-blue sky overhead, I wondered whether it was going to rain or snow. A chilly breeze drifted through the air, but I shut my eyes and raised my arms into a horizontal line. For one brilliant moment, a stream of light broke through and shined on my face. I had missed the sun, as I always did in the winter months. But this was different now. Everything had changed.

When dusty clouds rolled in again, I tilted my head back and watched the warmth disappear. Then I took a few steps further and glanced as far as the eye could see. We were surrounded by forest on all sides, an army of trees at our feet. Part of me figured that must have been a good thing, to keep us secluded and hidden away from our enemies. Then again, the opposite was true. If they couldn't see us from afar, then we couldn't see them either. Especially through the thickets of a dark forest at night.

I felt my cheeks turn pink as my teeth began to chatter. While I should have worn a jacket outside, I didn't exactly have access to my wardrobe in the dorm or back home. And I wanted to stay out here for as long as I could, instead of being holed up in that house. Besides, a storm was near.

"What are you doing out here?" Julian asked, even though I hadn't heard him come up.

Leaning forward, I crossed my legs beneath me and watched him come closer. Julian sat down facing my side with enough distance between us to prevent touching. I batted my lashes at him with a smile.

"Just wanted some fresh air," I confessed, toying with a piece of grass in the ground.

"I know." He leaned back on an elbow and watched me. "You love being outside."

I pinned my eyebrows together and turned to ask him a question, but he stopped me before I could.

"Outdoors, I mean," he explained. "Since you've been cooped up in there with me."

Searching for strength, I changed the subject and said, "I'd like to know if there is a time frame you're looking at, for when I can finally go home. For when it's safe to, I mean."

Julian looked away and then set his sights beneath him. "No," he dryly stated.

"No?" I shot him a look of displeasure and then pulled my knees into my chest.

"I don't know what kind of answer you were expecting," he chuckled. "I've already explained everything to you. Right now, the safest place you can possibly be is right here with me."

I chewed at the inside of my cheek and nodded. "And I'm supposed to believe this?

Coming from the man who was hired to kill me?"

"What?" His glittering blue eyes scanned my face in defeat. "You still don't trust me."

"I don't even trust myself anymore," I confessed.

And it was the truth. On one hand, I had a right to believe Julian. If he were going to kill me, wouldn't he have already done it? But the rational part of my brain butted against that theory. As mercurial as his emotions were, how could I trust whatever his mood may be at the moment? He was cold one minute and then burned me the next. But which side of the coin was the real Julian? Who was behind the mask?

"I'll tell you this," he offered, hunching forward. "What those men had planned for you is far worse than anything I would have ever done. Just because I'm—" he dropped off and then gazed into my eyes, fearing that I had already judged him. "Well, it doesn't mean I'm not humane about it."

I forced down the thick lump riding up my throat and turned my gaze away. "You mean..."

"I think you know what I mean," he countered, challenging my innate perception.

"Tell me," I pressed. "What would they have done to me if you hadn't been there? What were they planning on doing to me?"

Julian shifted so he could sit up straight and let his elbows dig into his thighs. "Are you sure you want to hear this?" He hesitated at first. But we were already closer, so I knew he must be interested.

"Yes," I hissed. "Tell me. I want to know everything."

He tilted his head to the side and scratched the stubble along his jaw. "Anna."

"Tell me, Julian," I demanded. "I don't want to be in the dark anymore."

"Fine," he agreed, turning his head from side to side. He scanned the length of the field as if he were worried that someone might overhear. I didn't know who could be out here swallowed up in the woods.

I braided my fingers together like I was about to say a prayer. Then I waited and listened.

"Well." Julian cleared his throat to begin. "Most of the girls that are on the—" he paused and searched for hatred in my eyes, "...list."

"What list?" I asked. "Like a hit list?"

"Yes." He pursed his lips and looked away, obviously ashamed. The guilt was written all over his face.

"Okay, so there's a hit list." I pretended to brush the matter off lightly, but it must have been clear how uncomfortable the term made me. Especially when my cheeks turned scarlet red. "Keep going."

"Well, most of them are taken care of." He looked up at me through his lashes to signify the meaning of those words. But I wasn't that oblivious. I knew what he meant.

"And the rest?" I inquired, pushing him onward in my quest for information.

"The rest are placed on another list," he revealed. "A list for the special ones."

"Special ones?" I echoed, quirking my brow.

With those dazzling blue eyes, he looked me up and down. "Young. Beautiful. Naïve."

"Like me?" I found the admission to be more insecure than vain.

"Yes," he breathed. "Like you."

I mashed my lips together and gazed out at the trees, threading my fingers through my hair.

"What happens to them?" I whispered. "To the special ones?"

"They're sold." He bowed his head and stared at the grass. "And the ones who haven't been touched?"

Scorching flames slithered across my skin as I dared to meet his paralyzing gaze. "Yes?"

"They sell for more," he muttered. "The most, in fact."

Feeling sick, I pressed the heel of either palm into my temples and struggled to breathe. When Julian grabbed my hand, I gasped. But there was something so pure in his eyes that made me stay still.

"I could never live with myself if I let them take you," he confessed. "They will never have you."

"And what about all those other girls?" I jerked myself from his grasp and stood up, fighting back tears. "How come no one was there to save them? Why didn't you do something? Instead, you just stand by and watch? Is that how this works? Is that what you do to earn a living?"

"Anna, I'm not proud of what I've done." He rose to his feet and touched my arm. "Yeah, I've killed people before. But what happened with those girls. I never condoned it. I never participated in it."

"You never did anything to stop it either," I bitterly remarked, getting in his face. "You let it happen."

"Anna! Dammit!" He took my face in his hands and pulled me close. "I didn't let it happen to you."

Deep down, something was drawing me to him. One day, all too soon, I wouldn't be able to fight it. But I could for now. So I glowered into those beautiful eyes and pushed him away.

"Is that why you didn't let the bartender kill me?" I asked, setting my hands on my hips. "Because you knew that's not what he was really going to do?"

Julian pressed his teeth together and studied the skyline in the distance. I had my answer.

"What about Bridgette?" I cried, unable to resist the tears now. "Was she—? Did they—?"

"No," he mutely replied, sensing my mourning. "She was just taken care of."

My mind scrambled backwards and forwards, while I took to pacing. Maybe my political connections as a former first daughter had landed me on that list. But why would Bridgette be on a hit list? Instead of asking, I skipped a step and phrased the question the way I should have been asking it all along.

"Who would place a bounty on my head?" My lower lip trembled as I withheld the urge to shudder.

Julian's eyes flitted over my face, and I knew. I knew he had the answer.

"Anna," he gently coaxed. "You wouldn't want to know. It's not healthy to think about."

I turned on my heel and longed to get away, but he was always just a few steps behind me.

"Anna!" Julian grabbed my shoulders and spun me around to face him. "Try to understand."

"How could you work for someone like that?" I croaked. Air was trapped at the back of my throat.

He gazed deep into my eyes and sighed. "I didn't have a choice."

"We all have choices," I announced. "And you think that you can just rescue me—save my life—to atone for all the bad things you've done in yours? What do you think I am? Some kind of reparation?"

"No, Anna!" he cried, holding on to my waist when I tried to pull away. "I genuinely care about what happens to you."

"Why?" I pushed against his chest to create some distance, but that only made him cling tighter.

He dropped his eyes away from mine for a moment. "I don't know," he softly murmured.

"That felt like a lie," I accused, hating him all over again. "So I'm guessing it probably was."

Julian relaxed his hold on my body as his shoulders sagged.

"Let me know when you want to start telling the truth."

And with the swish of my hair, I blinked the tears from my eyes and ran into the house.

Chapter 8

Anna!" Julian chased after me and reached for my arm. When he grabbed ahold of my wrist, I found myself falling into his rock hard chest. "I'm not the monster you think I am," he gasped.

I tried to flee, but he held me against him, relentless as ever. "Prove it," I said, testing him.

He looked over my face and blinked, as if something had just become astonishingly clear. Then he took my hand and traced the inside of my palm with delicate care. Just when I thought he was going to tell me my destiny, Julian looped his fingers through mine and led me down the hallway.

Once we reached the last door on the right, he fished a key out of his pocket to unlock it. Betrayal flashed through me at the realization of what he had done. His lack of trust in me was blinding.

"Come on." He took the stairs two at a time, dragging me behind him. By the time I was at the top, all I felt was the blood thrumming loudly in my veins. Julian released me and slipped his hands into his pockets, motioning towards the computer on the desk where the phone had once been.

"How do I know you won't stop me?" I declared. "Especially after last time?"

Julian pulled out a chair and turned the computer on. Even though I knew he was only doing this out of guilt, like a Jeanie in a bottle, he had granted my first wish. What did it matter why?

As soon as I took a seat and shook the mouse, the screen came to life. Anxious for news, I ignored the fact that Julian was looking over my shoulder and clicked on the Internet Explorer icon the moment I saw it. What I didn't expect to find were my parents, Mama and Daddy, crying on the front page.

Before I could scroll down to read the article, a video of the two of them began to play.

"Today, former President Walter James and former First Lady, Winifred released family photos to aid in the recovery of their only daughter, nineteen-year-old Anna James," the reporter announced.

"We want our daughter back." Daddy stood in front of a tall podium on a large stage. "She is all we have. What we hold most precious in this world." The silver in his hair looked white. "We are willing to pay however much money it may take. I just want my little girl back. Bring her back to me."

Tears welled in my eyes as Mama rubbed his back and took center stage.

"My daughter is a beautiful, smart, innocent young woman," she insisted, scanning the crowd with a ferocious pair of green eyes. "She does not deserve this! No one deserves this, but especially not our Anna. Whoever has taken her, we want her back! We want our daughter back!"

Silence emanated the crowd as Mama relied on her Louisiana drawl.

"I will not sleep until she is found," she declared. "I know she's out there. I can feel it."

"Please," Daddy butted in. "If anyone has any information..." he broke down in sobs as my mother joined him, both ultimately escorted off the stage where they could grieve in silence.

The screen flashed back to a news anchor at the front desk. "Anna James was last seen on Princeton University campus around nine thirty on the night of December tenth. The body of her roommate, Bridgette Eastwood, was found last week at the bottom of a lake, not far from the club they visited that night. If you have any information regarding the whereabouts of Anna James, please contact the number below."

Breaking down, I buried my face in my hands and cried. Before long, I slipped out of the chair and crumpled to the floor. Julian was by my side in an instant, cradling my body in his arms.

"Bridgette," I choked on the word, because that could have very easily been me.

"Shh..." Julian put my head on his chest and stroked his fingers through my hair.

"I was the one who wanted to go out. I was the one who made Bridgette go with me." I leaned back as Julian put his hands on my waist. "It's my fault. She's dead, and it's my fault."

"Shh... Come here." Julian picked my body up and set me down in his lap. As he consoled me, I let the emotions flood through me like a dam destined to break.

"It should have been me at the bottom of that lake," I decided.

"No!" Julian took my face in his hands and looked into my eyes. "You didn't do anything wrong. Do you hear me? You did nothing wrong! It has nothing to do with being in the wrong place at the wrong time."

Tears ran so heavy that I felt them on my chin. "What is happening?"

The world I knew before was gone. The one I had wanted to get out of. The one I had failed to appreciate. The one I no longer had. I had been so selfish that night, and now Bridgette was dead.

Somehow hearing it over the news changed everything. For once, I had confirmation of my roommate's ultimate end. But knowing that she had been tossed into a body of water like a used piece of trash—that lit a fire within me that I had never possessed before. A fire for bloodlust and vengeance.

"You're safe with me," Julian whispered. "Don't be afraid."

"I'm not afraid." I pushed off him and rose to my feet, while he stared up at me from the floor. "I'm not in control. Everything is completely out of my control, and I don't like it. I hate it!"

Julian leaned forward to stand up, contemplating the pressing matter at hand.

"And what about my parents?" I yelled. "We have to call that number. They have to know I'm all right."

"If you make any contact with your parents, you'll only be putting them in danger."

Fuming, I turned on my heel and glowered at him. "My parents are worried sick about me! You would let them go on not knowing whether I'm alive or dead? That's my mother and father!" I pointed at the computer screen and gritted my teeth at him. "You can't do that to them! You can't!"

Julian inched closer and held my gaze. "Even if it means they'll both be dead?"

"What?" I snapped, taking immediate offense at his words.

"If you reach out to them, then they're as good as dead!" he shouted, raising his finger at me.

"What am I supposed to do?" I argued back. "Let them think that I am?"

"Yes!" he shouted, sending chills down my spine. "It's the only way to keep them safe."

"I hate you." I glowered, slamming my palms into his chest until his back collided with the wall. "You never should have taken me! You've ruined everything!" I got in his face until our noses nearly touched. "And I'll bet you'll be standing by to collect the reward. Won't you? Won't you!" I screamed.

"Anna," he sympathized, lowering his voice. "You don't know what you're talking about."

"Leave me alone." I clasped his shoulders and pushed him away. "Get out! Get OUT!"

Julian walked backwards with his hands in the air until he finally descended the steps with his eyes on me. Once I heard the door click shut and knew that he was gone, I collapsed on the floor and cried out loud. I was mourning the loss of my friend, while reckoning with the guilt of her death.

Everything was my fault.

I must have laid there for the longest time, drowning in a pool of my own tears. But then a brilliant flicker of light switched on in my head. Julian was gone, and I had the computer to myself.

Seizing the moment, I hurried over to the office chair and sat down. The moment my fingers connected with the keys, I began typing his name into Google. But then I realized one minor problem that not even the most reliable search engine could solve. All I had was his first name. *Julian.*

Scrapping that thought, I logged on to Gmail and thought of another solution. My inbox was overflowing with countless emails, yet I clicked on "COMPOSE" immediately. In no time, I typed up an email to my parents which explained that I was safe and unharmed, but in hiding at the moment, as there were assassins after me. *An angel has found me*, I said. *He will keep me safe.*

While the email was intended to give them peace of mind, I worried that it might have the opposite effect. So I sat there contemplating the choices before me. What if Julian was right?

What if—by starting up communication—I was putting them both in danger? Surely, Daddy would come looking for me. He might even have someone trace the IP Address to find a location.

Doubt settled in the pit of my stomach, while the pointer hung over the send button and my finger lingered above the mouse. If I sent the email and either of my parents were harmed as a result, would I be able to live with that? I already had the blood of one person's life on my hands. I couldn't handle another.

But then the wooden stairs creaked, and my heart rate picked up. Someone was watching me. As I stared into the reflective pane across the screen, I flinched with the click of the mouse.

The blunt end of a baseball bat connected with the monitor, and I screamed. Ducking for cover, I crawled across the floor and shielded my face with my hands. Julian jammed the baseball bat into the computer again and again, until sparks were flying and fiberglass scattered all over the room.

When he finally stopped, I caught my breath, still gasping for air. The baseball bat rolled on the floor as he ripped the cord out of the wall and carried the machine across the room in his arms. He opened the window and tossed the computer out of it, where it joined the phone on the ground outside.

Hiding in the corner, I peeked between my fingers as Julian licked his lips and stared at me. His chest rose and fell with every loud breath, sending fear through my veins. Furious with me, Julian placed his hands on his hips and then wiped his mouth, contemplating his next move.

I opened my mouth but not to speak. I was trembling too much to afford words right now.

"Did you press send?" he asked, hot air flying through his nostrils.

My eyes dropped to the floor as I clasped my hands together and struggled to think.

"Did it go through, Anna?" he pestered. "The email? Do you know if it went through?"

I squeezed my eyes shut and hugged myself. "I don't know," I mumbled. "Maybe."

Julian cursed under his breath, but I heard every chilling expletive he said.

"Why did you do that?" I whimpered, still shuddering from his violent outburst.

"Do you really have to ask me that question?" Julian cocked his head to the side. "Have you been listening to anything I've been saying this whole time? Or do you just not believe me?"

I peered up at him with fear in my eyes. Julian tightened his jaw and snickered.

"Well." He took three slow steps forward and crouched down in front of me. "You will."

His eyes stayed on mine until he turned and took the stairs. I watched him leave and then looked around the room at the debris that remained. So maybe I had lied before. Julian *did* scare me. Especially now.

* * *

"It's supposed to snow tonight." Julian walked into the room with his hands in his pockets.

I sat in the bed with my arms crossed over my chest. While I desperately hoped that email had gone through, I feared the repercussions of such a cryptic message. If the IP Address were discovered, could that be a trail leading straight to us?

Whose hands would have access to that information? After all, we were talking about the Internet here. The World Wide Web. I could have just put more than Julian and me in danger. What had I done?

"Do you think that email went through?" I wondered at dinner. Julian had prepared canned soup, and to be honest, it was beginning to taste like poison. But how else were we going to survive? Especially when a horrendous blizzard was highly likely in the night to come.

"You better hope not." He ignored me and

lapped up the broth from his bowl.

"I just wanted my parents to know that I was all right." I pressed the flat of either palm against the table and searched his eyes, mainly because he wouldn't let me meet them. "It's not fair to let them go on worrying about me. Don't they deserve to at least know that I'm alive?"

"After that stunt you pulled today, you might not be for long," he growled, standing up from the table and taking his dishes to the sink.

I turned around in my chair to face him as he stomped away. "What is that supposed to mean?"

Julian tossed his bowl beneath the running faucet and then slung an empty pot in there as well. "I don't know what it's going to take for you to realize that I'm being honest, that you *are* in danger."

"*Why* am I in danger?" I demanded, marching towards him and slamming my fists against the counter.

Julian leveled his eyes at me with a glower. "Why don't you ask your Daddy?"

I crossed my arms over my chest and tightened my jaw. "Don't talk about my father like that."

"What? You think your Daddy was just having lunch with senators everyday on Pennsylvania Avenue and trying to establish world peace?" He took a step towards me, and I took one back. "You think he's a good man. You think he's different from every other politician, even though you despise them all."

"Julian, stop." I put distance between us, but that only made him inch closer.

"You think you're his little girl." He stalked towards me until my back was against the wall. When his hands landed alongside me, I felt trapped, caged in by the strength of his arms.

"Daddy is a good person," I defended. "He would never do anything to hurt anybody."

Julian shook his head, and I felt his breath on my lips. "Grow up, Anna. He's a crooked politician, just like all the rest of them." He lowered his face to mine until we nearly touched. "And you know it, too."

All the lights went out, and I shivered. The wind howled like a great white wolf outside the front door, as the shutters violently banged against the window. The storm had arrived, as snow came rushing down in a flurry.

"Stay right here," Julian whispered in the dark. The moment he disappeared into the hall, I found my way out of the kitchen and sat down on the mattress. With the blinds partially open, moonlight filtered into the room, though not nearly enough to make me feel brave.

Gathering a fresh set of clothes, I rushed towards the bathroom and practically tripped over my own two feet. But then Julian returned and reached out, snatching me up by the elbow before I could fall. When I stood up straight, his chest was in my face. His warm, strong, sturdy chest that felt like heaven.

"What are you doing?" He grabbed my arms to keep me upright.

"I need to take a shower," I confessed, gazing into his watchful eyes.

"Make it a quick one," he ordered. "The heater is out." He let go of me and slid his hands into his pockets, scanning my features as if he had pushed too far. "Looks like this storm could get pretty bad."

"Okay." I moistened my lips and nodded, turning around so fast that it made my head spin.

In the shower, I yelped when the water first kicked on. Somehow, tonight was worse than all the rest, because it felt like I was bathing in the sea that sunk the Titanic. Goosebumps raised across the surface of my skin as I showered in a flash.

When it was time to wash my hair, I thought twice about it, but then grabbed the bottle of shampoo anyway. Sure, there would be no blow dryer waiting for me afterwards. But with no heat in the house and a blizzard on the way, it was best to take a longer shower now in exchange for short ones later.

Since it was freezing, I put my bra back on and then pulled a long t-shirt over it. Julian had given me a pair of sweatpants for the night, which I presumed were his. For a minute, I called in to question everything about this place. Did Julian own the house? Did he come here often? Or did the structure belong to the entire team of assassins he used to work for?

What disturbed me most was the possibility that Julian had prepped the building ahead of time with clothing and essentials for us both. What if he had planned the whole mission out in its entirety? What if he had been expecting me? What if he had known I was coming? What if it was premeditated—his plan to bring me here.

Shaking it off, I dried my hair with a towel and tried not to think about what if. All that did was lead me down an endless rabbit hole. One that I had no means of crawling my way out of.

"We need to move upstairs," Julian announced, startling me when I stepped out of the bathroom.

"Okay." I put a hand to my chest in an attempt to catch my breath. "Why?"

"Because heat rises." Julian took my hand and dragged me after him. "And it's getting really cold."

Struggling to keep up, I clung to his shoulder and followed him behind a mysterious door that took us up another set of steps. There was one window above the landing in the staircase which revealed the heavy, whipping snow that was coming down outside. Julian jerked me away from the glass, and before I knew it, we were on the second floor with its own bounteous supply of rooms. I quirked my brow at the odd layout of this place, considering there were two hidden staircases and possibly a third.

Once we reached the top of the steps, Julian

led me through the first door across the hall. As with the bottom floor, there were many rooms I had yet to see. Rooms that I might never see. But I had grown accustomed to not asking questions. So when he tugged at my hand and pulled me into the bedroom, I let him.

Chapter 9

Julian drew the curtains back with the jerk of his arms, while I lingered in the doorway and watched the room bathed in moonlight. For an elusive moment, he put his hand on the wall and gazed out. Just what he was searching for out in the shadows of the forest, I would never know.

"We'll need plenty of firewood," he said, turning back on his heel. "Especially tonight."

"Okay." I hugged my body and shivered, warming the bare skin of my arms with either palm.

"Why did you wash your hair?" he criticized. "You'll be freezing."

I glanced up at him in displeasure and shot daggers at those pretty blue irises.

Sensing his fault, Julian took his jacket off and draped it over my shoulders. "Stay here," he whispered. His breath ghosted against the side of my neck, tingling and prickling every fiber of my being.

Before I could acknowledge his command, Julian was gone. So I ambled over towards the window and slipped my arms through the sleeves of his jacket. The fabric smelled like him, and I couldn't help drowning in the scent. It was all musk and pine, the way you would imagine a lumber jack to smell. But I snapped out of it and brushed the thought away before any danger could come of it. Who was Julian anyway? So far, he was nothing more than a mystery to me.

With a deep sigh, I leaned against the curtains and stared through the glass. Sheets of snow came tumbling down with violent force, kicking and stirring up everything below. As I peered through the pane, a sphere of light danced through the trees in the distance, fading in and out.

I pressed my palm to the glass with a furrowed brow. Had I lost my mind?

"What do you see?"

Gasping, I turned around to find Julian with his arms full of wooden logs for the fire. "You scared me."

"You didn't answer my question." He dropped the stack of wood into the fireplace with ease then lit a match just as effortlessly. When he rose from his crouched position and came towards me, I shuddered from the inside out.

Flipping my head back to the window, I searched what lay on the other side of the glass and pointed. "I thought I saw..." The beam of light had disappeared, as I began to wonder if it had ever been there at all.

"What?" Julian hissed, irritated with having to repeat himself. "What did you see?"

"I don't know!" I barked. When I turned my face towards him, we were mere inches apart. My chest rose and fell with every breath, and I could smell his manly aroma. It was more subtle and muted on his jacket. But standing before me, this was the real thing.

Julian pursed his lips with a complacent smile. "It's been a long day," he said. "Let's go to bed."

"What?" I snatched my hand from his hold. "I'm not going to bed with you!"

Julian lowered his voice and gazed into my eyes. "I didn't mean like that."

"Oh." I watched him take a pair of long strides and then close the bedroom door.

"To keep the heat in," he explained, recognizing the weary look on my face.

I swallowed thickly as wooden logs crackled in the fireplace, pulling my attention to the flames. Unsure of my position in the room, I sat down on the edge of the bed and pushed my palms into the mattress. I wore my vulnerability like a beautiful cloak, on display for all to see. Surely, Julian noticed it.

When I felt his eyes on me, I looked up with a crinkle between my brows. Julian picked at the hem of his shirt in a teasing gesture before dragging the fabric up his lean torso. When the garment went over his head, Julian tossed it on the floor and I felt all of the blood come rushing to my cheeks.

"What are you doing?" I demanded, inching back farther on the mattress. It squeaked at the added pressure, and I nearly jumped from feeling so out of my comfort zone.

"Getting ready for bed," he answered, fluttering those dark lashes up at me.

I licked my lips when my mouth turned dry, struggling for words or air, anything to keep me from losing my nerve. Julian held some kind of power over me, an ability to make me feel lightheaded and weak in the knees. Even now, lounging on the bed, I felt sure I was practically moments away from falling off.

Julian popped the button open on his pants and slid the zipper down, while I turned my head to maintain some sense of modesty. His pants must have hit the floor, because I heard the distant clink of his belt against the ground. Then there were footsteps, and his rough hand found mine.

"Are you ready?"

My eyes darted up to meet his, while I contemplated his possible meaning. "Ready for what?"

"To go to bed," he replied, caressing the back of my hand with his thumb. "To sleep."

"Julian, I—"

"We need the body heat," he interrupted.

"And it's not like you haven't let me hold you before."

My eyes scanned his figure from head to toe, eventually returning to those glittering blue gems of his. Julian had sapphires for eyes—that is the only way I have of explaining their elusive, liquid appearance that makes any sense.

"All right," I acquiesced, letting him take my hand and guide me.

Julian turned the covers down and motioned for me to slip beneath them. I let go of his hand and crawled over to the left side, lying down on the firm mattress. The one downstairs felt soft and springy, akin to the consistency of a cheap pull-out couch. But this bed was warm and inviting, like a steaming hot bath after a month long trek through the cold and snow and rain. It felt like sunshine.

When the bed dipped down, I opened my eyes and shifted to accommodate Julian. He tossed two large blankets over the mattress that he had just retrieved from the closet. With the fire as our only true source of warmth and the moon as our only light, it almost felt romantic.

"Take your clothes off," Julian instructed.

"What?" I snapped my head up so fast that I'm surprised my neck didn't crack.

Stern as ever, Julian narrowed his eyes at me. "I said take them off."

My eyes widened at the implication. Was this the cost of my safety? Julian had vowed to protect me, but I was beginning to wonder at the price.

Was he expecting the use of my body at his leisure in return?

"No," I boldly declared, my chin held high.

Disliking my answer, Julian grabbed my elbow and shucked the jacket off that he had lent me. When it fell to the floor, I knew what was coming next, and I panicked. Julian slipped his fingers beneath the green top covering my torso and hitched it up my body.

"Julian, stop!" I cried, bucking and kicking. "STOP!"

But he pulled the shirt over my head and threw it across the room to join the jacket on the floor. His eyes dropped to my jeans as he slipped his fingers in the waistband and unfastened the button above the zipper. When tears broke loose, I pushed against his bare chest and cried out. But Julian was much too strong, covering me with the weight of his body and pinning my arms above my head.

"If you would just calm down, it will only take a minute," he assured me.

"NO!" I screamed, wailing in panic and terror. I could taste my tears at this point, and they were salty.

"Anna, stop it," he scolded. The back of my head dug into the pillow as I turned my face and looked away. His long, calloused fingers smoothed against my thighs while he peeled the jeans away.

I was left lying there in a pair of underwear and my bra. Hopefully, it would all be over soon.

Julian dropped my jeans to the floor and then hovered above me, his breath against my skin. As I lay there, waiting to be taken, all I could think about were my mother and father. I had written them an email telling them that everything was all right, that I was being cared for, kept safe by an angel.

But Julian was no angel, and everything wasn't all right.

I was in hell.

Warm blankets covered my nearly naked figure, as Julian draped his arm over my stomach. I tensed at his touch and clung to the mattress, dragging my nails across the fitted sheet. This was it.

"Anna. What are you doing?"

Slow and steady, I peeled my eyes open to find Julian propped up on his elbow. He lay beside me on the mattress with anything but malicious intent etched across the planes of his face. I was confused.

"Is that it?" I sat up and pulled the bed sheet up to my neck.

Julian tossed his hand in the air and looked around the room. "Is what it?"

"You're not going to rape me?" I asked, still shaking from the likelihood of it.

"*Rape* you?" he echoed. "Why would I rape you?"

He held my gaze in the palm of his hand, those blue eyes the purest shade of innocence.

"Because..." I opened my mouth and drifted away, at a loss for words.

"If you don't take your clothes off, then we can't keep each other warm," he preached. "Remember the blizzard?" He pointed to the window and then looked at me like I had lost my mind. Maybe I had.

"Well then, why didn't you just say that?" I growled, angry at his lack of clarity.

"Because you have a funny way of not listening to things."

I hung my head and threaded my fingers through my hair. It had been a long day. I wanted to cry.

"God, Anna. Don't you get it?" He shook his head in frustration. "The last thing I want to do is hurt you."

As reality set in, I looked back over my shoulder at him, at the pained expression on his face. To be honest, Julian had never laid a hand on me, not in a sense that indicated abuse or violence. In fact, I was the one who had slapped him across the face.

But how could he expect me to fully let my guard down 24/7? One moment he was comfort and warmth. The next he was cold as ice. All the while, he was the one man, the only man to save me from those monsters, even if he had been one of them. Maybe he still was. Maybe that was my greatest fear. Regardless, Julian had made a choice to spare me. Even though that decision could possibly cost him his life. All so I wouldn't end up like Bridgette. Drifting at the bottom of a lake.

"Anna." Julian stroked the side of my arm, as I searched his eyes with the touch.

There was something so wholesome in the way he looked at me. It made me wonder how many nights he had been watching me when I didn't know it. He said two months was all the time he had been stalking, but I wondered if it had been longer.

"Trust me," he begged, gazing up at me sweetly. "Please."

Warm air passed through my parted lips, while I touched my hand to his cheek. Julian caressed my forearm and held on to my wrist, showing affection the way a lover would. I wondered what I had done to earn it. When he stared into my eyes like I was the center of his universe, I knew why I had told my parents an angel had found me. Because he looked like one.

"Okay," I breathed, struggling on the inside. "I don't know you. But okay."

Relaxing with relief, Julian pulled me into his arms and lay back on the bed. I put my head on his chest and tensed when his fingertips danced across my naked back. He sensed my unease and tilted my chin up in the palm of his hand. "I don't want you to be cold," he confessed. "Ever."

As my blood cooled, I tucked my head beneath his chin and wrapped my arms around him. Julian tucked us both in under the blankets, as if we were cocooned together. He was warm, and I found his manly scent to be just as enticing as the heat of his body. Julian kissed my forehead and ran his fingers through my hair, while I wondered at these hidden moments of affection. Always just before I drifted off.

I wondered if there was a place inside Julian that knew how to do more than kill.

I wondered if there was a place inside him that could feel.

I wondered if there was a place inside him that could love.

* * *

I stirred awake in the middle of the night, wrapped in Julian's embrace. Desperate to relieve myself, I slipped out of his hold and peeled his arm from my back. Julian jerked in his sleep, but his eyes remained closed. I laid his arm out by his side and softly slipped out of the bed, careful not to wake him.

As I tiptoed across the floor, the freezing chill nearly took my breath away. With the fire dying down, I hurried into my clothes and left the bedroom, anxious to return to Julian's warm arms.

Out in the dark hallway, I tried not to think about a scene from a horror movie. Bridgette and I had gone to the theatre just a couple months ago for Halloween, her zeal for the latest slasher flick dragging us there. While scary movies had never been my favorite, Bridgette was good at persuasion. So we saw the film, and I couldn't sleep for the next two nights. Hardly the best image to conjure up in my mind now.

Once I found the bathroom, I snuck past the door and jerked my pants down, sighing in relief on the toilet. There was a roll of toilet paper attached to the wall, which I had never been more thankful for. Just as I wiped, something creaked down the hall. Something that made the hairs stand up on the back of my neck.

My heart pounded loudly in my chest. So loud that I could feel it in my ears and throat.

I had probably just freaked myself out after remembering a montage of horror films in my mind. All that was left to do was wash my hands and get back in that warm bed with Julian. So I pulled my pants up and turned the faucet on quietly enough for a thin stream to drizzle out. As I rinsed the soap off, that haunting creak sounded down the hall. Only this time, it was louder.

Truly terrified now, I shut the water off and dried my hands on the front of my shirt. Then I shut my eyes and leaned against the wall, taking one slow breath at a time. If I pushed against the door, surely it would make a sound as I slipped out. But I could either stand here all night or make a move.

So I lowered my lashes and opened the door just enough to squeeze into the hall. Somehow, I had managed to accomplish the task in relative silence. Spotting the door to the bedroom, I padded down the dark corridor and hurried my way to Julian. But then I saw something flicker out of the corner of my eye.

There was a man on the staircase.

And he was waiting for me.

Chapter 10

I tried to scream at first. But no words came out. It was like I didn't have a voice.

The man was huge, likely twice the size of Julian. He sported a buzz cut, military style, like someone had peeled everything but the hide off his scalp. As I stood there paralyzed, he looked like one massive, bulging muscle, entirely capable of crushing a girl like me.

Tired of waiting, he charged up the staircase and grabbed me before I had the chance to run. My back hit the floor with a painful thwack, as he dragged my writhing body down the wooden steps. His large hands wrapped around the ends of my hair, pulling at them like my locks were a ponytail designed for steering. And that was how he brought me to the bottom floor, by the head of my hair.

"Ju—Ju—JULIAN!" I screamed, an agonizing

sound that ripped my ears in half.

The stranger kicked my legs once I landed on solid ground and then picked my body up in his arms only to toss me against the wall. I hit my head and felt blood pooling at the edge of my lip. But my attacker had no mercy, reaching around to retrieve an object from his back pocket.

"JULIAN!" I cried out, shaking like a leaf.

My tormentor dangled a steel chain over my head with an unforgiving glower.

"JULIANNN!" That was the last semblance of a word I got out before he wrapped the chain around my neck and squeezed. Cruel and ruthless, the monster clamped his hands around the cold metal links over my throat and lifted my body off the ground. My feet kicked against the wall behind me while he held me up against it, constricting every last ounce of breath like a deadly snake.

All of the blood rushed to my head, and my vision began to blur. I scratched his face with my nails and flailed my legs about, but there was no fighting his brute force and strength. It was hopeless.

Just as air began to slip away for good, Julian cracked him in the skull with a baseball bat. The man loosened his hands from my throat and collapsed, his body hitting the floor with a reverberating boom. But when he let go, I nearly turned my ankle as my body came crashing down.

Julian caught me and uncoiled the chain from my neck, while I coughed and gagged, unable to reckon with the burning. He cradled my head in his lap, his warm palm to my cheek, soothing my agony. But then the beast on the ground stirred awake, and I saw him before Julian did.

My eyes widened in terror, and since I could hardly speak, that was the only warning Julian received. When the man reached for the chain, Julian slid his stomach across the floor and grabbed the bat. Then he unleashed a side of him that I never should have seen, that no one should ever see, but that I saw.

Julian swung the bat and hit him in the head like it was a baseball. Blood splattered against the white walls, violent and gory. I tried to turn my head away, but lacked the strength to keep from looking.

Julian kicked the man in the chest and then cracked the bat against his face. I heard the sound of crushing bone and knew that the man must already be dead. But Julian had no intention of stopping anytime soon.

He tossed the bat aside and used his bare fists, pummeling my attacker until his face was one messy canvas of crimson blood and sagging flesh. When the man struggled for a final breath, Julian stood up and walked around him, dragging him all the way down the hall by his wrists. I leaned back on my elbow and stared into the distance, horrified by the sight of Julian lugging him through the door.

Traumatized and shaken, I wiggled around

until the wall supported my back. There was blood everywhere. All over the walls. All over the floor. When I looked down, I discovered that the sticky substance had seeped into my clothes. The green cotton of my shirt stained with red.

Someone screamed, a final cry of forgiveness. Trembling with fear, I staggered to my feet and limped my way down the corridor, failing to ignore the bloody mess we had made. A bright light rippled up in the sky, just to the left of the front door entrance. It appeared to dance from inside the house.

I leaned into the frame of the door and then stepped onto the front porch. Snow covered the land around us, as I recognized the likeness to a moat. That is, if the castle were surrounded by the aftermath of a blizzard rather than a flood.

Despite my pounding head, I stumbled down the steps and followed the yellow light. With so many inches of snow on the ground, everything looked different. A winter wonderland had formed overnight.

And then I saw him, standing over the dead man's body. Julian had soaked the man with lighter fluid and then set him on fire. It almost looked like a mirage—orange flames burning above the snow.

There was a trail of blood across the ground. A disturbing contrast of red on white.

Julian looked up and stared at me through the flames, his face and clothing covered in blood. In that moment, I respected and feared him. Part of me was forever indebted to Julian for saving my life. But there was a younger, more vulnerable side that saw the real monster hiding inside.

If he was capable of vengeful slaughter, what else had he done in his life? What else could he do?

It was the darkness within him that allowed Julian to save me. But that same darkness scared me. It made me shiver. It made me see him for the killer that he was.

Julian walked around the fire and took slow, careful steps towards me. As he came closer, I noticed a weeping gash above his eye and red marks on his skin. There was blood on the stubble above his lip that must have flown freely from his nose. Julian may have been hurt, but he was still alive.

"Are you all right?" he asked, his breath misting out like fog.

I stared into his eyes and barely had the strength to nod.

Julian traced my cheekbone with the pad of his thumb, and I flinched. His fingertips rested beneath my chin, as hurt raced across those glittering blue irises, so dark in the night. When he dropped his hand from my face and pulled away, I went weak in the knees and stumbled into his body.

Tears broke loose like a dam waiting to overflow, and soon I was shaking all over again.

Julian held me against his strong, muscular frame and circled his hand over my back. I cried into his chest and would have fallen, had he not kept me securely held within his embrace.

"Shh..." he gently whispered, petting my hair with delicate strokes.

I clung to Julian and peered over his shoulder at the burning body in the snow. But I didn't have to watch for long, because Julian draped his arm across the small of my back and led me into the house. I waited downstairs while he searched every room on every floor, ensuring all the doors and windows were locked. When he found me in the hallway, I was curled up in a ball rocking back and forth.

Without a word, Julian knelt down and lifted me in his arms. I put my hands around his neck and burrowed my face in his shirt, still crying over all that had happened. Julian carried me up the staircase and into the bathroom, setting my feeble body down by the sink.

I pressed the heel of my palm into the countertop as he lit a few candles, the snowstorm raging on in the night. Regardless of his own injuries, Julian cast his troubles aside and tended to mine. I sat still and watched him wet a washcloth beneath the faucet. I had never seen him look so calm and focused.

"Julian," I croaked, my voice hoarse and scratchy from the strangler's attack.

"Don't talk." He touched my hand and looked

over me. "I know it hurts."

Hanging my head, I obeyed and closed my eyes. Julian lifted my chin with his finger and wiped the blood off my face. There was a bruise near my temple that was particularly tender, but Julian made sure to be gentle. Various scrapes and stings rattled my insides, yet I fought against the pain.

My face was throbbing, and even the roots of my hair hurt. But nothing compared to the discomfort in my throat. It felt like someone had crushed the structure of it, and now that part of my body was attempting to regain its natural shape.

When Julian set the cloth aside, I drew in a breath of air and opened my eyes. He brushed my long blond hair back over my shoulders and placed his fingers on my neck. His hands were cold as he felt of the damage that had been done, but I held on to the counter to keep myself from shivering.

Once he was finished inspecting the bruises on my neck, Julian pulled my shirt over my head and observed the casualties to my upper body. He scrubbed away the blood that had seeped through the fabric and then re-bandaged the injury on my lower stomach, just above my left hip.

"Put your arms around me," Julian requested, lifting me off the counter momentarily. He slipped my pants down just enough to get them around my thighs, while I clung to his shoulders for support.

Once he took my jeans off for me, I was left

with my legs dangling over the counter in nothing more than my bra and underwear. Julian ducked out of the room for a moment that lasted too long. But when he returned, there was a comfy sweater and thick pair of sweatpants waiting for me in his arms.

Julian helped me into the new clothes, while I rose up and held on to his shoulders, slowly stepping into the pants. He even took the time to cover my feet with a warm pair of wool socks. When he stood up with his hands around my waist, I looked at him with gratitude in my eyes.

"I trust you now," I whispered, even though it hurt. "I really mean it this time."

Julian touched my hair as his lower lip twitched. "Save your voice."

In that one beautiful moment, I wanted to do and say so many things. But I couldn't.

"You should lie down," he suggested. "Let me help you to bed."

"No," I mouthed, shaking my head. "You're hurt. I want to help."

Julian lowered his lashes in disbelief. "Okay."

I tried to hoist myself back onto the counter but lacked the strength. So Julian picked me up in his arms and set me down by the sink again. Then his eyes locked with mine as he lifted his shirt over his head.

My eyes flitted over his bare, exposed torso in a series of lengthy looks. Julian was ripped by every definition of the word, his pecs hard and firm, his six pack abs chiseled to perfection, not to mention the muscles and veins embellishing either of his arms. When I looked up to meet his gaze, my cheeks flushed red with heat and desire. Julian was watching me.

Reverting my eyes to his torso, I grabbed a new washcloth and ran water over it in the sink. Julian set his hands on the counter along either side of my hips, while I wrung the cloth out to keep it from feeling soaked. Swallowing, I leaned forward and wiped the blood from his shoulders. Purplish bruises were starting to form along his arms and torso. But when I spotted the nasty scar along his right set of ribs, those bruises didn't hold a candle to the anguish he must have suffered in the past.

"It's okay," Julian admitted, interpreting my thoughts. "It happened a long time ago."

I parted my lips to speak, but then thought twice about it. Instead, I brought the washcloth to the side of Julian's mouth to collect the blood that had gathered there. He winced the moment it touched his lip and grabbed ahold of my wrist. "I'm sorry," I whispered, concerned that I might have caused him pain.

"I'm fine," he assured me, releasing my wrist so I could continue.

After washing the blood from his face, I dipped the cloth in cool water and pressed it to the cut above his eye. Julian stared at me with an intensity that burned right through my skin. I felt incredibly exposed, as if he were looking at my naked soul, no need to cloak my sins or fears, no need to hide.

Julian took the washcloth from my hand and dropped it in the sink. Then he gazed at the sweater he had given me and ran his palm over the fabric around my arm. I lowered my eyes for a split second, just enough time for him to move closer and stand between my legs.

When I looked up, his face was an inch from mine, his warm breath like a gentle caress over my mouth. If I lifted my chin ever so slightly, our lips would touch. Julian slipped his hands around my waist as I closed my eyes, remembering the way he had made me feel the first night I saw him at the club.

"We should be fine for a while," he said. "Snowed in. No one will find us. For now."

I exhaled and he took a step back, walking out of the room with his shirt in his hands.

* * *

After bundling beneath the covers, I watched Julian tend to the wooden logs in the fire. He crouched down and studied the flames for what felt like the longest time. When he turned back, I closed my eyes and pretended to be asleep. Sometimes, Julian made me feel like a child who might be due for a proper spanking. This felt like one of those times.

I listened to his footsteps and then opened my eyes to find him standing in front of the window.

He crossed his arms over his chest and stared out at the snowstorm howling in the night. In that moment, I would have given anything to know what he was thinking.

When he thought I was asleep, Julian slipped out of the bedroom and disappeared downstairs. After what had happened tonight, I couldn't believe he would leave me alone, unprotected. Equal parts curious and betrayed, I crawled out of bed and followed the path he had taken down the staircase.

Recent memory shuddered through me once I stepped into the hall. He had been waiting for me on the stairs. He had been waiting to kill me.

Casting my anxiety aside, I hurried down the steps as quietly as I could and passed through the door once I reached the bottom. At the sound of glasses clinking, I picked up the pace and walked into the room we had previously occupied. There he stood in the kitchen with a bottle of whiskey in his hand.

Julian tilted his head back and slammed another shot glass, sucking the alcohol down as fast as he could. I saw his hand shake with the force of his consumption. It was plain to see that Julian had demons he had yet to share.

"You shouldn't drink that stuff," I said, even though my voice was hoarse. "It'll kill you."

Julian froze the moment he heard me speak. He set the tumbler down and countered, "So will a lot of things."

"Julian." I took a step towards him as he wiped his mouth with his shirtsleeve and turned around.

"What do you want?" he barked, towering over me. "You shouldn't be in here."

I clenched my jaw and glowered, bold enough to hold my own. Spotting the bottle of whiskey on the counter, I set my sights on the target and moved. But Julian stepped to the left and blocked me.

"Don't," he demanded, daring me to test him.

While the bottle hadn't been full, it certainly wasn't empty. But Julian had taken one drink too many. I could tell by the look in his eyes. He was buzzed. And he enjoyed it.

"Is that how you want to end up? Some wayward drunk on the side of the street?"

Julian gritted his teeth and balled his hands into fists at his sides.

I swayed towards him and breathed on his face. "There's more to life than that."

"Like you would know," he bitterly remarked.

"What's that supposed to mean?"

"I've seen you," Julian announced, backing me into the counter. "All alone in your dorm room when you think no one is watching."

With every step he took towards me, I took another back. He smelled sweet. Like alcohol.

"You call that living?" he scoffed. "Hiding out. Hiding behind your books."

"You have no idea what it's like to be me!" I shouted, jabbing my finger at him.

"Oh, yeah." Julian pressed his lips together and nodded. "I'm sure it's really tough being the President's daughter."

"*Ex*-President's daughter," I corrected, even surprising myself.

Julian glided an inch closer, and we were standing chest to chest. "You don't even know how to live your own life," he scowled, sizing me up like I was nothing special. "Don't tell me how to live mine!"

Steaming with frustration, I took his face in my hands and sealed my mouth over his. At first, Julian remained cold and distant, stubbornly set on his side of the argument. I felt sure he would resist me, but that only made me fight that much harder for his attention.

When he growled, I leaned up on the tips of my toes and raked my fingers through his hair. Once I broke through the first layer of steel around his heart, Julian allowed the heat of my lengthy kiss to fully sink in. His hands settled along the small of my back, but I refused to submit, crushing his lips to mine.

Julian groaned as I tugged at the collar of his shirt, jerking him down to my level. His hands slid beneath my thighs as he lifted me onto the counter behind us, and molded his mouth to mine. I curled my arms around him and cherished every touch, over the moon that—whatever it was between us—he felt it too.

His hands slipped beneath the hem of my

shirt, his fingers dancing across my sensitive skin. I grabbed ahold of his shoulders and circled my legs around his waist to keep from falling off. My skin was hot and pulsing, the blood thrumming loudly in my veins. I had waited so long. Would it finally happen like this? Would I mind?

Julian teased me with his playful touches and planted kisses along my jawline. I dug my nails into his back and gasped, letting my eyes slide shut with gentle pleasure. I quivered when the stubble of his beard touched my face, but it felt so good. He felt so good. All around me. Everywhere.

When he buried his nose in my hair and inhaled, I captured his chin and covered his mouth with a delicate kiss. Julian hugged me close and pushed the full weight of his body into mine, trailing sumptuous kisses down my neck. Despite the bruises from tonight's earlier attack, his lips pressed against those places, and it felt nice.

"Julian," I whimpered, turning my neck into his face so his kisses would continue.

But just like that, Julian stopped. He lifted his head and uncoiled my legs from his waist, stepping back from me. I opened my eyes and stared, especially when he lengthened the space between us.

He caught his breath and ran his hand over his face. "Don't ever do that again," he said.

With the turn of his heel, Julian bolted out of the room and vanished from sight. I put my hands on the countertop and leapt down, feeling hurt and rejected. What had I done wrong?

Thankfully, the bottle of whiskey was still in the kitchen. But that was the least of my worries now.

I ran my fingers through my hair and stared at the floor. Why was he so repulsed by me? Was I a bad kisser? Was I not experienced enough? In truth, I guess I really didn't know what I was doing. But it had been hard to find dates who were comfortable with secret service men coming along.

Confused and flustered, I turned in a circle and looked out the door he had just walked through. That was the most passionate kiss I had ever shared with anyone. But now I was stuck back in his game of hot and cold.

Maybe I had let my imagination get away with me. But sometimes, I wondered if Julian actually cared about me. After all, if he was willing to risk his life and career, then didn't he at least *like* me?

Why else would he put himself through the trouble? What had he seen in me that made him want to go straight? Become a white knight after living so many years in the dark?

I would never know.

Chapter 11

For the next three days, Julian all but ignored me. He prepared my meals, guarded the front door, left blankets on the bed to make sure I was warm. But he never spoke another word about what had happened in the kitchen, what had happened earlier that night, what had happened to the body.

While living with Julian, I had learned not to ask questions. Sure, I had enough to fill a library full of encyclopedias. But they were all pointless if he had no intention of providing answers to them. So I kept to myself, stayed quiet, out of his way. I thought we might go on living under one roof in silence forever. Until the following night.

Due to the severity of the blizzard, we had been snowed in for days. But I could see the inherit protection in a situation such as this. If we had no way out, then they had no way in.

Regardless, my safety had been a pressing concern ever since the night I almost lost my life. The threat merely worsened the second time around, when that monster nearly strangled me to death with a chain. I could still feel the links digging into my neck, like cold steel designed for breaking bones.

I lay awake and stared at the ceiling, flinching from every little noise the house made. Since it was freezing outside, I approved of the second story bedroom equipped with a warm fireplace. But without Julian, I felt lost and afraid. He had been the one to save me before. If he hadn't come downstairs in time...

I didn't want to finish that sentence.

So I kicked the covers back and hopped down off the bed. Dancing red flames flickered in the fireplace, but they only made me feel more jumpy. In an oversized t-shirt that felt more like a dress, I walked into the hallway and stopped to use the bathroom.

Since my bladder was full, I didn't bother to shut the door. Julian would be downstairs all night, and I was about to dart back into the bedroom anyway. After relieving myself, I extended my hand for a roll of toilet paper. And that is when I heard it. That creaking sound. The same creaking sound as before.

My heart thumped loudly in my chest. I wiped and pulled my underwear up, wishing I had worn sweatpants over them. With my bare legs exposed,

I felt all the more vulnerable.

Taking a deep breath, I crept into the hallway and peeked around the corner. There was a man slowly making his way up the staircase. A man that looked nothing like Julian.

With stringy blond hair and a strong jawline, I couldn't help but notice that I had seen him somewhere before. Then he looked up and ascended the second set of steps. I spotted the tattoos spiraling around his arms, and it hit me like a bolt of lightning.

The bartender was alive.

In a flash, he reached the top of the steps and saw me. I tried to run, tried to call for help, tried to hide. But my legs felt rubbery, not quite the consistency of JELL-O. No matter how I moved, my feet wouldn't take me anywhere.

"JULIAN!" I cried out, praying he was sober enough to hear me.

But the bartender was fast. In a series of slick, cat-like moves, he grabbed my hair and slammed me up against the wall. When my ears began to ring, the only color I could see was blood.

"AH!" I yelped in pain when he kicked my ribs. "JULIAN!"

Just as I caught my breath on the floor, thinking he had given me a break, the bartender clamped his hand around my already tender throat and raised me in the air. My feet kicked the wall while he wrapped a rope around my neck. But then the rope turned into a snake, and I screamed.

"NO!" I wailed in terror, flailing against the beast. "JULIAN! PLEASE! HELP!"

Rough hands squeezed my shoulders. "Anna! Stop! Open your eyes. Open your eyes!"

I listened to the voice and peeled my eyelids back. Bits of ash crackled in the distance, as I recognized the fireplace, as well as the room surrounding me. Julian pressed the back of his hand to my forehead, and I turned to look at him. I was coated in a sleek sheen of sweat, but he didn't seem to mind.

"What happened?" I rasped, touching my hand to my neck to make sure the snake was gone.

"You were dreaming," he noted, nonchalant as ever. "How long have you been having nightmares?"

I would have loved to fall into his arms and let him console me. But things weren't like that between us anymore.

"I don't know." I ripped the sheets back and paced the floor around the bed.

"What do you mean you don't know?" he inquired. "You've either been having them or you haven't."

"Well, maybe if you still slept in here I wouldn't be having that problem!" I lashed out, smoldering with fury. Then I crossed my arms over my chest and faced the fire in an attempt to calm down.

Julian got off the bed and sighed. I felt sure he was headed for the door.

"We never talked about it," I declared, casting my eyes across the flames.

He lingered between me and the doorway, exhaling aloud. "About what?"

"The email," I replied. "It must have gone through."

Julian didn't say anything, so I had my answer.

"He knew where we were, because I led him straight to us," I realized, taking full responsibility.

"Anna," Julian began, but I cut him off before he could make anything of it.

"No." I slowly spun around to face him. "You were right. And what if there are others?"

"Anna," he scolded.

"They know where we are. They know how to find us." I stormed over to the window and gazed through the glass, remembering the sphere of light I had seen hours before the attack. "They want me dead."

The only response from Julian was the sound of his footsteps as he drew near.

"And I will be dead," I accepted, hearing my voice crack. "Just like Bridgette."

Tears broke loose and racked my body to the core. I shook with fear and placed my hand over my mouth, wanting to fall to pieces on the floor. *Her body was found at the bottom of a lake.*

As I stumbled backwards, Julian caught me in time for both of us to collapse on the floor. I sat between his legs and wept, while he pulled my back into his chest and put his chin on my shoulder. "Shh..." he whispered. "I won't let anyone hurt you. Not ever again." He nuzzled my neck. "I promise."

"What are you doing?" I turned around to face him and scooted back.

"Anna, I—"

"Stop messing with my head," I begged, sitting up against the wall by the window.

His eyes stayed on me, taking in every raw emotion that flitted across my face.

"You've got me so confused!" I buried my fingers in my hair and pulled. "First, you try to kill me. Then you think you're some kind of hero just because you let me go. But you lock me in this house in the middle of nowhere and won't let me contact my family. I can't tell if you rescued me, or if I've been kidnapped! You hold me close and then push me away," I continued, ranting on and on. "From one minute to the next, you're just as likely to love me as to hate me. And—"

Julian leaned in and brushed his lips over mine, interrupting me with a soft, tender kiss. Pleasure flooded my veins like an avalanche, stinging and exciting every part of me. When I opened my eyes, he was on his knees before me, resting his hand over my hair.

"I don't hate you," he clarified, leaning in for a feather light kiss. "Trust me."

I gazed up at him in bewilderment and stared. There was a coy smirk playing at the corner of his lips, like some inside joke that I knew nothing about. But that was the thing about Julian. He was a mystery.

"Why don't I sleep in here with you tonight?" he suggested. "Do you mind?"

Apart from all the hell he had put me through, I couldn't deny that whatever semblance of a life I had was better with him in it. Julian had saved my life. Twice now. So naturally, he made me feel safe.

"No," I breathed, still buzzing from his last kiss. "Not at all."

Julian smiled, and it was the most natural look I had ever seen on his face. When he extended his hand and helped me up, I wondered if he had a split personality. His mood swings were diagnosable.

Once he led me to bed and pulled the covers back, I slipped beneath them. He climbed in after me and turned my body so his chest aligned with my back. Before I knew it, his arm was curled around my stomach, and I could feel the warmth of his breath in my ear.

"Julian?" I hissed, knowing he was still awake in the night.

"Yes," he crooned, a subtle shade of amusement to his voice.

"What made you want to do this?" I wondered. Curiosity had been eating at me for days.

"Do what?" He sounded so comfortable here with me, as if our nights spent snuggling beneath the blankets in desperate need of body heat were a ritual that was all too familiar.

"Kill for a living," I bluntly stated.

"My father did it," he answered. "And his father before him."

"So it's a family business?" I guessed.

He thought about it and then finally decided, "You could say that."

"Doesn't it ever get to you?" I closed my eyes with my head on my pillow.

"What?" His palm ghosted across the sliver of skin exposed beneath the hem of my shirt.

"Taking lives," I murmured, sleepy even though I was interested. "Killing people."

"No," he clipped, and I knew that was a lie.

"You've killed men?"

"Yes."

I waited a beat and added, "Women?"

"Yes."

I almost didn't want to ask, but I had reached the point of no return and knew that I had to. "Children?"

His long eyelashes fluttered against the side of my neck before he uttered, "Yes."

I mashed my lips together and shuddered, afraid that he could sense my reaction.

"How many people have you killed?"

Julian blew hot air through his nostrils in frustration. "Do we have to talk about this now?"

"We're sharing a bed together," I argued. "I'd like to know. For my own peace of mind."

Julian sat up and removed his arm from my waist. Fearing his response, I rolled onto my other side and looked over at him from my pillow. He rubbed his palms together and faced me, fidgeting nervously.

"How many?" I probed, refusing to back down. I was digging my heels in on this one.

"After the last one." He pointed over his shoulder, referring to the monster with the chain who had nearly strangled me. "A little over five hundred."

My eyes widened in terror, as he studied the look of horror on my face.

"Five hundred," I repeated. "You've killed over five hundred people?"

He gave the slightest nod and confirmed, "Yes."

After staring at him for a full five seconds, I pressed my palms into the mattress and sat up. His Adam's apple bobbed as he swallowed, catching every emotion that flickered across my face. I leaned my back against the headboard and tucked my hands beneath my arms, letting the number sink in.

"How long have you been doing this?" I had to know.

Julian looked up at the ceiling and toyed with his fingers over the blanket. When his eyes shifted to the wall behind me, I wondered if he had ever had this conversation with anyone before. Had any other woman ever cared to ask?

"Since I was eighteen," he said. "They recruited me out of high school."

"Who did?" I had a pillow sandwiched between my arms and chest. All I could do was squeeze the mesh, even though I had no recollection of putting it there. I must have done it subconsciously. An involuntary gesture spawned from fear.

Julian gazed over me like a little boy, totally vulnerable and exposed.

Since he refused to answer the question, I moved on to the next. Julian hunched over on the bed with his knees tucked into his chest. There was a gaping distance between us, but maybe there should have been.

"Why now?" I muttered. "Why me?"

Julian furrowed his brow as his lips turned down. "What do you mean?"

"You spend your life as an assassin and suddenly you want out? Why?" I shook my head from side to side while blood pulsed loudly in my ears. I wanted an answer. "What changed?"

Julian looked deep into my eyes, and I swear he could see my soul. "You."

I stopped breathing. I stopped thinking. There was nothing in the room but me and him.

"What?" I hardly got the question out, but knew that he could hear me.

"You," he repeated, pinning me to the mattress with that one word.

I opened my mouth then closed it again. I

didn't know what to say.

"You changed everything."

I moistened my lips and swallowed. "Why me?"

"Because you're different," he murmured. "You're not like everyone else."

"So you just end your career and take me with you?" I accused. "Was that your plan?"

Julian leaned forward to prove me wrong, but I wouldn't give him the chance.

"Are we going to stay out here forever? Hiding from the world?"

"Anna, let me explain."

"Is that why you took me? To keep you company? So you wouldn't be alone?"

I was drilling him with questions, but I didn't care.

"Aren't you leaving out the part where I saved your life?" he countered, smoldering.

Heat spread through me like wildfire, and I had no idea how to reckon with the sensation. So I succumbed to my emotions and leapt out of the bed. "I don't—" I grabbed my pillow and threw it at his head, but Julian blocked the hit. "Belong to you!" I snatched his pillow up next, and he ducked before it even flew out of my hand. Then he grabbed my arm and pinned me on the mattress beneath him.

I looked up at him from the flat of my back and gasped for air.

"Now." Julian hovered above me and held my

arms over my head. "Let's not forget who's in charge here, Anna." He lowered his face to mine, as I watched his pupils dilate in a sea of blue. "You'll stay in this house as long as I like. And you won't leave until I say so. Is that clear?"

I tried to move my arms, but he held me down. "Yes," I snarled.

Noticing the hateful gleam in my eye, Julian said, "Is there anything else you would like to add?"

"Yes," I hissed.

Julian narrowed his eyes with intrigue, waiting for me to elaborate.

"I lied before," I confessed, glowering up at him. "You do scare me."

Julian lowered his gaze and regarded me quietly. Then he eased back on the mattress and released my arms. We watched each other for more than a minute, wondering who would make the next move.

Eventually, I lay down on his side of the bed and cried.

And that's when Julian got up and left.

Chapter 12

I slept for hours the next day, lacking the energy to drag myself out of bed. The sun never poured in through the window, blocked behind an overactive gathering of murky clouds. It snowed every day now, burying us deeper and deeper in inches of white powder.

There was a knock at the door, but I didn't even blink. The last thing I wanted to do was move.

I turned my head but didn't look back. After our last encounter, Julian had made me feel like a caged animal. While part of me believed he was keeping me here for my own protection—especially after I was nearly strangled to death—I wondered at the extent of his concern. Could he have taken me back earlier? Did he ever plan to? I didn't know. Either way, if I ever returned to my old life one day, would I be able to face it? After everything that had happened, how could I go back? Nothing would ever be the same.

Julian opened the door and came inside, his footsteps lingering at the foot of the bed. "Anna."

I stared at the wall and kept quiet, refusing to move.

"I made dinner," he announced.

I clung to the sheet in my hand and shut my eyes. Julian always made dinner. How was this different than any other night?

"Are you going to come downstairs?" he asked.

"Why?" I huffed, planting my hand firmly on the mattress.

"Aren't you hungry?"

I felt his searing gaze through my back.

"You've been in this room all day."

When I failed to answer him, Julian sat down on the edge of the mattress and touched my back. I should have flinched. I should have groaned. But all I did was sigh.

"Have dinner with me," he softly murmured.

"Do I have a choice?" I bitterly remarked.

"Yes." His hand left my back, and I sat up on the bed to face him. "You always have a choice."

"Liar," I accused, throwing the covers back at him as I dropped my feet to the floor.

"I'm not lying." Julian reached out to grab my arm, but the moment his fingers grazed my skin, I pulled away.

"Then take me home." I put my hands on my hips. "Get me out of here."

"It's not safe."

"Oh, and it's safe here?" I countered, tossing my hands in the air. "How many times are you going to use that line? I almost died the other night!"

"But you didn't." Julian stepped towards me and grabbed my arms. "I kept you safe. I'll always keep you safe."

Withdrawing from his grasp, I strode towards the window and looked out at the snow. "I want to know that I won't always be here."

"You won't." Julian came up behind me, and though he could have reached out to touch my shoulder, he didn't.

I crossed my arms over my chest and fumed.

"As soon as it's safe again, I'll take you back. I'll take you home." He hesitated, perhaps hoping I might have something to add. "I promise."

I spun around, and there was hardly an inch of space between us. "I don't like being kept in the dark, Julian."

"I know," he murmured.

"No, you don't!" I snapped back. My chest rose and fell, but he failed to move an inch. I could feel his breath on my lips. "You don't know me."

I shoved past him in pursuit of the bed, but Julian tugged at my elbow and pulled me back. "I know more than you think," he said.

Breathing hard, I stared into his deep blue eyes and glared. "Well, isn't that great?" I scanned him from head to toe. "You know everything, and I know nothing."

Julian took my face in his hands, so I tilted my head back and looked down my nose at him. "Have dinner with me, and I'll tell you whatever you want to know."

Searching his face, I inhaled and said, "Why?"

"Because maybe I don't want you to be in the dark anymore either."

I held my breath and swallowed, moistening my lips.

"Please," he begged, his long fingers in my hair.

"Fine." I gave in and pushed against his chest when he smiled.

But Julian ignored my aversion to him and took my hand, braiding his fingers through mine. He led me out of the room and down the staircase like a school boy dragging me to his playground. While I tensed my body and held on, Julian hauled me into the kitchen.

Once we crossed the threshold, Julian let go of me and lagged behind. Since the temperature was colder downstairs, I hugged my body and shivered. As he hung his jacket over my shoulders, I noticed a pair of candles on the table in the distance—the only light in the room.

I put my hands on my shoulders to keep the jacket from falling off, and Julian rested his hands over mine. With his breath on my neck, I turned around and let him hold the jacket for me, so I could fit my arms through the sleeves. When I glanced up at him, there was so much heat in his eyes that it took the chill away.

"Thank you," I whispered.

Despite the absurdity of it all, I did feel cherished. Especially when Julian pulled my chair out and then pushed it back into the table once I sat down. There was a plate of steaming spaghetti waiting for me on the table alongside a napkin and fork. Julian took a seat in front of an identical entrée and poured us each a glass of red wine. I looked out the window at the snow coming down and admired the fragile beauty of it all. We were in our very own winter wonderland.

"Why did you do this?" I asked after the first bite. Pasta was my favorite food, and I never realized how much I had craved and missed it until now.

"Not every night you spend with me has to be a terrible one," he said, stirring up a mix of emotions inside me. "I want you to remember at least one night with me that was good."

I furrowed my brow and looked down, twirling the tines of my fork through the noodles.

"So." Julian chewed at the meaty tomato sauce and then wiped his mouth. "What do you want to know?"

In many ways, it felt like we had already had this conversation. Surely, tonight would not be the first I had asked him lingering questions. While I couldn't say he hadn't answered them, I had a feeling that tonight would be the unguarded Julian, all of his walls down—maybe not for good—but down, even if it was only for a little while. I had to take advantage of this Julian while I could, mercurial as he was. I doubted that he would ever extend the courtesy to me again.

Gnawing on my lower lip, I toyed with the fork in my hand and appraised him. There was so much to ask, so much I wanted to know. "What were you like as a boy?" I wondered.

Julian took a sip of wine and then gave me his full attention. "Kind of nerdy, I guess," he muttered. "I liked science and math."

"You don't strike me as the nerdy type."

He narrowed his eyes at me with a snarky grin. "Yeah, well I guess I grew out of it."

"But you are smart," I noted.

"How do you figure that?" His elbows dug into the table as he leaned in closer.

"Well, you're an assassin, and you're not dead yet." I pushed the spaghetti around on my plate, avoiding his watchful blue eyes. "The fact that you've survived this long says something."

"Such as." He motioned his hand, enticing me to continue.

"Maybe you're too wise for your own good."

His blue eyes focused on nothing but mine, so much so that it almost scared me.

"I won't live to see thirty," he predicted.

"Julian," I scolded. "You shouldn't say things like that."

"It's true," he urged. "Both of my parents were gone before their twenty first birthday. I was raised by my uncle. He died when I was sixteen."

I slumped down in my chair and frowned, my shoulders sagging. "I'm sorry."

"Don't be." Julian shoveled a forkful of pasta into his mouth. "I'm used to being alone."

I thought to ask what had happened to them—his mother, his father, his uncle—how they had died. But by the look on Julian's face, that would be like tearing open old wounds. So I decided against it and took another bite.

"Why so quiet all of a sudden?" Julian kept his eyes on me. "You all out of questions?"

"I think we've covered enough for one night." The perplexed look on his face gave me a sense of purpose, like I had accomplished something truly great. "Why don't you ask me a question?"

Julian's confusion grew, spreading across his face in waves. "Why?"

I drummed my fingers against the table and replied, "Why not?"

Julian gazed into my eyes and then pushed his plate aside. "Okay."

When he folded his hands together, I took a glimpse and realized how large they were. Something about that was attractive to me. I couldn't explain it, but I didn't need to. Maybe it was primal.

"What do you like to do for fun?" Julian set those eyes on me, and I couldn't look away.

"Books," I plainly stated.

He snorted at my response, though not in jest. "Studying," he mused. "Is that all you ever do?"

"No." I shook my head, because he had clearly failed to understand my meaning. "I like to read."

"Oh." He glanced away momentarily, sticking his lower lip out. "I see."

"When you were spying on me in my dorm room, I guess you couldn't tell the difference between a text book and a novel." I leaned across the table and tilted my head from side to side in a flirty gesture.

Julian shot me a complacent grin. I trembled at the way his smile eclipsed his frown.

"What's your favorite?" He rested his fist beneath his chin and admired me, as if he were posing for a portrait.

"Story?" I found his fascination to be just as intimidating as it was endearing.

"Mmm-hmm." Julian nodded to show me that he was still listening.

I pressed my palms together and touched the ends of my fingers to my lips. My eyes circled the room, pondering the question at hand. I already knew the answer, but wasn't sure if I wanted to share it.

"You'll think it's stupid," I decided, gazing at him from the corner of my eye.

"No, I won't." He shook his head just once. "I promise."

I tucked a lock of hair behind my ear and

confessed, "*The Gift of the Magi.*"

"What?" He leaned in closer, almost touching my hand, but caught himself before we made contact.

"You've never heard that story before? When you were a kid? In school? Or growing up?"

"No," he admitted. "Never."

Feeling guilty, I leaned back in the chair and looked down. While I had been off living the privileged life of a politician's daughter, there was no telling what kind of Christmas Julian had grown up with. As an orphan, who had taught him about Rudolph and Santa Clause? With the life he led now, did he even celebrate it?

"Why don't you tell me about it?" he suggested. "What happens?"

I tugged the sleeves of his jacket down to cover my hands and folded my arms over my chest. Even though it was cold, I knew the real reason for my shivers. Julian was my only way to get warm.

"A woman cuts her hair and sells it to buy a chain for her husband's watch. But when she gives it to him, he has already sold the watch to buy combs for her hair." I searched his face as thoughts fluttered through his mind, behind blue eyes. "They each sacrifice their most valuable asset to get each other a Christmas gift."

"But the gifts are useless," he insisted. "Without his watch or her hair."

"No, the gifts show how much they love each other, how much they are willing to give up for each other. For the wife, his Christmas gift was more important than her hair. For the husband, her Christmas gift was more important than his watch. In the end, what they treasure most is each other."

Julian sucked his cheeks inward, drawing attention to his taut, angular face. "Sounds like a paradox."

"It's not," I declared.

"Really?" Julian failed to blink, supporting his side of the debate.

Feeling shy, I looked down at the pasta on my plate and blushed. "It's love."

Julian lowered his gaze and then looked over me, while I squirmed in my seat from the examination. When I was least expecting it, he rose from the table and walked over to the closet. As he rifled through the contents, I silently scrutinized my glass of wine. Curiosity got the better of me, and I eventually took a sip. But the bitter liquid tasted rotten and sour, which was just as well, since I suppose it was.

My head popped up when music began to play. It was the familiar sound of gifted hands dancing across the piano, swiftly followed by a melancholy harmonica crying out for all to hear. Julian stepped away from the turn table he had placed on the dresser, while I watched the vinyl record spinning round and round. People my age didn't experience music like this anymore, and I was mesmerized.

Julian slipped his hands in his pockets and approached me at the table. "Would you like to dance?"

I glanced down when he extended his hand, surprised that he had not given me a command. He wasn't telling me to dance with him, he was asking me. And I liked that.

So I set my napkin down and put my hand in his, rising from the table. Julian pressed his palm into the small of my back and pulled my body close. I inhaled with a silent gasp and placed my free hand on his shoulder. Then I looked into his eyes and held my breath.

Julian clasped my hand in his as we swayed from side to side, drifting to the soft, calming tune that I couldn't quite place. I had listened to it on the radio before in the car, always transfixed by that haunting harmonica. But I never could place who the singer was. It was a familiar song, one that I liked, even though I had never known the name.

"Who sings this song?" I looked up at Julian as he led me around the room in slow circles.

"Billy Joel," he replied, taken aback. "You don't know who Billy Joel is?"

I shook my head in bashfulness. "I've heard the song, it's just—"

"Well, Miss James, you have lived a sheltered life," he noted, holding my gaze with intrigue.

"Not by choice," I returned. His hand slipped farther down my back, but I didn't protest.

"It's your life, Anna," he said, "however you

want it."

I thought about that for a moment and let the soothing music pour through me. "I haven't heard this song in so long," I confessed, feeling our warm bodies inching closer. Before long, our torsos pressed together without a sliver of space between us. His breath gusted down my neck, and I shuddered.

Feeling sleepy, I put my head on his shoulder and closed my eyes. He smelled exactly as he had that night I first saw him in the club. I had returned to that scenario in my mind so many times and wondered how matters might have unfolded differently. If we had just been two college students in need of wild, crazy, no-strings-attached sex. But who was I to talk about casual flings? I'd never had any kind of fling. Not even a one night stand.

But when Julian held me tight, some sick and twisted part of me liked that whatever it was between us had lasted for more than one night. Despite everything he had done and could do, I liked him. As we swayed together that night, I felt myself being drawn to him like never before. He was like a spider, weaving his web and luring me into the trap. But maybe I wanted to be lured. Maybe I wanted to be trapped.

When the song ended, Julian braided his fingers through mine and stepped back. "It's getting late."

"Yeah." I nodded with a yawn, sleepy from all

the pasta. "Dinner was delicious."

"I'm glad you liked it." He clenched his teeth and bit the corner of his mouth.

I stared into his eyes and marveled at the absurdity of it all. Had I just been on a date with an assassin? The same man who had been hired to kill me? The same man who had sacrificed everything to save me?

Not a word was spoken as he led me up the staircase and stopped in front of the bedroom door. When he let go of my hand, I lingered, balancing on one foot and then the other. "So umm..."

"You don't have to say anything." Julian shoved his hands in his pockets. "I know how you feel."

His tone of voice indicated doubt, disappointment, displeasure. He thought I hated him.

"You don't know anything." I crossed my arms over my chest and caught the gleam of hope in his eyes. "Thanks for tonight, Julian. I really needed it. I really needed something normal."

Julian did everything but nod, turning to move away from me.

"Julian?" I called him back, relieved when he gave me his undivided attention.

"Yes." He watched me with so much focus that I couldn't help turning red.

I bit my lower lip and looked away. "Will you stay with me?"

Julian tilted his head to the side, perhaps contemplating our love/hate relationship.

"Please," I begged, raising my eyebrows as I procured my best puppy dog look.

"Okay," he agreed. "Let me clean up downstairs first."

"Okay," I echoed, confused about why I was smiling so much.

When Julian turned to go down the stairs, I watched him leave.

An overwhelming sensation flowed through me like a cool brook in the forest. I spun around and skipped into the bedroom, just as confused by my emotions as you probably are right now. But something warm and beautiful was blossoming in the pit of my soul. Through his darkness, I was starting to see the light. Our time together in this house didn't have to be miserable if I didn't want it to.

When Julian returned, I shut the door behind him and walked over to the bed without a word. Stripping down to nothing more than a long shirt, I slipped beneath the covers and leaned back on the mattress. Julian stood on the other side of the bed and dragged his shirt over his head.

Unfurling with desire, I dragged my bottom lip between my teeth and inhaled. Julian kept his eyes on me as he stepped out of his pants, tossing them across the floor. When he climbed in beside me, I lay down on my side and rested my head on the pillow.

Even though we had done this before, something about this time felt new, fresh. Julian reclined on the flat of his back and stared up at the ceiling, perhaps worried that we would return to the dark places we had been before. But I wasn't angry with him anymore. Something deeper was taking hold. Something strong. Something that I no longer had the ability to resist or control.

When Julian rested his hands behind his head, I reached out and rubbed my hand over his chest. He pressed his lips together and looked down at me, his breath catching at the back of his throat. There were so many questions behind those puzzled blue eyes, but he didn't ask any of them.

Gaining trust, I moved closer and eased my way onto his side of the bed. My intentions were clear: I wanted to cuddle. What did it matter why?

"Is this okay?" I whispered, tracing my finger over his sternum.

Julian breathed aloud and moistened his lips, brushing the stray hairs from my face. "Yeah."

Brimming with happiness, I draped my arm across his stomach and nestled my head at the juncture of his shoulder and neck. Julian brushed his fingertips down the length of my arm, and it already felt like we were lovers. Somehow, I had always known we would be. There was no stopping it.

Any attempt at disrupting fate was as futile as tossing pennies in a bottle.

We would come together like a toxic, raging

storm. Hearts would crush. Bones would break.

And there was nothing either of us could do about it.

Chapter 13

When I stirred awake in the morning, Julian was nowhere to be found. So I rolled out of bed and tugged my clothes on, nearly tripping on my way over to the window. Sunlight streamed in through the glass, though I knew the warmth was not strong enough to melt the snow.

Grinning down at my winter wonderland, I drew pictures in the frosted glass and then blew warm breath over the condensation. For a moment, I felt giddy, like a child again. I chose to forget about what had happened and the reason why I was here. I wanted to enjoy this—whatever it was—because who knew when I would get it back again?

There was a knock at the door as Julian stepped inside. I turned around and smiled, gliding towards him with some kind of magnetic force, a power I could not control. Julian glanced down at me and grinned, delicately clasping my hand. Despite his darkness, despite his rage, I marveled at the feeling.

"Do you want to go outside?" He regarded me from beneath his lashes, and it was almost hypnotizing.

"Yeah." I bit my lip and nodded, squeezing his hand. I hadn't been this excited about something in a while.

Julian chuckled as he pulled me out of the room and down the stairs with him. He was amused by my enthusiasm for a day playing in the snow, but I couldn't remember the last time I had done it. Born and bred in the north, I loved the freezing white powder. But the life I led had never allowed much time for relishing it. Or rather, the life my father led had set a precedent for everything else.

Downstairs, Julian opened a closet in the hallway filled with winter gear. I shivered in place as he rifled through the clothing and accessories. For an instant, I had a flash of my father helping me dress for the winter cold. It was a distant memory, because he had helped me get ready for school only once in my life. I wondered what he was doing now, and whether or not my mother was scared.

Julian pulled a red ski jacket off one of the hangers and turned around, slipping the sleeves over either of my arms. I stood up straight as he zipped the jacket up to my neck, looking over me in a protective manner. Blush heated my cheeks as I lowered my gaze, seeking comfort in his presence.

When he turned back to look in the closet, I put my hand on his back. It was an involuntary gesture, but I wanted to make sure he was warm. I felt the separation between his shoulder blades as he returned to the task of dressing me. My hand dropped from his back, while he tugged a knit cap over my head. Our eyes met and I leaned in closer, desperate for a feeling I could neither grasp nor explain.

Sensing my passion, Julian stuffed a pair of leather gloves in my hands and said, "Put these on."

I did as he said, squeezing my fingers through the tunnels of material designed for them.

Julian put on a black leather jacket with faux fur around the sleeves and collar. Matching gloves were next, while he pointed to a pair of winter boots that were a little bigger than my size. I stepped into them but before I could tie the laces, Julian knelt down and did it for me.

"Thank you," I murmured once he was done.

Julian touched my leg and stood up, searching my face with those glittering blue eyes.

I cupped his cheek in my hand and dragged my thumb across the stubble. Julian parted his lips and clasped my wrist, recognizing the lack of distance between us. I could taste his breath.

"Let's go." His gaze shifted from my eyes to

my mouth as I gave him a slight nod of approval.

When Julian opened the door, I stepped out into the freezing cold and climbed down the front porch steps. Snow crunched like gravel beneath my boots, reminding me of a time when I was young and cotton topped. Before Daddy became the President. Before Mama became the First Lady. Before I became a target.

As I sauntered through the yard, Julian stayed close behind me. Frost covered the land, rising higher in other places according to the transition from hills to flat land. I trekked through the snow and stuffed my hands in my jacket pockets, spinning around to eye Julian.

He shot me a devilish grin and I ran, searching for refuge behind the nearest tree. But since the wilderness was at a distance, I reached over to mold a clump of snow into a ball in my hand. Julian tossed one at me before I could beat him to it, so I turned to face him and chucked a snowball in his direction.

Julian dodged the sphere of snow and chased after me, while I squealed with excitement. I kept tossing snowballs at him until one finally smashed into his chest. He held still and smoldered, sending a prickle of fear through me.

Giggling like a little girl, I brushed the bits of pearl white powder from my gloves and watched him. Julian took off and I screamed, rolling another ball in my hands. This one grazed the top of his head, and I jumped for joy at the victory.

Julian shook his head and charged, while I darted away from him. "AH!" I yelped once he looped his arms around my waist and tackled me to the ground. There was a mound of snow behind my head that doubled as an outdoor partition, obscuring our visibility from anyone who might see.

Breathless, I gazed up at Julian from the flat of my back. He hovered above me, holding his weight with the strength of his arms. His eyes danced across my face, taking in every inch of skin.

"Is this okay?" he asked, echoing my words from last night.

"Yeah," I whispered, falling under his spell.

Julian brushed his thumb across my cheekbone with the lightest touch, as if he were afraid I might break. Then he lowered his face and brought his mouth to mine, in what felt like our first real kiss. I closed my eyes and swooned, tugging at his jacket.

His lips were cold, but I fell slack beneath him and cooed. Julian tasted like cinnamon and spice, his warm breath pouring into my open mouth. I curled my hand around the nape of his neck and tugged at his hair. Julian growled in response, scraping his teeth against my bottom lip.

When he pulled away, I sighed at the bitter parting, gazing deep into his eyes. Our breath materialized in the air before us, resembling fog. Julian clenched his jaw and looked away, as if he were displeased about something. He rocked back on his knees, and I touched his shoulder.

"What is it?" I wondered.

But he leaned his head back and sighed, his breath misting up like smoke from a chimney.

"Nothing." Julian took my hand and watched me, but there was no smile. "Let's go inside."

With the furrow of my brow, I leaned into his weight and let him help me up. Even though we had just come out here, I was hungry for breakfast. Maybe it was time to go back in the house and bundle up.

As we headed inside, Julian held my hand, but his fingers weren't tangled through mine. There was resistance on his end. He was holding back, just like he always did. On the edge of revealing his true colors, but never really willing to let me in.

"Julian?" I stopped in my tracks and tugged at his arm.

He looked back over his shoulder and waited for me to say something.

"I, umm..." I turned my head to the side and fluttered my lashes. I wanted to say something, but I didn't know what to say. Everything felt so strange, like it could all slip away in one incandescent flame.

Julian lifted my chin, and I reveled in the closeness of his touch. "I want to show you something."

Pressing my lips together, I hung on to his every word and forced a smile.

"Come on." Julian led me through the front door and closed it behind us, fixing the latch to keep our enemies out. When he wiped his boots off on the mat, I followed suit. I took my gloves off next, and he stored them in the hall closet along with the ones he had worn, the knit cap, and both of the jackets. In a way, it almost felt like we had a home together, living out here in the wilderness alone. I guess you could say we were roommates.

I followed Julian into the kitchen as he walked over to the table by the window. There was a red box wrapped in ribbon waiting there. When Julian picked it up, I leaned into the counter and frowned. He turned back to face me and held the box out in his hand, his eyes focused on nothing but me.

"What is this?" I took a few steps towards him to close the distance between us.

He placed the box in my hands and murmured, "This is for you."

Confused, I pinned my brows together and stared at the gift in my hands. "Julian, I—"

"Open it," he interrupted, egging me on. "I want you to have it."

After scanning his features, I glanced at the box and eyed it carefully. Since there was no way around it, I sat down at the table and untied the ribbon. Once it fell away, I lifted the lid off the box and found a sterling silver bracelet inside with one dainty charm in the shape of a heart.

"It was my mother's," Julian explained. "My

father gave it to her for her sixteenth birthday."

As I handled the bracelet, the metal felt cool to the touch. But it felt wrong to wear it, because such an heirloom surely should have been saved for someone else. So I placed it back in the box and stared.

"Why are you giving this to me?" I looked up at him, desperate for answers more than ever before.

"I know it's not much." Julian set his hand on the back of my chair and looked from the bracelet to my face. "It's not nearly enough." He held my gaze, and I would rather die than look away. "I just wanted you to have something to open on Christmas."

My heart sank as I eased further back in the chair. "What?" I squeaked.

Julian kept his eyes on me, but I rose from the table and panicked.

"It's Christmas?" I sounded very small, like a mouse burrowing into a hole in the wall.

"Anna." Julian reached out for me, but I pushed past him, shoving his shoulder in the process.

"It's Christmas," I croaked, while my pulse thrummed rapidly in my ears. My hand went over my mouth to cover the painful sound coming out. "It's Christmas," I cried, breaking down in shaking sobs.

Julian grabbed my elbow and turned me around to face him. His hands moved up and down my arms, soothing and caressing. But I shuddered at the comfort and pushed his love away.

"What about Mama? And Daddy?" I sniffled, running my fingers through my hair. "It's Christmas, and they don't even know where I am! They could think I'm dead! It's their first Christmas without me."

"Shh... Anna, they'll see you again. I promise. All of this is temporary. It's not forever."

"But they don't know that!" I paced the floor and wept. "And what if we don't make it out of here alive? What if I never see them again?"

Julian grabbed my arms and shook me lightly. "Listen to me! You will make it out of here, Anna. You will have a life after this. You will survive!"

"No." I hung my head as a fresh flood of tears came raining down. "And Bridgette."

"Bridgette's death is not your fault," he demanded. "It's mine."

"What?" I looked up at him despite the blurring water in my eyes.

"I should have done something," he said. "I should have saved her. Like I saved you."

Sadness enveloped me, and I let it come through in waves. "I'm never going to see them again."

As I pulled away, intending to draw farther into myself and mourn, Julian braced my shoulders and backed me into the wall. "You will see your family again, Anna," he vowed. "You will. I promise."

Struggling against him, I placed my hands on his chest and pushed, trying to shove him away. But Julian grasped my wrists and clamped his mouth over mine. I relaxed beneath his tender touch and sighed as he held me against the wall. When I glanced up at him, he was staring at me with longing and desire in his eyes. Heated and vulnerable, I tilted my head forward and kissed him back.

That was all it took for sparks to fly. Flames ignited between us like someone had just struck a match. I lost my balance and sank into his warm embrace, while Julian secured his hands at the small of my back.

My fingers tangled and twisted through his hair as I leaned up on my tippy toes to reach him. Julian gasped for breath between kisses, groaning when I pressed the full weight of my body into his. His hands smoothed up and down my back as he squeezed my torso, clinging tightly.

Julian hoisted me up in his arms, and I curled my legs around his waist. His mouth left mine in search of new territory, roaming across my neck and jawline. When I took his face in my hands and silenced him with my lips, he stumbled back and lay me down across the bed, hovering above me.

The heel of my boot dug in to his belt as Julian pressed my body into the mattress. When he slipped his hand beneath my shirt and crushed his lips to mine, I whimpered at the delightful sensation. His nose skimmed from my jawline to the hollow at the base of my neck. I struggled to catch my breath as he fumbled with the buttons on my shirt, swiftly unfastening every last one.

"I shouldn't be doing this," Julian exhaled. "But I can't resist you anymore."

Unraveling at his words, I tilted my head back and moaned. Julian wrapped his hand around my waist and trailed kisses down the fine line between my breasts, soft and tender. Tensing up, I fluttered my dark lashes and clutched the bed sheet in my hand. When his lips reached my stomach, I was breathing in and out so fast that I could hardly speak, much less think straight.

"God, you're beautiful." He tugged at my lower lip as I sat up to help him remove my shirt. Once it was off, Julian traipsed his fingers along the sides of my arms. He kissed the end of my earlobe and whispered, "Your skin is so soft."

All my life, I had denied myself this part of me. Sensuality. Sexuality. Everyone has it. I had just refused to let myself experience it. Even so, I was glad that I never wasted the moment.

I had been waiting for Julian.

"We don't have to do this if you don't want to." He stilled above me and waited for my response.

"I don't want to wait anymore," I revealed. "I've waited long enough."

Julian sat up on his knees to pull his shirt off.

But I was impatient, so I rose with him and slipped my fingers beneath the garment, tracing my palm over his abs and chest. He lifted his arms in the air and kept his eyes on me, while I tugged the shirt over his head and tossed it to the floor.

"Are you sure you want to do this?" He lifted my chin with his forefinger and thumb, hesitating.

"Yes," I replied, looking deep into his eyes. "I want you to do it. You're the one."

His nostrils flared as the depth of my words sank in. While I had chosen him for the task of claiming my virginity, I wondered if Julian would ever understand what I truly meant. For me, being with Julian was so much more than some hot romp in the sheets. I cared about him. And I thought he cared about me, too. After all, he must feel something. Why else would he sacrifice so much of his life to save mine?

Julian stroked my cheek and then tucked a lock of hair behind my ear. "Okay."

If there had ever been a more voluntary expression of consent, I had never seen one.

Julian leaned in for a tender kiss, and I placed my hand against his chest. Over his heart. He lowered his head and took my hand, pressing his lips to the back of it. A mixture of wonder and light flashed across his eyes, and I prayed that nothing would ever take him away from me.

Taking it slow, Julian covered my mouth with his and slowly lowered my body back onto the mattress. I closed my eyes and tried to relax, sighing as he traced every curve of my figure with his hands. Julian knelt down and untied the laces on my boots, pulling them off and then peeling my socks away.

When he returned to me, I moistened my lips and swallowed. Julian took my face in his hands and kissed me softly to alleviate any stress. My heart hammered against my chest as he unbuttoned my jeans and then slid the zipper down. He stuck his fingers in my belt loops and eased the jeans off my hips, slowly peeling the fabric away from either of my legs.

Goosebumps spread like wildfire across my body, while I yearned for him desperately.

Julian touched my thigh and searched me from head to toe. "You can tell me if I need to stop."

I nodded, even though the information was fruitless. I had no intention of telling him to stop.

"Just don't crush me," I whispered. It was my only request of Julian.

His hand slipped farther up my leg, and I knew there was no going back. We had reached the point of no return.

"I won't," he promised.

Those were the last words spoken until we were both under the sheets.

Julian kissed me as his hands searched my naked body. I was more than willing to let them roam, giving myself over to sweet desire. When he stroked my bare torso and planted his lips on my neck, I stuck my fingers in his hair and whimpered. He was so warm, yet gentle and soft, all around me. I didn't want any of it to end.

As he gazed down at me, I bit my lower lip and turned my head to the side. Julian held himself above me with his arms and leaned down to whisper in my ear. "It's okay," he soothed. "Breathe. Relax."

So I followed his instructions and exhaled, feeling the bristle of his whiskers against my neck. Once my lips parted to inhale, Julian molded his mouth to mine and braided our fingers together. He drove the back of my hand into the mattress and squeezed my palm achingly tight.

With my free hand, I ruffled my fingers through his hair and tugged at the dark strands. Julian grazed his teeth over my chin and rubbed my bare shoulder, soothing the nerves that would soon be long gone. When a gasp escaped me, several more followed in quick staccatos. I was so overwhelmed and excited, reeling with pleasure at the newfound sensation, and whatever it was building towards.

"Julian," I whimpered, searching for something to hold on to. I felt myself slipping—losing grip—and it scared me. So I dug my nails in and scratched his back, even sinking my teeth into his shoulder when it became too much. Julian covered my mouth as I cried out his name, silencing me with a kiss.

While I closed my eyes and trembled, Julian moved away from me and sat down on the edge of the mattress. Once I recovered, I held the bed sheet to my chest and looked over at his bare back. Julian put his clothes back on and stood up, taking long strides to the door. He failed to acknowledge me even once before he left.

I had never felt so empty and alone.

The moment was gone. And so was he.

Feeling utterly used, I lay in bed and stared at the door he had walked through. What had I done wrong? Despite the initial discomfort, that was the best human experience of my life.

But Julian obviously didn't feel the same way. We were back to the shock treatment he loved. Very hot to very cold. With no room for anything in between.

My legs felt like JELL-O, and I didn't want to move a muscle. But he had just punched a hole straight through my heart. I had given him everything. And he had given me nothing. Like always.

I thought of all the girls he must have been with, how much better they probably were than me. But for now, Julian was mine. I wanted him more than ever before, because I knew whatever physical attraction had formed between us was temporary. After all, I could die tomorrow. So could he.

We had found good love. Why waste it?

Determined to have my way, I draped the covers around my body like a cloak and left the room. The front door was cracked at the end of the hall, and I could see the screen from where I was standing. With my hair tumbling over my shoulders in messy tangles, I pushed against the door and stepped out on the frosty porch in my bare feet.

Julian sat on the steps with his back to me, looking out at the sun. He folded his hands together and rested his elbows at his knees, dropping his gaze to think. Even though I knew he must have heard me, Julian made no effort to glance in my direction.

"I shouldn't have let that happen," he confessed. "I never should have let it go that far."

"Julian—"

"I shouldn't have let it happen," he repeated, shaking his head and rubbing his jaw.

I walked closer and put my hand on his shoulder. "But I wanted it to."

Julian pursed his lips and said, "So did I."

Longing to ease the sting of his current mood, I sat down beside him and huddled beneath the covers.

"What are you doing out here in that? You'll freeze." Julian stood up to take me back inside the house where it was warm.

"No," I protested, jerking him back down to my level. He sat on the steps and sighed, running his fingers through his hair.

I grabbed ahold of his arm and studied his handsome profile. "Be with me," I whispered.

"No, Anna." He looked into my eyes, and I

noticed the sorrow etched into the planes of his face. "It's wrong. I've done enough bad things in my life." He parted his lips and groaned, as if he were trying to convince himself. "It's wrong."

Digging my heels in, I leaned closer and said, "Then why does it feel so right?"

Julian stared at the ground and sighed, freezing up when I wrapped my arms around him. "Be with me," I begged. "I want this. I want you."

He touched my arm and whispered—almost painfully—"I want you, too."

Euphoric, I put my head on his chest and squeezed tight. Julian rubbed my back and threaded his fingers through my hair. When I lifted my chin to look up at him, Julian pressed his lips to mine. It was a soft, gentle kiss in a league of tenderness all on its own. I opened my eyes and he watched me, tracing the edge of my jaw.

"You're so young," he murmured.

Beaming, I settled in Julian's lap and sealed my mouth over his. He returned the kiss and slipped his hands beneath the blanket, searching my warm skin. As I curled my arms around his neck, he pressed his palm into my back, tugging me closer.

And so our love affair began.

Chapter 14

We lay tangled in the sheets as I hooked my leg over his and rested my head on his chest. Julian combed his fingers through my hair while I shut my eyes, relaxing from the gentle massage. The fireplace crackled in the distance, since we somehow found ourselves in the upstairs bedroom again. It was a dark, chilly night. But it had been a day I would never forget.

"How do you feel?" Julian asked, running his hand down the side of my arm and back.

"Good," I giggled, kissing the stubble along his jaw.

He turned my face up in the palm of his hand and smiled without showing any teeth.

Wanting the moment to last forever, I snuggled close and touched his stomach. There was a raised scar along his right set of ribs that looked rough and pink. Julian tensed when I traced my finger over it, and I pulled my hand away.

"What happened there?" I wondered. Curiosity had been eating away at me since the first time I saw it. But it never seemed appropriate to ask about it until now.

"Years ago," he began, "I got in a fight."

"What kind of fight?" I listened to the beat of his heart. There had never been a prettier sound.

"Kill or be killed." His fingertips dug into my back as he mulled over the memory. "I won."

When I shivered, he tightened his grip and held me close.

"I don't want you to be afraid of me."

"I'm not." I leaned up on my elbow to get a better look at him. "Not anymore."

And it was true. As sick and twisted as it sounded, Julian made me feel safe.

The assassin made me feel safe.

Julian kissed the end of my nose and caressed my arm. Then he dragged his thumb across my cheek, and I bit my lower lip with a smile. We studied each other for a very long time, never able to know what the other was thinking.

"What left a mark like this?" I eyed the raised scar but never touched it again.

"A broken beer bottle," he answered.

"Did you need stitches?"

"Probably," he mused. "But I never got them. Too risky."

I nodded and lay back down, cuddling in his arms. While I truly believed Julian wasn't that man anymore, his past did frighten me. What he had done. All the people he had killed. It was crazy, but I trusted him with my life. He had already saved it more than once.

For the first time, I had no idea what my future might hold. I didn't know how much time we had, when it would be safe to leave, if we had any chance of escape. But there was beauty in the uncertainty of our doom. Every time he touched me could very well be the last.

So I closed my eyes and kissed his neck, wrapping my body all around him. Julian stroked his hand along my spine and let me hold on for dear life. There was a tenderness to his touch that had not been there before. Because he had claimed a part of me that no one else ever would.

"Merry Christmas, Anna," he soothed.

"Merry Christmas, Julian."

I drifted off in his arms, accepting the cold reality that they might not always be there.

* * *

I found Julian downstairs the next morning making breakfast. As I swayed my hips into the kitchen, my body felt achy in places that it never had before. I blushed at the soreness and bit my lip the moment I saw him.

"Hey," Julian cooed, reeling me into his warm embrace.

"Hi." I fluttered my lashes up at him and turned my cheek when he made me feel shy.

Julian kissed my forehead and wrapped his arms around me. I relished the rare hug and squeezed tight.

Sweet music bounced about the place as I waltzed into the adjoining room. A vinyl record spun round and round on the turn table, lifting my spirits with delight. Even though Billy Joel's name was written across the front, the tune sounded remarkably similar to the fifties.

While Julian stood by a pan of steaming bacon, I took the moment of distraction and leapt onto the bed. Billy crooned about his "Uptown Girl," and I had never felt more like Julian's. My heels sank into the mattress as I bounced up and down, provoking Julian with a wicked grin.

"Anna," he scolded. "Stop that. Get off the bed. You're going to hurt yourself."

Shaking my head, I spun around in a circle and giggled like the devil. Julian turned the heat down on the stove and stalked towards me. My blood thrummed violently in my veins as his smoldering gaze connected with mine.

Julian charged and tackled me to the bed while I screamed, crashing to the flat of my back. Once he had me pinned to the mattress, I curled my arms around his neck and whimpered. Sinking his fingers into my flesh, Julian dragged his lips down my throat and I closed my eyes, running my fingers through his hair.

I loved this. The way it felt. The way my whole world kept spinning out of my control.

I loved him.

As he tugged at my waist, I hooked my leg around his hips and held on to his shoulders. Julian smoothed his hands over my stomach and covered my mouth with his, his heated breaths racing down my neck. As his soft lips traced a line of tender kisses along my jaw, I turned my head and sighed.

The song ended as the record kept spinning on the turn table. Julian pushed me deeper into the mattress and held my hands against the pillow above us. When he braided his fingers through mine, I peered up at him through my dark lashes and saw the fire in his eyes. I loved it.

A single gunshot echoed in the distance. And that was all it took to ruin everything.

Julian snapped back and hopped off the bed, peeking through the curtain over the window. My heart was beating so fast that I could hardly breathe, much less move. When Julian turned on his heel to look back at me, I had never been so scared in my life.

"Stay here," he ordered, marching towards the door.

Terrified, I leapt out of bed and ran after him. "No! Julian, don't go," I cried. "Don't!"

Julian placed his hands at the small of my back and kissed me like he knew it was the last time. When he pulled away, I was trapped in a daze, struggling to get out. As I opened my eyes, Julian slipped through the door and locked it behind him. Helpless, I hurried to catch up and beat against the wood.

"Julian, let me out!" I begged. "Don't go, Julian! Don't go!"

"I have to," he said through the door. "Stay here, Anna. Stay here."

I pressed my ear to the wall and heard him rifling through the closet in the hallway. My heart throbbed against my ribcage, feeling swollen and lost without him. I tore my fingers through my hair and paced the floor, shivering when he slammed the front door and I knew he was gone.

Rushing over to the window, I knelt down on the floor and peered behind the curtain to see through the glass. Julian crouched low and then jumped off the front porch, sneaking around the back of the house. As sweat brimmed along my brow, I sank my fingertips into my temple and tried to think.

A few miserable moments passed where I could do nothing more than curl into a ball on the floor. I tucked my legs into my chest and rocked back and forth, nearly cutting my tongue with my teeth. When someone fired a gun, I shut my eyes tight and forced a deep breath. Whose bullet was it?

Gathering up my courage, I got to my feet and made my way towards the door. At the sound of another gunshot, I nearly froze in place. But then the sheer torture of not knowing did me in.

As I failed to kick the door in for the third

time, something sparked in my mind, like the flash of a lightbulb. One night, Bridgette and her bad girl ways had taught me how to pick a lock. We had been out past curfew and snuck into the dormitory with a single bobby pin. Despite being pressed for time, Bridgette made me do it, saying that it might come in handy one day. "You never know when," she had mused.

Reaching into my jean pocket, I retrieved a bobby pin, and my eyes lit up with hope. I pounced on the opportunity and toyed with the needle enough to jimmy the lock. Once I heard that beautiful sound and the handle twisted freely, I threw the door open and ran into the hall.

One more gunshot, and I stumbled to the ground. How many more until someone was dead?

I opened the front door and crept across the snow-covered porch. Then I did what only a fool would do. I perked my ears up and listened for the direction of the next bullet. And then I followed it.

Crouching down low, I swung off the porch and trekked across the land. I saw two figures fighting in the distance. I ran with everything I had in me, willing to give up my own life if that's what it took to see Julian one last time. The closer I came to the men, the more I realized that neither could see me.

Since there was a light blanket of snow coming down, my approaching figure was obscured. But that proved to my advantage with every pounding step I took towards them. Just before the edge of the wilderness, I saw a silver gun resting in the snow. There was a man on top of Julian, holding him to the ground as they wrestled between two trees.

When I knelt down before the gun, the man punched Julian in the mouth and his blood splattered across the snow. Swallowing, I held my breath and studied the obvious. Julian was losing.

The man kept beating Julian, and with every nasty blow, I saw his head snap back as he groaned in pain. When Julian lacked the strength to fight anymore, the man wrapped his hands around Julian's throat and squeezed, choking him, constricting the supply of air to his lungs. Julian kicked his legs and my heart stopped, my hand unknowingly reaching for the gun.

Just as the man dug his heels in—his last real effort towards strangling Julian—I put my finger on the trigger and fired. The bullet pierced his skull and lodged its way into his brain. He lurched forward and loosened his grip around Julian's neck, rolling to his side with his shoulder in the snow.

Julian forced the man's weight off him and rose to his feet, snatching the gun out of my hand. Then he turned back and shot the man in the chest three times. At that moment, I actually looked at the man. His main features: his hair, his face, his eyes.

He must have been a few years older than Julian, mid-thirties at the oldest. His dark hair was buzzed to the scalp, his icy blue eyes drifting into the distance. I saw him for the human he was, or rather the human he had been. I watched his chest until it stopped moving, and then I could breathe again.

Julian knelt down and searched the man's pockets, stealing a wad of cash and a knife. Then he rolled the man to the flat of his back and placed his dead hands over his blood-soaked shirt. I fell to my knees and trembled, feeling lifeless and cold. I could not stop shaking, and it had nothing to do with the weather.

I thought I saw Julian whisper something to the man, because his mouth started to move. Then he rocked back on his heels and grabbed a lighter from the man's coat. As I wrapped my arms around myself, Julian found a pack of cigarettes in the same pocket and lit one.

"Do you know him?" I asked, shivering in place.

Julian pressed the white stick to his lips and took a drag. "I did." Then he dropped it on the man's shirt along with the flaming lighter and exhaled, blowing smoke up in the sky. "I did."

Rising to his feet, Julian took one last look at the man on the ground and then took a few shaky steps towards me. I touched his arm and observed the blood coating his face and clothes. This was him, Julian the Assassin, his true colors red and loud, bright enough for even the blind to see.

He pressed his lips together and sighed, cupping my pale cheek in his dirty hand.

"Are you okay?" he muttered, rubbing the edge of my earlobe with his thumb.

I parted my lips to speak, but a lonesome teardrop skirted my face instead.

"Let's go," he ordered, tugging at my elbow as he led me back to the house.

I looked over my shoulder at the man burning in the snow, even though I shouldn't have.

When Julian pulled me inside and locked the door, I could hardly move. I knew what was happening. These men weren't going to give up anytime soon. Whatever part Julian had played in my fairytale was over. Then again, it had never been a fairytale. Julian wasn't Prince Charming. He was a monster.

In the kitchen, I followed Julian into the bathroom and sat down on the edge of the tub. He peeled his jacket away and then slipped his shirt over the top of his head. Then he pushed the shower curtain back and hung them over the rod. I stood up and watched him rinsing the blood from his face. Crimson circled the drain and I swallowed, because the sight of Julian wounded in front of the mirror was all too familiar.

Julian splashed water on his neck and chest, dabbing at the streaks of blood there. He reached for a towel and dried himself off, running cold water through his hair. Then he set his hands on the sink and appraised his reflection in the mirror. I wasn't sure if he liked who he saw.

"Come here," Julian called, stepping to the side.

I stood up and approached him with my eyes down. Julian turned my shoulder so I was directly in front of the mirror, but I didn't want to look. There was blood on my clothes, too. That man's blood.

Julian took a wet washcloth and rinsed my face off, cleaning my hands next. Then he picked at the hem of my shirt and inched it up my torso until I wasn't wearing it anymore. There were cuts and bruises all over his face and chest, and his lip was swollen. But Julian acted like it had simply been another day at the office. For him, I guess it was.

When Julian shed the rest of his clothes, I followed suit and took mine off as well. He said we should take a shower and get cleaned up, wash the blood off our skin, rinse the murder away.

But no amount of soap could ever scrub it away—the reality of what I had done. Perhaps Julian had grown used to the feeling, numb to the act of taking life. But it was new to me. My first time.

As Julian turned the shower on, I lifted my eyes and studied my figure in the mirror.

I didn't like who I saw.

So I turned and took Julian's hand, stepping beneath the icy cold water. The truth hurts. And as Julian closed the shower curtain and grabbed the soap, I understood that my pain had just begun.

Dying is one thing. Living with yourself and all the things you've done is another.

His hand stroked the length of my arm as I leaned my head back, closing my eyes. He kissed my neck and caressed my skin, putting his hands on my stomach. When his teeth sank into my earlobe, I reached behind me to thread my fingers through his hair and shivered.

Julian was a killer.

But so was I.

Chapter 15

The clock was ticking. Our time was running out. Julian scarfed down dinner, while I could hardly eat. There was a bundle of nerves in my stomach, preying on what we had done. While Julian was right about us having no choice, I had no idea how the law treated assassins when it came to self-defense.

Then again, we were talking about an illicit group of trained killers. They were above the law. They made their own law. There was no law. I didn't know which one was true.

"Is it true?" I stared at Julian as he swallowed the canned tuna in his mouth.

"What?" He took a swig of water and furrowed his brow. There was a cut above his eye.

"My father," I declared. "What did he do? Why is there a bounty on my head?"

"Do you remember when he was almost

impeached?"

"I was thirteen," I remarked. "Of course I remember."

"Do you remember why?" Julian searched my face while I looked away.

At the time, I tried to block it from my mind. The press had been particularly brutal that year. Mama took me to a therapist every week, worried about the effect the media would have on me.

"Something about leaking government secrets," I finally said. "That's all I could get them to tell me. I wasn't allowed to watch TV when all that was going on. They didn't want it to mess with my head."

Julian chuckled. "They were the only ones messing with your head."

"Who? My family?"

"Your mother and father," he said.

I seethed, glaring at him.

"Why then?" I snapped. "Why did he do it?"

"Because of your mother." Julian leaned across the table and squared his jaw. I hated it when he was like this: self-satisfied and smug, all too sure of himself.

"My mother?"

"Yes," he hissed. "There was a videotape of your father with the press secretary. They were having an affair."

My entire body froze, while simultaneously filling with heat. "What? No." I shook my head. "Daddy would never cheat on Mama."

Julian stroked his jaw and set those glittering blue eyes on me. "What makes you so sure about that?"

"No, he wouldn't," I insisted, shaking my head again. "He just wouldn't."

Julian lowered his gaze and stared at the table, drumming his fingers.

"So what?" I inquired. "Even if he did cheat, what does that have to do with anything?"

"Someone held the affair—and that tape—over his head. It was blackmail."

"Who?" I wondered, digging my nails into the palm of my hand.

"An enemy," he revealed, running his fingertip around the rim of his glass.

"But you're not going to tell me which one?"

"Foreign affairs," he flatly replied, taking another sip of wine.

"But—"

"Enemy X wanted to take down Enemy Y. But Enemy Y also happened to be an ally of your father's," he explained. "So Enemy X blackmailed your father into revealing information about where members of Enemy Y were located. Are you following so far?"

"Is there a reason why you're making this sound like a math equation?" I grumbled.

Julian laughed, and it was the truest laugh to ever leave his mouth.

"Enemy Y suffered casualties," he went on. "Women. Children. And they blame your father."

I stopped moving as all the pieces fell into place.

"You don't know how many men were killed, along with their daughters."

I took a silent breath and moistened my lips.

"They want revenge, Anna," he said. "An eye for an eye."

"So the one that used to be an ally—"

"No." Julian waved his finger. "No allies anymore, Anna. They're both enemies now."

Rising from the table, I staggered forward and leaned against the kitchen counter. I felt sick.

"Why do you know all of this?" I placed my hand at the base of my throat, hardly able to breathe.

"Why do you think?" Julian returned, approaching me from behind.

He was the one hired to do the job. Of course he knew the particulars.

"I don't want to believe you." Tears streamed down my eyes as I clenched my jaw.

Julian curled his arms around my body and rested his head on my shoulder. "Then don't," he whispered.

"Are you ever going to do it?" I turned back to face him and gazed into his eyes. "Why don't you do your job?" I pushed, testing him. "Why don't you do what you came here to do?"

Julian looked taken aback, his eyes scanning my figure up and down.

"I'm tired of hiding," I confessed.

Julian pursed his lips and swiped his thumb across the tears raining down my cheeks. Then he brushed his fingers along my jawline and planted his hand at the base of my neck. I felt the warmth of his skin inching up my body until he clasped my entire throat in the palm of his hand.

"This is what you want?" he checked, holding his thumb over my throbbing pulse point.

Breathless, I closed my eyes and forced my body to relax. "Yes."

"Okay," he answered. "This is going to be quick and painless. I promise."

"Thank you." I looked at his beautiful face one last time. The face of the man who had haunted and saved me. The beautiful stranger. My killer. My lover. My friend.

"Close your eyes," he gently whispered, his hand preparing to clamp down on my throat.

Trusting him with my life, I shut my eyes and exhaled, slightly tilting my head back. Julian inhaled and leaned in for the kill, something he was trained to do, something he was designed to do, something he was meant to do.

As I waited for him to snap my neck—surely a less cruel fate compared to what my father's enemies and Julian's ex-employer had planned—his lips landed on my throat instead.

"You have such a pretty neck," Julian noted, his breath ghosting across my face like a warm caress.

Confused, I opened my eyes and found him

staring at me. Slowly but surely, he withdrew his large hand from my throat and let his fingers settle on my shoulder. I flicked my tongue out to moisten my dry lips, my chest rising and falling with each uncertain breath.

"I could never kill you," Julian confessed. "I want you too much."

He crashed in to me, threading his fingers through my hair as he sealed his mouth over mine. I leaned up on my tippy toes and grabbed the collar of his shirt, returning every kiss like it was air I needed to breathe. His hands slipped into the back pockets of my jeans, as he drew me into his warm body.

Heated and desperate, I curled my fingers at the back of his neck and relaxed into his hold. Julian molded his mouth to mine, our lips brushing like paint over canvas and sticking together like glue. When I whimpered, he lifted me in his arms with a breathy groan that felt trapped at the back of his throat.

His hands slid beneath my thighs, as I locked my legs around his waist, sitting up in his strong hold. Julian nipped at my earlobe and then dragged his lips down my neck. The same neck he could have snapped in half. He was a strong man, Julian. And he could kill me with his bare hands. He had said so himself.

Ravenous with desire, I ran my fingers through his hair and then took his face in my hands, nibbling on his lower lip. Julian walked towards the bed and lay me down across it as I pulled him on top of me. His knees slid along either of my hips, and I squirmed beneath his hard body, cherishing every minute of it.

Julian slipped his hand under my shirt and traced the sensitive skin over my back until goosebumps were rising up everywhere. Unlike our rushed encounters, he took his time kissing me, adoring the curves of my lips. One of my hands lay limp on the mattress as I leaned my head into the pillow. My eyes fluttered with every touch of his mouth to that pulsing point in my neck.

After tugging my top over my head, Julian squeezed his hands behind my back and lowered his face. Sweet kisses danced over my ribcage while I balled the sheet in my hand, biting my lip. When he returned his mouth to mine, his touch had never tasted so good, and we hurried to shed our clothes.

Julian hovered above me and pulled the covers around us, resting his elbows along either side of my face. I loved how close we were, huddling beneath the sheet and blankets as if we had pitched a tent. It felt like our own personal space that no one had access to. A lock without a key. A bubble not ready to pop. Like the walls of Troy. Unable to be breached. For now.

When I gasped, Julian placed his open mouth over mine. I reached out for something to grab on to and sliced my fingernails across his naked back.

I knew the scratches must have hurt, but he didn't seem to mind. Instead, he braided his fingers through mine and gazed deeply into my eyes.

Right then, I saw his soul. The real Julian. Scars and all. Those blue sapphires dilated, and I spotted a flicker of light in the dark. A fallen angel trapped between heaven and hell. My fallen angel.

Julian pressed his chest into mine, as I wrapped my arms around his bruised, battered torso, holding him in the most intimate embrace. He buried his face in my neck and I touched my warm palm to his bare back, pushing down so hard that I must have left an imprint. When Julian lifted his head to look at me, his hair was a mess, sticking up in every direction, evidence of my fingers tangling and twisting their way through his dark locks. He held his upper body up with his arms and remained above me, staring.

All it took was one look, and his face fell.

I was crying.

Averting his eyes, Julian put as much distance between us as possible and put his clothes back on. Still quivering, I covered my body in the bed sheet and watched him walk away. It hurt more than anything else to see him withdraw deeper into himself like this, especially after what had happened today.

"I love you, Julian," I blurted out as he headed for the door.

He stopped in his tracks but refused to turn around and face me. I was forced to confess my feelings to the shirt over his back, because that is what he had done. Turned his back on me when I needed him most.

"I love you," I repeated.

Julian turned to the side enough for me to see him shut his eyes and clench his jaw.

"I know that I'm just some girl you saw that made your conscious clear," I admitted. "And maybe by sparing me, it's some form of retribution. But I don't care what you've done. I don't care about your past. I don't care how many people you've killed." I shook my head and pulled my knees into my chest, tucking the bed sheet around me. "I'm in love with you, Julian," I murmured. "I love you."

"Stop saying it," he commanded, twisting on his heel in anger.

His eyes connected with mine, and I had never felt so wholly exposed.

"But I want to," I murmured, another tear streaking down. "I want you to know how I feel."

"Stop, Anna!" He took a step closer, but there was still too much distance between us for my liking. "Stop it!" His voice sounded strained, almost like he was begging at this point.

"I love you," I croaked.

"Well, I don't want you to love me!" He came towards me with the words, placing his hands on his hips. When I shivered with fear, he ran his hands over his face and took to pacing the floor.

"Why not?" I leaned against the headboard

and clasped the sheet over my breast.

He dared to look my way and gnawed on the inside of his cheek. "I'm a bad man, Anna. I've done things. Terrible things. You don't want to love someone like me."

I gazed up at him like a sick puppy and whimpered, "Too late. I already do."

With a resounding sigh, Julian took a seat on the edge of the bed and held my hand. He flipped it over to expose my palm and then looked into my eyes. "You're good and innocent and pure." He cupped either of my cheeks in his hands and brushed the fallen pieces of hair out of the way. "Don't you understand?"

"No." I put my hand over his and shook my head. "All I know is that I love you."

Julian ducked his head and swallowed, wiping my tears away. "Did I hurt you?"

"No." I pursed my lips and smiled, still trying to reckon with the intensity of his lovemaking.

He shut his eyes only to open them again. "This is wrong. What we're doing. It's been wrong this whole time. But I kept on doing it because—" he hesitated, swiping his finger across my palm.

"You want me too much," I answered, recycling his earlier confession.

"Yes," he accepted, placing my hands in my lap as he turned to leave again.

"Why can't you just be with me?" I touched his shoulder and waited for him to reply.

Julian tucked a lock of hair behind my ear.

"Because you deserve more."

"I don't want more," I said, angling my cheek into his palm. "I want you."

Julian removed his hand from my face and sighed. "I'm sorry."

"Am I not good?" I wondered, considering my lack of experience in bed.

The light returned to his eyes momentarily. "You're more than good, Anna. You're perfect."

I sank my teeth into my lower lip as a furrow formed between my brows.

Julian kissed my forehead and then left. As he disappeared, I lay down and placed my hand over the mattress. Deep down, I knew what the problem was. Time. There was never enough of it. Especially for us.

The end was near.

* * *

I fell asleep alone in the bed where Julian had taken my virginity. I wondered if that was what had set him off—the significance of what had happened between us in this room. But then again, maybe it was the tears in my eyes. Tears born out of the way he made me feel. I had heard about girls enjoying sex with someone they loved to the point that it actually made them cry. Now, it was an emotion I could understand.

Stirring awake in the darkness, I attempted to shake off any thoughts of Julian and what he had said. But that was impossible. He had been running through my dreams all night.

As I stumbled out of bed, I looked up at the ceiling and cocked my head to the side. Was that a piano?

Despite what had happened in these halls after dark, I made my way up the staircase and followed the music. Someone was playing the song Julian and I had first danced to after that one romantic dinner. The Billy Joel record. The one I should have known the name of but didn't. *Piano Man.*

When I reached the top floor, I strolled down the corridor until the sound grew louder. As soon as I found the door it was coming from, I pushed against the frame and let myself inside. Julian sat in front of an antique piano on a wooden bench, his long fingers dancing over ebony and ivory.

I stood in the doorway and watched him play, amazed that I never knew he had such a talent. After being so intimate with him, it felt like something I should have known, something he should have told me, a level of comfortable exposure that we should have reached.

Julian hit the last key and stared straight ahead, letting the tone reverberate through the walls. He must have known I was in here, because he perked his ears up to listen to what I had to say.

"Who taught you how to play?" I wondered, dressed in a long night shirt and nothing else.

"My mother." Julian pulled the cover down over the piano, shutting it with a noisy thud.

Before he could get up and run away, I sat

down beside him on the bench and showed him the bracelet on my wrist. Julian touched my arm and took the heart charm between his fingers, examining the smooth surface. "I'm glad you're wearing it," he noted.

"Why did you give me your mother's bracelet, Julian?" I asked.

He exhaled through his nostrils and admitted, "Because I wanted you to have it."

His answer was good enough. But there must have been a reason why he would give me something so precious. Why me? Surely, I was nothing more to him than a warm body to touch and lie with in the night, a shot at redemption.

"What time are we leaving in the morning?" I put my head on his shoulder and hooked my arm around his elbow. I wasn't stupid. Two assassins were dead. Surely there were more to come. We couldn't hide here. Not now. Our safe house wasn't safe anymore. It hadn't been safe for a while.

"Dawn." Julian slumped forward and let his shoulders sag. I wondered if he was overcome by the same sense of dread I was. Whatever had happened between us out here in the woods, it was over.

I nuzzled his neck in response, hugging him close and memorizing his scent.

"Anna," he warned, tightening up.

"I don't care," I muttered against his shirt. "I love you. And you're going to love me tonight."

Julian looked over me with equal parts shock and amusement. But I didn't care what he thought. Tonight might be all we had, and while I had no clue what I meant to him, he meant a hell of a lot to me. This could very well be our last night together. *Ever.* And I'd be damned if I let him waste it.

When Julian failed to make the first move, I tugged at his shirt and clamped my mouth over his. In no time, his hand settled at the back of my head, easing over my long blond hair. At least I had two advantages. One: Julian was a man. Two: He wanted me too much.

So I twirled my fingers through the hairs at the nape of his neck and climbed into his lap, dominating our rendezvous for a change. Julian sank his fingertips into the small of my back, his large hands breaching the hem of my shirt. When he consumed my mouth, I pushed against his shoulder and we tumbled to the ground.

"Sorry," I giggled, collapsing on top of his chest.

Julian grabbed my wrist and gazed up at me from the flat of his back. "It's okay."

Grinning like a Cheshire cat, I leaned down and claimed his mouth, cradling his head in my hands. Julian smoothed his palms up and down my back and then grasped my hips, smirking up at me. With my newfound experience, I felt like a vixen, rousing him in the night to fulfill his every wish and desire.

Julian held my body tight as I kissed my way down his wounded torso. Hesitant at first, I placed my lips to his raised scar and then clamped my hand over the muscle in his arm. He responded to my every touch, never one to withhold a gasp or groan. Especially not tonight.

He let me love him.

Right there on the floor by the piano.

Nothing had ever felt like a more thoughtful gift.

I kissed him on the mouth one last time and then curled up in his arms. Instead of pulling away, Julian rubbed my back and held me against his chest, our warm bodies pressed together in the night.

Despite the tear trickling down my cheek, I cuddled closer and tangled my legs through his. Julian kissed my forehead and pushed the messy hair over my shoulders and out of my face. Then he pressed his lips to the end of my nose and tucked my head in the space where his shoulder met his neck.

I closed my eyes, but I didn't want to sleep. I wanted to taste him, drink him in. I wanted to remember the way he smelled, the way he felt, the way he kissed, the way he loved. I wanted to remember it all.

So I stayed awake until he dozed off, watching the way his long lashes fanned out across his beautiful face. When the tears came, I sat up and swiped them away. They were blurring my vision, obscuring my last night of being able to look at Julian. After this, I might not ever see him again.

When he shifted in his sleep, I worried that I had woken him. But then he parted his lips and said my name. "Anna," he called out, almost painfully. "Anna. Come back. Please don't go away."

Even if he was asleep, I knew a man's subconscious didn't lie. He was dreaming about me.

Despite the feelings he was quick to deny, I had heard him loud and clear. Julian didn't want me to go. Maybe he would never confess what he truly felt for me. But for now, his confession in the midst of a dream was enough to stay with me for a while. It meant something. More than he was ever willing to reveal.

Putting my head on his chest, I lay with Julian in the dark as my tears puddled on his skin. Then I leaned back on my elbow and ran my fingers through his hair, doing all the things that I might be doing for the last time. Admiring his features, I smoothed my thumb across his forehead, down his nose, over his cheekbones, chin, and every other plane of his face.

I saved his lips for last. With the pad of my index finger, I traced the upper curve and then the plush, fuller one beneath it. While he was asleep and dreaming of me, I touched my lips to his mouth and then sat back to gaze down at the only man to ever love me. Even if it was only in the physical sense.

Either way, he was the only man I had ever loved. For the slightest of seconds, my mind raced back to that night in the club when I first saw him. I was drawn to him from the start. His curly dark hair. Those sweet blue eyes. A body that was meant to do nothing but love and protect me.

When the tears became too much, I placed my ear to his chest and took a breath. As long as that heart of his was still beating, I could get through whatever path lay ahead of us. Even if a fork in the road developed and took him away from me. One thing was for sure.

I wasn't ready for tomorrow.

Chapter 16

The man we killed had arrived in a car. An old Volvo with a low hanging bumper that was some mixture of beige and tan. Despite stalling out in the snow, Julian fixed the vehicle and fudged with the license plate enough to allow us a decent chance at escape. But even if the odds were in our favor, I had a hollow feeling in the pit of my stomach and the depth of my soul that was eating away at me.

I didn't want to leave.

"Anna." Julian tugged at my arm in the entryway to the kitchen. "We have to go."

"I know," I murmured, raking my eyes over every square inch of our temporary home.

"I thought you hated this place," Julian mentioned. "Shouldn't you be running out the door?"

Turning on my heel, I looked back at him and

pouted. Julian took my hand and rubbed his thumb across the back of it, but that only amplified the pain to come. Leaving this place meant abandoning all that had happened while we were here, leaving it all behind.

I couldn't do it. I didn't want to. Because as soon as we left this abandoned house in the wilderness, Julian and I were over. It was only a matter of time before life came crashing back in like a hurricane and ripped him away from me.

"Anna." Julian turned my chin up and then grasped my shoulders.

"I don't wanna go," I whimpered, sounding like a child.

Julian hung his head and sighed, hot air passing through his flaring nostrils.

"It's over?" I wondered, searching his eyes when they averted me. "Isn't it?"

Julian twisted his mouth into an indecisive expression and stared at the wall.

I had my answer. It wasn't over now. But soon, it would be.

"No." I backed away from him and retreated further into myself. "I can't let it go. I can't, Julian. I can't." I shook my head from side to side and clamped my hand over my mouth to stifle the sobs.

When I turned around, I saw the bed where he had laid me down and done what he wanted with me. Not that I hadn't wanted any of it in return. I collapsed on the mattress and buried my face in the sheets, weeping for the home we had found in each other's arms. How could I leave it behind?

"It's not safe here, anymore, Anna," Julian declared, giving me the space I needed.

"I know," I cried, inhaling his scent from the pillow. "I understand."

"Do you?" he barked, turning sour all of a sudden. "We have to leave. Now."

Death was what I feared most. But not mine. His.

In the middle of nowhere, we had some sense of protection. So two assassins had breached the thickets of the forest. Did that mean others would? Did that mean we had to thrust ourselves out on the open road? Where his killer friends would surely be waiting for us? Like hitchhikers ready to slit our throats after climbing inside.

I wanted to stay here and be with Julian. There had been days when I felt truly happy out here alone with him. I knew he could protect me. I knew he would protect me. But how could he protect himself?

"You will see your family again," he said. "I'll get you home safe. Like I promised."

I dragged my hand across my eyelids and looked back. "Maybe I don't wanna go home anymore."

Julian squared his jaw and came towards me, circling his arms around my waist. When he set me down on the floor, I huffed at his unnecessary force and glared. But he had no time for patience.

Tugging at my elbow, Julian led me out into the hall and towards the front door. But I withdrew from his grasp and ran, reaching for a world that didn't exist, a fantasy that had never been real, a man that wasn't quite whole, quite human, quite anything but truth and darkness.

Julian snagged my shirt and I tripped as he collapsed alongside me. "No!" I cried out.

"If you won't come willingly, I have no problem throwing you over my shoulder." Julian kept his eyes on me while I gazed into those glittering blue depths with a round of heaving, shaky breaths.

"Julian," I pleaded.

"I will drag you out of here if I have to," he promised. "It's for your own good."

"Do you even love me, Julian?" I asked, struggling for breath on the floor. I had to know.

Julian looked away and then clenched his jaw, fixing his smoldering gaze on me. Desperate for him to bare his soul like I had so willingly bared mine, I parted my lips and held my breath. When he failed to respond right away, my lashes fluttered as I scanned every inch of his beautiful face.

The beautiful face of a beautiful stranger.

"No." He pursed his lips and frowned. "I don't love you."

Pain ripped through me like a dagger to the heart. As hurt flitted across my features, I sat up and pressed my back into the wall. Julian reclined on his elbow and reached out for me, but I had no desire for his touch. "Anna," he gently cooed. "I never meant to hurt you."

"Good job." I got to my feet and glanced down at him with pure pity in my eyes. "You did it anyway."

Julian studied me with a pair of wide blue eyes, and for a moment he almost looked like a boy.

"Let's go," I urged, turning my back on him. "You don't need to throw me over your shoulder."

Hardening my heart, I slammed the front door open and stomped out into the dreary cold. In no time, Julian was at my heels with winter boots and a hooded jacket. I snatched the clothes out of his hand but refused to put them on until we reached the car.

Julian started the engine and blasted the heat, asking if I was cold. But I fastened my boots and pulled the hood up on my jacket, shamelessly ignoring him. As we drove away, I looked out the window at the place which—only now that we were leaving—suddenly felt like home.

I knew we would never be back.

* * *

Dozing off in the car, I lost track of time. I have faint memories of Julian pulling over for what felt like hours at a time, paranoid of who might see us in broad daylight. I felt dead, like I hadn't slept the night before, probably because I hadn't. But when he pulled into a motel later that night, I squinted my eyes and groaned from the tight muscles and kinks in my neck that refused to relax.

"Stay in the car," Julian commanded, taking the keys from the ignition. "In fact, lay down in the back seat."

"What?" I cocked a brow at him and scowled.

"I said lay down." He pointed to the back and glowered until I did what he said.

"Fine." I sprawled my legs out and put my head over my hands on the cloth seat.

Julian tossed a blanket over me like he was trying to cover up a dead body. Then he slipped out of the car and locked me inside. Thankful for the warmth, I turned my head towards the back of the seat. Then I picked at the cushion with my fingernail and tried not to think.

No. I don't love you.

How could those words be true when every action led me to believe otherwise? If Julian really didn't love me, then why had he gone through all the trouble? To save me. To spare me. To take me home.

Deep down, I knew it must be true. Of course he had taken advantage of the situation, my inexperience, my feelings. After all, Julian was ten years older than me. And I didn't even know his last name.

Someone knocked on the window and I startled, flinching at the pain in my neck. It was Julian.

"Come on. Let's get inside." He opened the back door and urged me on. "Hurry."

I stepped into the cold night with the blanket draped around me and pulled my hood up. When Julian led me inside, I almost resented the fact that he held the door open for me. Only a true gentleman would do such a thing. And Julian was certainly no gentleman.

His large hand settled at the small of my back as we walked down the dark hall. This was a seedy place, but inconspicuous enough to be attractive for our circumstances. Julian opened the door to our motel room and twisted every lock in sight once we were both safe inside.

Crossing my arms over my chest, I took a few steps forward and observed our less than stellar living conditions for the night. There was only one bed, meaning we would have to share, meaning I would have to sleep beside a man who had knowingly admitted that he didn't love me, even though I was helplessly in love with him. But it was so much more than that.

I was crazy about Julian. But maybe that's all it was.

Crazy.

"We should be safe here for the night," he noted, checking the ceiling for cobwebs.

"I'm hungry." I threaded my fingers through my hair and winced at the throbbing migraine that was starting to make my eye twitch. We had only stopped once to eat in the car, and all I had managed was one square of Rice Krispies Treats. Julian was so paranoid about being spotted, with me being an Ex-President's daughter with a bounty on her head, that food had been placed on the back burner for the day.

"Okay." Julian set his hands on his hips and looked me over. "Why don't you lie down and rest?"

Scoffing, I slid beneath the sheets and put my head on the pillow. "Like you care."

"What?" Julian waited for me to clarify, but I had no intention of making things plain.

"All you want is to tell me what to do," I announced with my back to him. "I'm sick of it."

"Anna." He sat down on the edge of the mattress as I rolled my eyes. "I'm trying to protect you."

"Then stop making me hurt so much." I bit my lower lip and clung to the pillowcase.

Julian reached out and put his hand on my arm.

"Go away," I barked. "Don't touch me anymore."

Turning quiet, Julian pulled away and got off the bed. "I'll go get you something to eat."

"Okay," I grumbled, sniffling all the while. When he finally left, the dam broke and tears came rolling down in wet streaks. I hoped that he hadn't heard me before walking out the door.

The last thing I wanted Julian to gain satisfaction from was the agony of him not loving me.

Once I let it all out, sleep came fast and peaceful. Even though Julian was gone, I didn't feel afraid. It was impossible to dream, but I tried to conjure up a world where he actually loved me.

In what felt like five minutes, Julian shook me awake and rustled a paper sack in his arms. After rubbing my eyes, I sat up enough to detect the delicious smell of cheese and bacon. My stomach growled, and when Julian perched himself on the edge of the mattress this time, I didn't even care.

"Thank God. I'm starving." My mouth watered at the sight of cheeseburgers and fries. Julian emptied the bag on the bed, while I lunged for the first item I saw. Within seconds, I ripped the protective paper off and sank my teeth into what must have been a quarter pound of beef.

"That one was for me," Julian butted in, though he wasn't terribly harsh about it.

"Too bad." I took a huge bite and glared. My heart was for him as well. But he didn't want that. He didn't care.

"What's with the attitude?" Julian unwrapped a smaller burger with a single thin patty.

"I don't have attitude," I sassed, talking with food in my mouth.

"Yes, you do." When I ignored him, Julian set his measly hamburger down on the paper sack and leaned forward, taking a bite out of the opposite end of mine.

"Hey!" I swallowed the meat and bread in my

mouth and sent daggers in his direction.

Julian confiscated the burger and finished it in three bites. Refusing to be patronized by him, I shoved a handful of fries in my mouth and moaned. Two could play that game.

"What are you doing?" Julian froze in place, as I watched his Adam's apple bob.

As I reached for another cheeseburger, Julian grabbed my arm and pinned my body to the mattress beneath him. I swallowed and gasped, my breath catching at the back of my throat. He framed my hair around my face and gazed into my eyes, trapping me with the guarded, sultry gleam in his.

Despite the way I was unraveling on the inside, I withheld my emotions and raised my chin at him. "You don't love me, Julian," I reminded him as he narrowed his eyes. "So stop torturing me."

His cheek twitched, and he chewed at the inside of his mouth. Because I was right.

Still starving, I pushed against his hold and sat up in bed, stuffing a few more fries in my mouth. When I unwrapped the next massive burger, Julian made no attempt to steal it from me. Instead, he offered me ketchup and even squeezed some onto the inside of a container when I agreed.

We ate in silence until not even a drop of food remained. Julian threw the empty sack in the trashcan and then headed into the bathroom. While he was gone, I stripped down to nothing more than a t-shirt and underwear. Then I circled the hotel room and swiped my finger over the trail of dust left behind.

Julian returned to find me peeking out the window, despite his warning to stay away. Furious with me for disobeying an order, he clasped my wrist and pulled me back. The curtain fell over the glass as he released his hold on me, looking my figure up and down. "We should go to bed," he decided.

I folded my hands behind my back in an attempt to hold my own. "Well, I think you should sleep on the floor." I didn't mean to bob my head in the process, but even my hair sashayed with the motion.

Julian snorted at the idea and took a step too close. "Do you now?"

"Yes." I moved backwards until I ran into the wall. "I do."

"Well, since I'm the one who will be driving tomorrow, I think I need the bed more than you do."

"Is that so?" I countered, ignoring the throbbing pain at the back of my head where I hit it.

"Yes," he hissed, caging me in with his arms. "It is."

"Well, what are you going to do about it?" I was secretly hoping to provoke him, stir up the passion inside, so he would be forced to reveal everything he was feeling for me. Even if it wasn't love.

"It's late." He blinked slowly enough to be mesmerizing. "And we have an early start tomorrow. Go to bed, Anna."

"Who do you think you are?" I snapped. "My father?"

Tired of my resistance, Julian took my hand and dragged me over to the mattress. Then he turned the lights out and pulled me into the bed alongside him. While I could have protested, I was tired and drained from a sleepless night. All I really wanted was for him to hold me in his arms.

Once I was situated beneath the covers, Julian lay there without touching me, and we both stared up at the ceiling. My heart thrummed loudly in my chest, while I longed for him to pull me close. Regardless of his lack of feelings for me, I still wanted Julian, I still desired him, I still *loved* him.

"Anna," he groveled, his voice vibrating all around me.

"Yes?" I folded my hands over my stomach and made sure our elbows weren't touching.

"Why do you fight it?" he questioned, sending prickles and shivers up and down my spine.

"Fight what?" I growled. It felt like he was teasing me, dangling the bait.

"Do you really want me to sleep on the floor?" he waited for me to answer, but all I did was breathe.

"No," I finally said. What was the point in hiding it? He could see straight through me.

"Then come here." He opened his arms and waited for me to sail into them.

Even though I loathed him for toying with me, I knew how badly I needed his comfort. So I sighed at the defeat, because he had won the battle tonight. Truthfully, I couldn't comprehend why we had declared war on each other. For me, it started the moment he told me he didn't love me.

There were bullet holes in my heart. Where he had pierced straight through with his gun. After the honeymoon we had shared in hiding, how could he take everything back in one breath? Like it didn't matter—what we had done. I didn't matter. Nor did the love I felt for him.

But that was just the thing. I loved Julian, and he knew it.

So I put my head on his chest and wrapped my arms around his torso. Julian rested his hand on my back and ran his fingers through my hair, gently coaxing me to sleep. As I drifted off, a small part of me wondered if Julian would miss me when I was gone.

Chapter 17

I woke to find Julian as blond as a California surfer. At first, the sight startled me and I fell off the bed, scared that I had been hijacked by his flaxen doppelganger. If he had an evil twin, that was saying a lot considering the fact that Julian was an assassin trained to kill without mercy.

"Julian," I startled, blinking more times than I could count. "What happened to your hair?"

After helping me up, Julian led me into the bathroom without warning. "You're next."

There was a pair of sharp scissors by the sink, and I swear they glimmered in the light. "No!" I turned on my heel to get out of there and slammed into Julian's rock hard chest. His eyes were morose.

"Anna, you have to." He pushed my hair over my shoulders. "You have a famous face." Then he lifted my chin in the palm of his hand and tenderly stroked the edge of my jawline. "You'll get recognized."

Seeing his point, I lowered my gaze and studied the grout. "You're right."

Julian braced my shoulders and led me to the mirror. I held on to the edge of the counter and took a deep breath, feeling my heart begin to race. For years, I had valued my beauty as a woman according to the thickness and length of those blond locks. My father told me to never cut my hair. Some verse from the Bible. But maybe I didn't have a choice. Like Samson, maybe a lover had convinced me otherwise.

Instead of preparing me for the moment, Julian gathered all of my hair into a loose bunch at the back of my neck. Then he brought the scissors to the makeshift ponytail and cut. It was one resounding snip that sent a mountain of hair falling to the floor. When I felt it gather at my feet, I held my head high and dared to look in the mirror. What had once skirted past my waist now barely touched my shoulders.

I turned my head to the side and shut my eyes. Somehow, I knew that this wasn't over yet.

Julian stretched a pair of plastic gloves over his hands and shook a clear bottle full of dark dye. After squeezing the substance on his palms, he rubbed them together and then began running the color over my pale locks. As he applied one coat and then another and then another, I saw the old Anna slipping away. A new Anna had replaced her. A dark, foul creature desperate to run away and hide.

When my hair was covered in black from root to tip, Julian tossed the gloves and waited for the dye to set. Afterwards, he rinsed my hair out in the sink, and it kind of bothered me how comfortable he was with this. Like changing his hair color and adopting a new identity were things he did often.

"All right." Julian finished drying my hair. "All done. Do you want to look?"

I peered into the glass and resembled a frightened puppy. Picking at a random lock, I let the reality sink in, even though I would always expect something else—or rather, someone else—every time I looked in the mirror. "I look like a witch," I noted, loathing the raven black.

"You'll get used to it." Julian wrapped his arms around my stomach and planted a kiss on my temple. "You still look beautiful to me."

Despite all the many ways he had hurt me, I touched his arm in a reassuring caress. Maybe Julian didn't love me. But surely I meant something to him. Perhaps I could forget what he had said and just enjoy what time we had left together. After all, it was inevitable. We both knew time was running out.

"Here." Julian handed me a navy blue baseball cap, but I failed to move. "We have to go."

I dragged my fingers across the glass and muttered, "I don't even know who I am anymore."

Julian put the hat on my head and untucked

the hair behind my ears so it hung loose, further masking my appearance. "You're Anna James. Student of Princeton University. Ex-President's daughter."

"No, I'm not." Shaking my head, I turned around and touched the stubble on his face. "I'm not any of those things anymore." I set my piercing green gaze on him, and he held still beneath my touch.

When I feathered my fingers through his newly blond hair, Julian put his hands on my hips and drew me into his embrace. Something flashed across his sapphire eyes, nearly aquamarine. Was it heat? Lust? Certainly not love. Regardless, just like the first time I discovered what he was, I wanted him anyway.

Julian rested his forehead against mine, and my eyelids slid shut. As the end of his nose skimmed my cheekbone, I trailed my fingers down his neck and inhaled. He smelled so wonderful. Fresh and clean. Right out of the shower. With my eyes closed, I still pictured him with dark hair and smiled.

As Julian honed in on me, I felt his warm breath across my lips.

"I can't do this," I spoke under my breath. "It hurts too much."

When he exhaled, I opened my eyes and studied his demeanor, searching for answers.

"You're never going to love me." I inquired. "Are you?"

"That doesn't mean I don't want you," he defended, slipping his hands beneath my shirt.

"Wanting is not good enough, Julian." I peeled his arms from my waist and turned away.

"It has nothing to do with you," he said, touching my shoulder. "I've never loved anyone."

Stopping in my tracks, I sighed out loud and looked back at him. "Anyone?"

"No." He shook his head and slowly came closer until I was pressed against the wall. "Not anyone."

"Well." I moistened my lips and focused on the task of drawing air into my lungs. "There must have been someone, sometime in your life. A family member. A friend. A woman."

"You're the only one who has even come close," he insisted, cupping my cheek in his palm.

A furrow formed between my brows. "Are you just saying that so I'll sleep with you?"

"No." He pressed his thumb to the soft flesh beneath my chin and clenched his jaw. "You mean a whole lot more to me than that. More than I'll ever let you know. It's not in my nature to be kind."

"But you are kind, Julian." I placed my hand over his heart, and it skipped a beat. "When you want to be."

"No, I'm not." He threaded his fingers through my black locks with tender care. "I'm a monster."

Breathless, I rubbed the dark stubble on his face and murmured, "We both know that's not true."

Julian searched my eyes and sank his teeth into his bottom lip. Heat blossomed between us as I grew weak in the knees. No matter what he did, that man held a power over me that no one else ever would.

"We should get out of here." He stepped back as I noticed the rise and fall of his chest.

I pouted at Julian with a groan and wilted against the wall, needing him desperately.

When he turned on his heel and left me alone in the bathroom, I approached the mirror and traipsed my fingers through my new hair. In a way, I suppose it was ironic that we had switched. Now Julian was the blond, and my chopped off locks were pure black.

"Where are we anyway?" I said over my shoulder.

"Vermont." Julian tossed my jacket in the air, as I reached out to grab it. "Let's go.'

As we headed out to the parking lot, I slipped into the Volvo and pulled the hood of my jacket over my head. Julian checked out of the motel and met me at the car, sliding into the driver's seat without a word. For the next three hours, the silence between us failed to change.

We stopped at a gas station in New Hampshire, not thirty minutes from the Massachusetts state line. While Julian filled up the tank, I used the restroom and walked around the convenience store. Julian had chosen a spot off the map, and since it was the middle of the week, there was no one inside but the owner.

Letting my hair down, I waltzed over to a rack of sunglasses and tried a few pairs on. The doorbell chimed when Julian stepped inside and headed to the front to pay with cash. Our eyes connected across the way and I turned on my heel, ambling towards the back of the store.

My eyes flitted over several shelves of Coke products before something caught the corner of my eye. There was a painting hung on the wall, at the back of a gas station of all places. Stopping in my tracks, I scanned the contrast from dark to light and was forced to drink it in.

The painting was of a canoe drifting through a stream in the woods. No one was inside of it.

Slipping my fingers into the collar of my shirt, I thought about how closely that resembled Julian's life. Never settling down. No permanent roots. No wife. No kids. Just murder. Just death. Just pain.

I felt sorry for that lone canoe, doomed to wander from stream to stream. A different body of water every night. Never able to stay in one place for long. Never able to stop.

What must that be like? I couldn't think of a better analogy for hell.

"You can have that if you want."

I glanced back to find the owner pointing a finger at me. A tall, stocky man with balding gray hair, he could have passed for mid-to late sixties. When he walked around the counter and came towards me, Julian stepped close enough to stand between us.

"That won't be necessary," Julian declared, taking my hand.

"Some local painter brought it in one day." The owner put his hands on his belt and stared up at the canoe. "No one will buy it. I can't ever seem to get rid of the thing."

"It's beautiful," I noted, glancing up at the blues and greens of the river one last time.

I felt the owner's eyes settling on my face as blush stained my cheeks. Julian squeezed my hand but I stood still, unable to move. It was like cement had been poured over my feet, gluing me to the spot.

"Hey." The old man tilted his head to the side. "Do I know you from somewhere?"

"I don't think so," I muttered, lacking the courage to look him in the eye.

"Just passing through," Julian butted in. "Thanks for the gas."

"You're sure you two haven't been here before?" The owner cocked a brow at us.

"Nope." Julian locked his fingers through mine, headed for the door. "Take care."

"Hey, where are you two headed?" The owner stared at the back of our heads.

Julian pushed the door open as it chimed, making me cross the threshold first. Then he turned back to the owner and replied, "West."

"New York," the man declared, brightening

up.

"Yeah." Julian crossed the threshold and touched my shoulder. "New York."

Blood thrummed in my ears like the sound of drums. Julian opened my car door and waited for me to get in, while the old man watched us through the window. I moistened my lower lip and buckled my seatbelt as Julian walked around the front of the car and climbed inside.

Julian started the ignition and stepped on the gas, slowly pulling away. When we were farther down the road, his eyes stayed on the rearview mirror. I pulled my hood up and tightened the strings, nervously chewing at my fingernails until he finally had something to say.

"What did we talk about?" Julian scolded. "You don't look at anyone. You don't talk to anyone. You don't say *anything*."

"What was I supposed to do? Ignore him? He was looking right at me!"

"You're America's sweetheart and a former first daughter. Right now, the whole country is looking for you." He jabbed his thumb over his shoulder, back at the gas station we had just left. "Including that guy."

"I'm sorry, but what do you want me to do? I don't even look the same anymore." I adjusted my seatbelt and turned to face him head on. "You cut my hair and then dyed it black," I pointed out.

"It's not your hair, Anna." His knuckles turned white around the steering wheel. "It's your face."

"What is that supposed to mean?" I furrowed my brow and waited for him to acknowledge me.

"Like it's not bad enough that you're recognizable. You're attractive, too."

"What's your point, Julian?" I remarked, an edge of bitterness to my voice.

He shocked me by looking into my eyes and then the road. "You think attractive people don't get noticed more often? You think they don't get more attention than the average person?"

I braided my fingers together in my lap and grew uneasy, looking out the window.

"This is stupid!" He beat his fist against the door. "I don't know why I ever thought it would be a good idea to take you back in broad daylight. We're going to have to start driving at night."

If we drove straight through, we could make it to DC by an hour or two after sunset.

"As soon as we get to Springfield, we're pulling over and staying in a motel."

Selfishly, I breathed a sigh of relief for the delay, and the fact that Julian had been taking back roads for most of the morning. While I understood his reasons for flying under the radar, I hoped the decreased risk of being caught wasn't the only one for his behavior. I wanted to milk every last second we had together on our journey home. Deep down, I wondered if he did, too.

* * *

When we reached Springfield, Julian found a

vacancy at a motel on the outskirts of town. We ate packaged snack foods left over from gas station stops along the way but hardly said a word to each other. While Julian was taking a shower, I turned the TV on and climbed into bed.

The curtains were drawn, blocking out every strand of sunlight. So even though it was early afternoon, the room was full of darkness, alluding to the inevitable night. But I felt safe at the motel, protected from the outside world, as if we were hiding out in a cave. Like a vampire in a coffin.

A picture of me flashed on the screen as I unmuted the television and sat up straight.

"The hunt for Anna James continues. Former President Walter James and his wife, Winifred have yet to discover whether or not the email sent from Anna's personal Gmail account to her father is in fact, from Anna herself. The message indicates that Anna is safe, in hiding, and being looked over by 'an angel.' Further investigation continues as we all await the return of the former first daughter. The only child of President and Mrs. James, Anna was in her sophomore year at Princeton University when she disappeared one night over three weeks ago with her roommate, Bridgette Eastwood. Police officials believe..."

I muted the television as the newscaster rambled on. While I had been living in a bubble with Julian, the whole world was out there looking for me. Was it selfish that I wanted to stay in the bubble just a little longer? That I wanted to live in a magic snow globe where nothing but the two of us mattered?

When Julian came out of the shower, I turned the TV off and set the remote down on the nightstand. There was a towel wrapped around his waist and nothing else. Droplets of water trickled down the contours of his chest and abdomen, rippling over the muscle. I leaned back on the mattress and wondered if the sadist in him was coming out. Was he trying to tease me?

"Julian," I called, biting the edge of my lip when he turned around.

He dressed in a flash, as if he didn't want me to see any part of him. I couldn't understand why. So I stood up and approached him as he buttoned his shirt all the way to the top.

"I'm driving you to New Haven tonight." He pulled a sweatshirt over his head and failed to look at me. "Someone there is going to take you the rest of the way home."

"What?" I grabbed his shirtsleeve and jerked him towards me. "Why can't you take me home?"

Julian pressed his lips together and sighed. "Because you're not safe with me anymore."

"But with a stranger, I am?" I motioned my hands at the absurdity of it all.

"Anna, I've got it all taken care of," he griped. "Now I need to make some phone calls."

As he turned on his heel to leave, I stared after him. "Julian!"

He stopped in his tracks and looked back at

me, his face lacking emotion.

"I want you to take me home. I want you to drive me to DC. Please." I moved towards him and struggled with the painful lump rising in my throat. Somehow, a treasonous tear slipped through anyway.

"I don't care what you want," he firmly declared. "I'm doing what it takes to get you home safe."

My lower lip trembled as I cried. "Am I ever going to see you again?"

Julian looked over me and then his calm blue eyes met mine. "No."

I stared up at him despite the fresh flood of tears coating my face with moisture.

"Anna." Julian squared his jaw. "Don't look at me like that."

"Like what?" I took a step closer and got in his face. "Like I care? Like I'm in love with you?"

"Anna," he scolded, putting more distance between us.

"Maybe this isn't hard for you," I sobbed, choking on my tears. "But it's ripping me in half."

Julian pressed his fingers against his chest. "You think this isn't hard for me, too?"

"I know it's not!" I yelled, gritting my teeth for the pain he was putting me through.

"You don't have any idea what you're talking about." He slowly shook his head.

I took a gasp of air and buried my face in my hands. "I don't know," I cried, shivering and shaking.

I was so confused about everything. Especially my life. The one I had left in the wilderness. The one I had left in the city. Which one I would return to. And then there was Julian.

We had been given so little time together, and now to have it all taken away at the drop of a hat...

It was too much. I couldn't cope.

"Shh..." Julian grasped the top of my shoulders and wrapped me in his arms. As he rubbed my back, I buried my face in his chest, drowning in his heavenly scent. I never wanted to forget the way he smelled.

When Julian lifted my chin with his fingers, I looked into his eyes and sobbed. "I love you," I whimpered. "I love you, Julian. I love you so much." I could hardly get the words out but knew that I had to, no matter how I was shaking. "Even if you don't love me. It doesn't matter. I'll love you forever."

"Things change," he reminded me, dragging his thumb across my cheekbone. "People change."

"Nothing will ever change the way I feel about you right now," I mumbled.

"I'm going away, Anna." He held my gaze, as I hung on to his every word. "And I won't be back."

"Can't I go, too?" I pleaded, utterly desperate now. "Please, take me with you."

"No." He scanned my face, registering every look I sent his way. "It wouldn't be safe. You don't know who I am, what I've done." He looked down and then returned his gaze to me. "You belong in DC with your family. With people who love and care about you. You belong back at Princeton, Anna. You had a great life before me. And you'll have an even better one when I'm gone."

"No." I stepped away, knowing that he wasn't backing down. He never did.

"Anna."

"I hate you!" I lashed out, stabbing my finger at him. "For saving me and protecting me and making me love you! I hate you! I hate you! I hate you!" I pounded my fists against his chest like a child.

Julian grabbed my wrists and held them away from his body. "Would you rather be dead?"

"Yes!" I hissed. "I would rather have you kill me than treat me like this!"

"Stop it, Anna! Calm down." He pinned my arms to my sides. "Someone is going to hear you."

"I'll bet your blond friend would have done it," I bitterly declared. "I'll bet he wouldn't have had a problem pulling the trigger. But you, you couldn't stop shaking. It was like you had never handled a gun before."

"If you don't shut up—"

"You couldn't kill me, because you didn't have it in you. So just say it!" I stalked towards him, turning into the closest thing I had ever seen to a witch. "Say it, Julian. You're a cowar—"

Before I could get the word out, Julian slammed my back into the wall and sealed his mouth over mine. I whimpered at the tingling touch of his lips, especially when he grabbed my thighs and lifted me in his arms. My legs wrapped around his waist like a pair of magnets that couldn't help but attract.

I toyed with the hem of his sweatshirt and Julian lifted his arms, helping me take it off. Once it hit the floor, his button-down shirt was next. Impatient and greedy, I twirled my fingers through the ends of his hair and brought his mouth to mine.

Julian struggled with the buttons, eventually breaking them all as he ripped through the fabric to get his shirt off. I smoothed my hands over his shoulders and biceps, pushing the garment to the floor. His hands slipped beneath my shirt, and I gasped at the sensitive contact.

When his lips landed on my neck, I tilted my head to the side and shut my eyes. I wanted this. I wanted him. *Forever.* But knowing that it wasn't going to last—that it was almost over—well, that just made me want it even more.

Julian pulled the sleeve of my shirt down and ran his teeth across my shoulder. Shivers ran over my spine as the back of my head lolled against the wall, my weight resting in the strength of his arms. When he pressed his hands into my hips and spun around to land on the bed, I squeaked at the bounce.

I lay beneath Julian with my head on the pillow, as he straddled my waist. His fingertips picked at the hem of my top, so I put my arms up and gave him the green light. He caressed every inch of my skin on the way up my body, slowly easing the fabric over my torso and head.

Julian kissed his way across my stomach, gently pressing his lips to each of my ribs just to make me squirm. My hand tightened around the bed sheet as he slid his palms along the curves of my waist. When he brought his mouth to mine, I wrapped my arms around him and squeezed so tight.

I think we both knew this would be the last time.

Julian peppered kisses all over my face. A slow, soothing gesture that was out of character for him. He smoothed his fingertips along the inside of my arms, and I shivered, desperately wanting to hold on to this moment forever. But maybe that was what made it so special. Ephemerality.

The moment was beautiful, because I knew it wouldn't last. I knew it was going to die. Just like us.

"Julian?" I looked into his eyes and traced my hand over his back as he held still and watched me.

"Yeah." There was a furrow between his brows. A beautiful furrow between his beautiful brows.

I wanted to tell him how much I loved him, but he already knew that. In fact, he was probably sick of hearing it. All of this lovey dovey talk, and I still had no idea if he would ever feel anything for me. Other than lust.

"I don't care if you don't love me," I confessed. And it was true.

Sorrow flitted across his features, but Julian let me continue.

"I just want to be with you," I whispered, bearing my soul. "One last time."

Julian held himself up on the mattress, his strong arms on either side of my face. He exhaled through his nostrils and watched over me, lowering his face to mine. "One day, you're going to make some man very happy."

As dread shot through me like the bullet from a gun, I shut my eyes to conceal the single tear that trickled down. Love is pain. Love is agony. Love is torture.

Oh how I wanted that man to be him.

Julian pressed a sweet kiss to my lips and then stopped. Confused by his hesitancy, I blinked my eyes open and leaned my head up. But Julian pulled away before I could reach his mouth.

"I can't do this." Julian dropped down from the bed and picked his clothes up off the floor. He was still wearing his pants, so all he had to do was slip into the clothing that remained.

"What are you doing?" I whined, sitting up on the mattress with terror in my eyes.

Julian ran his fingers through his hair and pulled the end of his sweatshirt over his pants. As he adjusted the collar of his button-down shirt beneath it, his striking blue gaze settled on mine.

The kind that caught your eye from all the way across the room.

"Won't it just hurt more?" he questioned. "Afterwards? When I'm gone?"

Maybe he was right, like he always was. But I didn't want to think about how I was going to feel tomorrow. All I cared about was this moment, and the fact that it was slowly slipping away. Like steel cut diamonds sinking to the depths of a clear, endless sea. Apparent enough to see drifting away, but never close enough to reach, never close enough to bring back again, never close enough to touch.

"I don't care," I admitted, gazing up at him with pouty lips and pleading eyes.

Julian stuffed his hands in his pockets and asked, "Haven't I hurt you enough?"

Clever, I considered what he was saying and mused, "Maybe I want you to hurt me some more."

"No." He frowned and headed for the door. "You deserve better than that. Better than me."

I sat helplessly on the bed, as if someone had shackled me to the frame. In a way, I guess he had. That man owned me, body and soul. He walked out the door and took my heart with him. And the worst part?

I wanted him to.

Chapter 18

I watched the streetlamps blurring by until it made me drunk. We crossed the state line around midnight, not long after Julian woke me up and said that it was time to go. If the choice had been up to me, I would have stayed in bed all night, wallowing in my misery. But it was time to leave. So we did.

We were in Connecticut now, a state whose spelling had been the cause of some taunting in my youth. At six, how was I to know that the second *c* was silent? I still thought it sounded better that way. More intriguing at least.

It had been awhile since we crossed the state line, and my palms were starting to sweat.

"I'm sorry about what I said to you earlier." I stared at my hands in my lap and then looked out the window. "I didn't mean it. The part about hating you and wishing you had killed me."

"I know you didn't." Julian kept his eyes on the road, which was just as well.

"I was acting like a brat," I added, owning up to it. "And I'm sorry."

"I'm sorry, too." Julian ran a hand through his hair as his knuckles tightened around the wheel.

"For what?" I turned to the side and studied his handsome profile. "For saving my life?"

"If I had it to go over again, there are some things I might have done differently."

"Not for me, Julian."

He looked my way for no more than an instant, but I cherished it.

"I wouldn't change a thing."

When he clenched his jaw and smoldered, I looked back out the window and crossed my arms over my chest. Even though we were driving south, it was getting colder. Julian leaned over to turn the heat up, and I shivered.

Silence ruled the rest of the car ride, while I wondered if those would be the last words we would ever say to each other. I was glad that I told him what I needed to get off my chest. No matter how much I was hurt by his unfeeling heart, I loved him. I would always love him. And he needed to know that.

Julian pulled into a bar on the wrong side of town, while I questioned his judgement. Scanning the parking lot, I saw nothing but drunks and drifters. My intuition told me to run, yet Julian looked over at me with a reassuring nod. So I swallowed my fear and opened the car door. I trusted him.

As I walked around the front of the car, Julian crept up behind me. "Put your hood up," he instructed, tightening the strings. I turned to face him head on, and he pulled my hair around my face, so it hung in a messy, obscuring fashion. Then he put his hand on my back and said, "Let's go."

Paralyzed with fear, I clung to his side and let him lead me through the entrance. The doors were clouded with smoke, and when they opened I gagged. Julian clamped his hand around my arm and steered me through the crowd until we reached the bar at the back.

I couldn't tell if this was a restaurant, bar, or brothel. From the looks of it, perhaps it was some combination of the three. When Julian put pressure on my shoulder and sat me down on a stool, I touched the cool counter and looked around the place. No one had noticed me. Yet.

Regardless, I breathed a sigh of relief and tried my best to relax. A tall, stocky man emerged from behind the counter and exchanged a handshake with Julian. The man had stringy black hair tied back in a bun, honey-colored eyes, and a gorgeous smile. He was the bartender.

As I turned to flee, Julian draped his arm across my shoulders, and I leaned into him.

"Anna, this is Jordan," he said, raising his voice over the booming music.

"Hi there!" Jordan extended his hand as I spotted a dimple in one of his cheeks. "I'm Jordan."

"Hi." I took his hand, only because Julian was there.

"Thanks for helping us out, man." Julian leaned over the counter. "I really appreciate it."

"No problem. Anything for an old friend. Can I get you a shot?" Jordan asked.

"Yes." Julian grinned like the devil, and I felt like puking.

I slid my hands beneath my legs and sat on them, despite the shortness of breath. Something about this place reminded me of the night Bridgette and I were taken. What was it with the good looking bartenders? Was that their ploy? What they used to suck the girls in?

"Can I get you anything, honey?" Jordan filled a shot glass with whiskey and slid it across the counter. When Julian slung the amber liquid back and asked for another, I lowered my gaze and paled.

"No," I muttered. "Thank you."

Jordan took a tequila shot and raised it in the air. "To beautiful women."

"To beautiful women," Julian echoed, clinking glasses with the man who might very well kill me.

I really wanted to cry. Especially when a suspicious pair of eyes settled on me. They belonged to a drunken man with grey whiskers and a sloppy demeanor. He dragged the back of his hand across his mouth and took another slurp, eyeing my well-hidden figure up and down.

"Well, I better get going." Julian set his shot glass down on the counter and bumped fists with Jordan. "Call me when you know she's safe," he said. "I owe you one."

"No problem, man." Jordan slapped Julian on the shoulder. "I should have her home tonight."

"Good." Julian looked at me once and then turned on his heel to walk away.

Panicking, I slipped down off the bar stool and followed him. "Julian, wait!"

He spun around at the sound of my voice and lowered his face to hear me better.

"Don't make me go with him," I begged, clasping his hands with mine.

"You'll be safer with him." Julian tilted my chin up in the palm of his hand.

"How? I don't even know him." I shook my head. Stalling. Plotting. Renegotiating.

"Because Jordan doesn't have a bounty on his head," he revealed.

"You do?" I widened my eyes, wondering why he had never chosen to share this with me until now.

"Yes." He rested his hands on my shoulders and smiled. "That's what happens when you steal the President's daughter."

Before I could correct him with the word *Ex,* Julian took my face in his hands and planted his mouth on mine. I held on to his arm and returned the kiss, lengthening it the best I could. But, of course, it was never enough. It would never be enough. What we had was not the stuff life is made of.

It was a stolen winter.

"I've known Jordan for a long time," Julian assured me. "You can trust him."

"Will we ever see each other again?" I damned back the tears, so unbearably ready to flow.

Julian brushed his thumb along my bottom lip and then let go. "Open your eyes."

Confusion marred my features, because my eyes were already open. But Julian saw no need to explain. He simply took a step back from me. And then another. And then another.

I fled the scene before he was gone, unable to bear the sight of him walking away. When I returned to Jordan at the bar, he flashed me a bright white smile, and I shuddered. His teeth reminded me of a wolf.

"Where is the bathroom?" I shouted over the pop techno tune that rattled my eardrums.

Jordan pointed me in the right direction and stirred a mixed drink. "I don't get off until two."

It wasn't ideal, but I would take it. "Can we leave after that?"

"Yeah." He nodded and then slid the drink across the counter to a pretty young blonde.

"Thank you." But Jordan didn't hear me. He had already returned to bartending.

On my way to the bathroom, I looked over my

shoulder, searching the building for Julian. But he was nowhere to be found. I hung my head and sighed, unable to hide my disappointment.

Someone bumped into my shoulder as air hissed through my teeth at the discomfort. I entered a dark corridor illuminated by black lights. There was a line to the bathroom a mile long, so I stumbled down the hall and found a door that was unlocked.

Dying to pee, I let myself inside and bet on the chance that a single unisex stall was waiting for me. But I found an empty room instead with stale carpet and blinding fluorescent lights. "Hello?"

As my eyes adjusted to the brightness, I turned my head from side to side. There were a handful of fold-up chairs in the room, all of which were empty. I spun around once, then twice. But the chairs looked the same at every angle. It was then that I realized they formed a large circle.

One that I was standing in the middle of.

"Hello?" I held my hand over my head to shield my eyes.

Someone dimmed the lights, as a familiar face stepped into view.

"Jordan," I sighed in relief. "I thought you were working until two."

"Have some trouble finding your way to the bathroom?" he asked.

"Something like that," I joked. "There's a *really* long line."

"Yeah." He stepped into the circle and rolled

his sleeves back, revealing his tattoos.

I honed in on the permanent ink, and my eyes saw what I expected them to.

Snakes and barbed wire. Spiraling out from the wrist to the forearm, just shy of the elbow.

My throat felt dry all of a sudden, so I licked my lips and swallowed to moisten it.

"How is it that you know Julian again?" I held my arms behind my back and forced a smile.

"Oh, we go way back." He moved closer and I froze. "He's an old army buddy of mine."

"Really?" I looked down as he paced the floor. "I didn't know Julian was in the army."

"It appears that there are a lot of things you don't know about him, Miss James."

"Oh really?" I faked a laugh. "Like what?"

"Like the real reason he brought you here tonight."

My body stiffened as I turned still as a statue.

"I'm sure you know by now that I'm not taking you home."

He hovered around me like a circling shark. And when he leaned his head over my shoulder, I took a breath and closed my eyes. His hand hooked around my waist, and I felt his chest against my back.

"What are you talking about?" I played dumb, innocent, naïve. Like that pretty blonde he had tended to at the bar. Maybe he would show me sympathy if I played the part.

Jordan pulled the hood off my head and

wrapped his hand around my throat, his thumb digging into the hollow at the base of my neck. "You've got smooth skin," he noted. "That's nice."

"What are you going to do?" I challenged, hardly able to breathe. "Kill me?"

He loosened his grip and then let it go altogether, standing in front of me while I coughed. He watched with intrigue as I fought to regain air in my lungs. It was like he enjoyed it.

"Well, maybe you know more about Julian than I thought," he declared.

"So, what are you going to do to me?" I stared into his eyes without blinking, something I had picked up from Julian. It was an intimidation tactic, but unfortunately, one that Jordan used as well.

"For someone who needs to be escorted home to Mommy and Daddy by a babysitter, you sure don't seem very afraid." He took to pacing again, lapping around my figure more than once.

When he said it, I realized that he was right. I wasn't afraid. At least not as afraid as I should have been.

But my heart had just been ripped out. The love of my life was gone. I would never see him again.

What else was there to be afraid of?

"No. I'm not going to kill you," he finally said, answering my earlier question. "But you'll want me to."

What had Julian done? A fate worse than

death? Surely, I had died and gone to hell.

"And why is that?" I turned my head to the side as he circled back, drawing a line down my throat and across my chest with his finger. Then he took my shoulders and got in my face. I could smell his breath, and there was more than alcohol reeking on the sour buds of his tongue. "Because you're special."

"Special," I repeated. I didn't question the word. I accepted it.

"Yes, Anna." His breath rained down my neck as he sized me up. "You're a special one. And I'm never letting you go." He petted my hair like I was a cat and then tucked a lock behind my ear, leaning in close enough to whisper, "You're the President's daughter."

Just like that, something inside me snapped, and I popped my fist against the bridge of his nose.

Jordan cursed and curled his fingers around his nose, feeling the blood that dripped out.

While he was distracted, I grabbed a chair and cracked it over his back. Then I kicked the rest of the chairs on top of him and tossed one accurately enough for the feet to hit him in the head. When I looked down at him breathless and bleeding beneath me, nothing had ever given me a greater sense of power.

Jordan curled his lip with a wicked smirk. "You think I do this gig alone?"

Before his words could resonate, the back

door flew open and a handful of men filed out.

As fight-or-flight took hold, I turned and ran, shocked that the door I first came through was still unlocked. Using the night club to my advantage, I sprinted through the gyrating bodies and pulled my hood over my head. When I made it outside, my breath fogged out in front of my face. I searched for Julian as lightning struck in the distance, a flash of electricity in the sky. His car was gone.

Part of me refused to accept the fact that he had truly left me. Julian had abandoned me. The one man who supposedly gave his life, his career, his safety to protect me. But where was he now?

For some reason, I thought he would have stuck around, in case something went haywire. I had no idea he had been so anxious to leave. If there was a bounty on his head, what about the one on mine?

We were in this together. Both wanted. Both missing. But now I called in to question everything he had ever told me. It was all a game, and he was playing both sides. Like always, Julian had won.

With the assassins hot on my heels, I took off running and darted down a dark ally. Little did I know that it would come to a dead end in the form of a brick wall. There must have been five of them in the pack, excluding Jordan, armed and dangerous. I heard them approaching, their footsteps like cleats on a set of bleachers, and nearly melted into a pool of blood and sweat. But then I spotted a ladder along the wall that reached all the way to the roof.

Frantic with terror, I swung my foot onto the bottom step and scaled my way to the top. Once I reached the roof, my hands were trembling and there was a metallic taste in my mouth. I ducked behind the brick border around the edge and lifted my head when the rain came pouring down.

Thunder rumbled around me, though I was already shaking in my boots. I heard shouting down below, and shivered as sheets of rain soaked my clothes and hair. The voices grew louder and I pulled my knees into my chest, planning out my next move. I would have to seek shelter once they left.

"Julian?" a worried voice called out in the night.

I heard one gunshot and then another. "WHERE IS SHE?"

My heart pounded beneath my chest, a quickening staccato that took my breath away.

"WHERE IS SHE DAMMIT?"

Gathering up my strength, I eased into an upright position and peered over the rooftop. I saw the back of a very blond head, the outlier in the group. He punched Jordan in the mouth and then kneed him in the groin. The remaining men just stood around and watched as Jordan crumpled to the cold, wet ground.

"I don't know, man," Jordan rasped, squeaking like a hamster. "She ran off."

"Ran off where?" Julian jerked Jordan up by the collar and slammed him into the brick wall.

"I don't know, man. I don't know." Jordan held up his hands. "Come on. Don't you trust me?"

"Not anymore." Julian shot him three times in the chest and took a step back.

My breath hitched at the back of my throat as he turned on the remaining men. Even though they had him outnumbered, every single assassin was afraid of him. I couldn't figure out why.

"Where is she?" Julian cocked the pistol and maneuvered the three who were left against the wall.

"I don't know!" One of them cried. "Really, I don't!"

In a matter of seconds, Julian blew them all away. He was quick and efficient in his manner of taking lives, careful not to waste any bullets. And when the last man crumpled to the ground, I gasped.

And that was when Julian looked up and saw me.

My heart sank to my stomach as I jerked away, ducking behind the brick. The rain came pouring down in buckets, and I tugged at the jacket strings to tighten the hood around my head. My breathing picked up, a series of harsh, painful gasps. It felt like the wind had been knocked out of me. And when Julian called my name, I shut my eyes and pretended that it was all a dream. A very vivid, very bad dream.

"Anna!" he yelled from the alley down below.

I knew he was coming for me. Only this time, I didn't know if I wanted him to.

"Anna!" His voice sounded closer. Like he was climbing his way up the ladder. "Anna!"

I had to get out of here.

I had to get away from him.

Before he killed me.

Relying on instinct alone, I rose to my feet and hurried across the rooftop. But the cement was slick, so I skidded across the slippery surface and tripped. I caught myself with my hands, but my knees dug into the hard ground in a way that made me wonder if I had damaged any bones.

When I looked back, Julian was already at the top of the ladder. I crawled backwards on my hands and knees, terrified at the mere sight of him. I didn't know whose side he was on.

"Anna!" He stepped onto the roof and came running towards me.

I turned around and leapt to my feet, sprinting as hard and fast as I could.

I would not let him catch me.

I would not let him beat me.

I would not let him kill me.

Julian called my name, and there was a pleading desperation to his voice. But I didn't trust it.

"Anna!" He caught up with me in a flash, clamping his hand around my elbow. "Anna.

Stop."

I cried out in anguish and slowed my steps, fleeing to the wall at my side for shelter. As fear flooded my veins, I pressed my palms into the cement and let the rain wash over me. After catching my breath, I turned around with my back against the wall, eyeing Julian up and down.

"Anna." He took a step towards me, and I cringed.

"Don't come any closer!" I held my arm out, as if that would really keep him away.

Disappointment fluttered across his features. "Anna. It's me."

"I know." I held my chin high and backed into the wall as far as I could.

Julian set his hands on his hips and looked off in the distance. He was drenched in rainwater, his blond locks darkened by the moisture. For a moment, he almost resembled the Julian I had known.

When he pulled the gun out, I sank down to the ground and curled into a ball. After watching him kill so many men without mercy, it was hard to do anything but shake. So I rocked back and forth, shivering from the rain, shivering from the cold, shivering from my inevitable death.

The gun slid across the pavement and stopped at my feet. I turned my head enough to look down at the weapon and then darted my eyes over to Julian. He knelt down in the rain and watched me.

"Why did you bring me here? Why did you

give me to Jordan?" I questioned.

"Because I thought he would get you home safe. Safer than I could," he confessed.

I tucked my wet hair back behind my ears. "He wanted to sell me. Like those other girls."

Julian clenched his jaw and snarled. "I'm never going to let that happen."

I blinked up at him through my tears. "But he said that's the reason you brought me here."

"Jordan did?" Julian cocked his head to the side. "Would you like to go ask him?"

When his eyes settled on me, I buried my face in my hands and wept. He spoke of death so casually, as if he hadn't just murdered his friend. Despite the fact that he had destroyed the men who were after me, there was something extremely unsettling about his nonchalance.

He had just killed four men in the span of thirty seconds.

And he didn't even care.

"Anna." Julian reached out and cupped my cheek in his hand.

I trembled at his touch and looked away.

"Anna, they would have killed you." He withdrew his hand from my face. "Or worse."

I gazed into his eyes and swore I saw the truth. He had the face of an honest man. For a moment, I wondered if he ever could be honest, if he ever had been, if he ever wanted to be.

"I thought I was protecting you," he murmured. "And I'm sorry."

I pulled my knees into my chest and braided my fingers at the back of my head. When my cheek brushed against the jean fabric over my legs, I sniffled and then opened my eyes to find him staring back at me.

There was a ring of truth to his words. And while I wanted to believe him, I knew the spell had already been cast long ago. There was no *wanting* to believe him. I did believe him.

And everything he had to say or possibly ever could say. Why?

Maybe it was because he saved me. Maybe it was because he was willing to put his life at risk for the sake of sparing mine, to an extent that I had never witnessed before. Maybe it was because I loved him.

"Anna, you're cold. It's freezing out here," he gently crooned.

I looked over at him and quivered. The blond hair. The blue eyes. Perhaps I had it all wrong. Maybe he wasn't evil and wicked. Maybe he wasn't a heartless killer. Maybe he was my guardian angel.

"Come on." Julian stuck out his hand, as I stared into the bed of his palm.

Of all the opportunities Julian had to kill me, he still hadn't done it yet. In fact, he took more lives than were necessary. He turned his back on fellow assassins and put my safety ahead of them all.

"I'll find us a warm place to rest," he offered,

enticing me along.

Trusting him implicitly, I put my hand in his and tingled at the feel of his touch. Julian rose to his feet and helped me up, even when my shoes slipped against the cement. As I stumbled forward, Julian locked his arms around me and steadied my balance, never letting go of my hand.

With a simple nod, Julian steered me to the end of the rooftop, and we climbed down the ladder. Thunder rumbled in the distance, as the rain failed to let up. When I reached the third step, the heel of my shoe slipped against the slick metal and my legs flew out from under me.

"AH!" I screamed, especially when my hand started losing grip.

Julian secured his arm around my hips and held me against him. "It's okay. I've got you."

Trembling with fear, I clung to that metal bar and flinched at a thunderous bolt of lightning.

"Just let go, Anna," Julian encouraged. "I've got you. I won't let you fall."

So I coiled my arms around his neck and held on tight. And Julian scaled down that ladder with one arm like it was nothing. Once he set me down in the alleyway—just like the one on the other side of the building, except this one had no dead bodies—I took a step back and caught my breath.

"Come on." Julian grasped my hand and braided his fingers through mine.

I loved the closeness of his touch, as we ran through the rain in the night, drifting from building to building, climbing ladders and darting across rooftops. It wasn't as if we could simply stroll along the sidewalk in search of a place to sleep. So when Julian found an abandoned warehouse where no one would come looking for us, I took a leap of faith and prayed that it would be a safe shelter for the night.

We were both dripping wet, soaked through our clothes. My hair looked like I had just been dunked beneath the rapid waters of a frigid river in the winter. I was exhausted and shaking, but happy to be alive. After everything that had happened, it would be ungrateful of me to feel otherwise.

Julian opened the metal door caked with rust, and I followed him inside.

Chapter 19

It was a cold, barren place. No heater. No fire. No warmth. I shuddered at the sight of a leak in the roof and stood off to the side from the main entrance. Julian swung the heavy metal door closed and lowered the latch across the frame, effectively locking us inside.

When he turned around to face me, our eyes connected in a moment of primal lust. I lunged for him and crushed his lips to mine, while he wrapped me in his arms. My mouth moved with and against his like an ocean in a storm, pushing and pulling, tugging and ripping, searing and scorching.

His long fingers threaded their way through my hair as his tongue slipped in to meet mine. I clawed at the back of his neck and gasped at the intimate contact, growing weak in the knees. Julian consumed me, body and soul, lifting me in the air as his hands squeezed and kneaded my thighs.

As he slammed my back up against the wall, I remembered a similar encounter in the hotel room. When he had denied me what I wanted most. Maybe it was the prolonged tension, risk of dying, or some combination of the two that had my fierce heart pounding with the need to seize the moment.

We might never have a night like this again.

Julian tugged at my knees until I wrapped my legs around his waist, writhing with want and desire. His cold hands slid beneath my shirt and raced up my naked back in a frantic attempt to unhook my bra. I gasped at the temperature shock on my skin and tilted my head to the side as his mouth worked over my neck, leaving sweet kisses and bites. Even when it hurt, it still felt good.

When he sank his teeth into my shoulder, I cried out in ecstasy. There was pleasure to the pain. A dull ache that would surely leave a mark. I hoped it would scar. I wanted to remember this night. Forever.

Julian trapped my body between him and the wall, rolling his shoulders back to take off his shirt. As he struggled with the buttons, I pushed his hands away and ripped through the fabric. Buttons scattered across the floor as I shoved the shirt down his arms, shucking it to the floor.

With one hand cupping my cheek, Julian kissed me again and trailed his fingers up my spine. I whimpered against his lips, craving the feel of his stubble against my face. When he tugged at the hem of my shirt and jerked it over the top of my head, I curled my arms around his back and squeezed him tight.

His fingers dug into the back of my head while I sealed my mouth over his. There was something so intimate in our embrace, standing there chest to chest. I could feel his heart beating with mine, the same rhythm, the same panic, the same desire. Maybe Julian knew that it was our last night, too.

He moved away from the wall and laid me down on a hard surface that sent goosebumps racing across my skin. Loathing the distance between us, I reached out for him and whined until he drew near. With a devilish smile, Julian planted a hand along either side of my face and crawled over my body. He groaned in satisfaction the moment his lips returned to mine, and I had never heard a more pleasant sound.

We were frantic and rough, hurrying through the motions. But Julian touched his nose to mine and cherished me with a tender kiss. There was a deep level of affection in the warmth of his mouth, like he was bearing a side of his soul that he had never shown anyone before.

"You don't know how long I've dreamed of this, dreamed of you." He left a trail of kisses across my cheek, down my throat, along my jawline. When his lips touched my shoulder, I sighed.

"You don't have to dream anymore," I

whispered, knotting my fingers in his hair. "I'm right here."

Julian slipped his hand beneath my back as I sat up, hugging him to my frame. As his mouth worked against mine, urgent and greedy, I grasped his shoulders and struggled for air. His fingertips sank into my ribcage, working their way up my spine. When he pulled me closer and nibbled at my ear, I leaned my chin over his shoulder and pressed my cheek into the top of his back.

My eyes slid shut as I absorbed the moment, memorizing every single sensation he was making me feel. From the shivers down my legs to the tingles in my toes. My breath hitched at the back of my throat, and I raked my nails across his back to reckon with the pleasure.

When my body began to tremble, Julian laid me back down on the table as flickers of light danced across my vision. He covered my mouth with his to silence the scream that would have left me horse, before my head fell to the side. For several seconds, I lay there trying to catch my breath and eventually licked my lips and swallowed.

Julian lay down beside me and caressed my warm cheek with his hand. When I opened my eyes, he pressed his thumb into my chin and then dragged it across my lower lip. I was drowsy and drunk, flooded with the sweetest dose of euphoria—the kind that I might not ever get back again.

But there was a sense of calm in his clear blue eyes. As I placed my palm on his chest, Julian admired my face as if I were a work of art, refusing to look away. He stared at me for a very long time and combed his fingers through my hair, searching every inch of my blushing face.

My eyelids grew heavy, and I thought I might drift off. But then Julian spoke up in the night.

"Anna," he said, smoothing his fingertips along the curve of my shoulder and neck.

Fluttering my lashes, I looked up at him and furrowed my brow.

"If anything should happen to me—"

"Shh..." I mumbled, slurring my words. I covered his mouth and uttered, "Don't say that."

Julian kissed the inside of my palm, and I felt the smile on his face.

"Let's go to sleep." I curled my body into his, and my head fit perfectly on his chest.

Julian wrapped his arm around my back. "I won't let anyone hurt you, Anna."

"I know you won't." I yawned, nestling into the warmth of his strong body.

He tucked a lock of hair behind my ear and then flattened his hand between my shoulder blades.

"I love you, Julian," I whispered in the dark, moving my lips against his collar bone.

He waited a beat and sighed. "I know you do."

As he left his legs tangled through mine, I snuggled closer and adhered to him like a child clings to a teddy bear. Julian guarded my body and kept me warm, not minding when I squeezed too tight. Even while I dreamed, I could feel him there, watching and breathing beside me.

In many ways, it was the best night of my life.

Maybe because—like my grandmother used to say—all good things must come to an end.

* * *

"Anna," a soft voice tickled my ear.

I mumbled in my sleep and groaned, pulling my eyebrows together in frustration.

"Anna." Rough callouses skirted over the side of my arm, a pair of lips at my throat.

Adjusting to the soreness of a new day, I tilted my head to the side and grumbled.

"Anna." Teeth skimmed against my earlobe in a teasing fashion, amplifying my irritation.

"What?" I whined, sounding like a toddler as I tsked my tongue against the roof of my mouth.

"You're grumpy in the morning." A large hand slithered down my spine and around to my stomach.

"Ju-li-an." My eyes shot open as I looked up at the tempting smirk on his face.

He was leaning over me fully dressed, while I lay beneath him with his jacket over my body.

"We have to go." His expression turned rigid and stoic, his posture serious.

Propping up on my elbows, I watched him clench his jaw as he tossed me my clothes.

"Get dressed." Sweet and sensual Julian was gone. Stern and rigid Julian had replaced him.

I slid down off the table and stepped into my jeans, swiftly tugging my socks on afterwards. It was cold in here. The outdoors still fresh with rain from the night before. The sun almost rising. After slipping into my shoes, I avoided the usual method of putting on a bra and left the strap gaping open in the back.

"Can you fasten that?" I turned my head over my shoulder and smiled like the devil.

Julian cleared his throat and approached me from behind, his footsteps hard and concise.

He knew what I was doing.

His knuckles traipsed against my bare flesh as he hooked the bra strap in place. I mashed my lips together and held still, counting on the slight chance that he might touch me again. But morning Julian was all business, no time for play. So even though his breath ghosted across the nape of my neck, he took a step back and kept his distance while I remained half-dressed.

"We need to get going," he pressed. "Hurry up."

"All right," I snapped, angry that my attempt at claiming affection from him had been thwarted.

I shoved my arms through the sleeves of my shirt and then tugged it on over my head. My hair got stuck in the collar, and when I reached back to grab it with my hands, I couldn't get over how short it was. But there was no time to waste, and

Julian was watching my every move like a hawk, the clock ticking.

With my jacket on, I tightened the strings and yanked the hood over my head. Julian looked about the place and then grabbed my hand, leading me to that heavy metal door. When he swung the latch open and let me out, I turned to look inside the place one last time. But he was at my heels, pushing me forward so he could close the door that much quicker.

I never got my last look inside. Even though I had really wanted to.

We would never be here again.

As mist lifted from the pavement with the coming dawn, Julian clamped his hand around my wrist and led me along the side of the street, journeying in and out of alleyways. When he found a decent sized dumpster, Julian opened the lid and checked back over his shoulder. "Get in," he ordered.

"What?" I watched his eyes, but they were searching the street for people.

"Get. In." Julian gritted his teeth and growled at me, dragging me towards the heap of trash.

"I'm not getting in there," I protested, failing to jerk my arm out of his hold.

"Yes, you are," he hissed.

Before I could say another word on the subject, Julian picked me up and hauled me into the dumpster. I clung to his shoulders as he grasped my waist, setting my feet down at the bottom of the trash.

"Julian, this is ridiculous." I looked up at him while he put my arms down at my sides.

He left a quick peck on my lips and confessed, "I need to steal a car."

My mouth dropped wide open. But Julian would never see me gaping, because he closed the lid and ran off. Bathed in darkness and foul odor, I ducked down and crossed my arms over my chest. It smelled horrible in here, and I didn't know how long I would be able to stand the stench.

As time passed—minutes that felt like hours—I pinched the end of my nose and breathed through my mouth. When the whiff of a dead rodent pierced my olfactory receptors, I gagged, praying that Julian would return soon. The atmosphere was sour enough to make me shut my eyes. But then the lid lifted and light poured into the nasty heap. Julian grabbed my arm and pulled me out, impatient as ever.

The next thing I knew, he was shoving me into the driver's side of a stolen car and sliding in beside me. His eyes flashed to the rearview mirror as he stomped the gas with no prior warning. Before I could split my head open on the dashboard, I fumbled with my seatbelt until it was fastened and secured.

"Where are we going?" I braced myself as he darted out of the alleyway and eased into the start of early morning traffic. "Did anyone see you? Are there people coming after us?"

"What is it with you and all the questions?" His knuckles tightened around the steering wheel until they turned white. He looked so different as a blond, his golden locks illuminated beneath the light.

"You just stole a car, Julian!" I shouted. "You don't think someone might have noticed?"

"Well, do you have a better idea for getting us out of Connecticut alive?"

I leaned my head against the window and sulked, my heart pounding every second of the way.

We didn't say much to each other over the next hundred miles, quiet as a mouse. When we stopped at convenience stores, I was only allowed to dart in and out of the bathroom while Julian was paying the bill. To my surprise, he bought two White Chocolate Macadamia Clif bars and a mango banana smoothie, plopping the bag full of goodies down in my lap once he climbed back in the car.

"These are my favorite," I chimed, staring with wide eyes at the familiar wrapper.

"I know." Julian started the car and we left the gas station behind, on the road again.

"Eight weeks, my ass." I tore the foil wrapper back and sank my teeth into the gooey bar.

"What?" Julian turned his head to the side and then focused on the road ahead.

"Before," I mumbled, talking with food in my

mouth. "You said you had been watching me for eight weeks."

"Yeah?" He waited as I held the smoothie bottle between my legs and twisted the cap off. "So?"

"I don't believe you." I took a swig of the tangy puree, and nothing had ever tasted so sweet.

"Why not?" he wondered, sounding more curious than normal.

"I think you've been watching me longer than that." I set my green gaze on him, daring him to test me.

As the side of his mouth twitched, Julian drove off the main highway and took a direction far away from interstates and street signs. In less than twenty minutes, I found myself riding beneath a canopy road. All of the leaves were missing, as I studied the branches of thin, tall trees.

The snow must have melted before we got here. Last night, I had been surprised to find the rain instead of white flakes coming down from the sky. But we were moving farther south, and the temperature of our general area (while still cold) was increasing every day.

"What are we doing here?" I inquired when Julian parked at the end of a field beneath a large tree. From the looks of it, we were in a national forest that visitors rarely frequented in the winter.

"You said a bad word, Anna."

"Excuse me?"

"And I'm going to punish you for it."

"I don't understand."

"You said the word *ass*, so now I'm going to spank yours."

I laughed at the proposition. "You're joking, right?"

"No, I'm afraid I'm not, Anna." He removed the keys from the ignition and opened his car door.

"You know, you were much nicer before you went blond." Julian chuckled and walked around to my side of the car, making my heart thump and race. When he opened the door, I shielded my eyes from the sun and winced. "Julian, please. This isn't *Fifty Shades of Grey.*"

"Your name is Anna. Isn't it?" He grabbed my wrist and pulled me out of the seat.

"Yes, but I spell mine with two n's. And my name doesn't stand for Anastasia either."

"What does it stand for?" he asked, even though he already knew the answer. "Annabelle?"

"It's a family name," I murmured, feeling small as he shut the door. "My grandmother."

Julian flicked his tongue against the roof of his mouth until it made a noise. I kept my back against the door as he crossed his arms over his chest, intimidating me with his stature and size. Sunshine broke through the clouds and picked up the flecks of yellow golden in his newly bleached hair.

"So why Anna?" He cocked his head to the side and regarded me with intrigue. "Why not

Belle?"

"What, now you think I should have been named after *Beauty and the Beast?*"

"It's just a question." He narrowed his eyes with a dangerous smile that lifted at the corners.

"That's what everyone called her. Anna." When he looked confused, I said, "My grandmother."

Julian nodded, his eyes drifting across the open field. "Would you like a head start?"

"What?" I cringed, still thinking that this was a joke. "Julian, you can't actually be serious."

"Oh, I'm very serious." He raised his chin and towered above me. "*Annabelle.*"

Clenching my jaw, I glowered up at him and said, "I'm not going to let you chase me."

Julian lifted his finger and traced the edge of my jawline. "Oh, yes you are."

Sending daggers up at him, I pushed his hand out of the way and smoldered.

"I'll give you a head start," he patronized, just to toy with me. Like a cat with string.

Stewing with anger, I walked around Julian, but not without brushing his shoulder. Blood hammered in my veins like the rhythm of drums. My eyes lifted to the sky as I shivered, shoving my hands in my jacket pockets. One foot landed in front of the other, but I had no intention of running. Especially after last night.

My legs were sore and achy, a pulsing tenderness that seared my flesh to the bone. Lazy and tired, I slowed to a stop and looked up at the gray clouds drifting through the sky. Feeling his eyes on me, I turned my head and looked back at Julian over my shoulder. He was running towards me.

Caught off guard, I turned on my heel and bolted for the trees. Despite his arrogance, I had honestly believed that he was joking. Why would Julian want to chase me? Capture me? Spank me?

It all seemed out of character for him. Then again, at times his personality was so split, that maybe I should have expected it from him. I was frozen one minute and burned by his touch the next. With a man as mercurial as he was, his current mood was as predictable as the weather.

When I heard him breathing hard and fast, I picked up the pace and spotted a large tree with low hanging limbs. I ran towards it and crouched down behind the trunk, slowly backing up as I slipped out of his peripheral vision. But then my back collided with a surface that felt hard as a rock.

Julian linked his arms around my waist and grabbed me from behind, slamming my shoulders into his chest. He clamped his hand down over my mouth when I screamed and pinned my arms to my sides. The pulse point in my neck was throbbing, as I bucked and kicked against him.

"If someone attacks you from behind, what do you do?"

His words made no sense in my ear, a warm

whisper that felt like a chilling caress.

I stuck my elbow out to jab him in the ribs, but Julian was too quick for that. When I stomped my foot down on his shoe, he swayed backwards and pinned me up against the tree. The hem of my shirt rode up with the motion, and the rough bark scraped against my sensitive skin.

"Or if someone wraps their hands around your throat." Julian touched his palm to my neck and splayed his fingers out, yet never applied any pressure. I attempted to beat him in the chest and kick him in the stomach, but Julian blocked every hit. Defending myself against him was impossible.

When Julian released me and took a step back, he set his hands on his hips with a sigh.

I struggled to catch up, drawing air into my lungs as I caught my breath. "What?"

"You can't fight to save your life," he noted. "I need to teach you how to shoot."

"So all of that," I leaned towards him and pointed at the tree behind me. "Was just pretend?"

"No. It was practice." Julian rubbed his jaw where I must have scratched him. "You only needed to think that I was coming after you," he explained. "How else will I know how you would actually react?"

I pondered for a moment as my heart rate returned to its normal beating.

Julian chewed at the inside of his mouth and pulled out his gun. "Come here," he instructed.

"I know how to use a gun." I stayed by his side and out of the line of fire. "Did you forget about—?"

"That was one time," he argued, butting in. "And you got lucky."

Taking offense, I narrowed my eyes at him and glowered.

"Now, come here." He showed me the gun and all the many pieces. The handle, the trigger, the bullets and where to load them. It felt like a safety course on how to use fire arms. "Here. Hold it."

I took the gun in the palm of my hand, as he told me to get a feel for the weight of it. Julian removed the bullets and then loaded them back in, forcing me to learn the difference. So I would be able to tell whether or not the gun was loaded just by holding it in my hand.

"This is an automatic," he coached, touching my hand. "Do you know what that means?"

"Just because I'm nineteen doesn't mean I'm stupid," I fired back.

Julian rolled his eyes and looked off into the woods. "Do you see the leaf up there on that tree?"

When Julian lifted his hand, I glanced in the direction his finger was pointed. Since it was winter, most of the trees were barren. It was the only leaf on that particular tree, making it pretty hard to miss.

"Yes," I hissed, biting my tongue to keep from

saying something nasty.

"Now." He lingered behind me and placed his hand on my back. "Let's see if you can shoot it."

Swallowing my resolve, I lifted the gun in the air with both hands and pulled the trigger. By some miracle, I actually aimed at the target and shot it. When the bullet pierced the leaf, it split into flakes and scattered.

"Well, I guess it's safe to say you know how to use a gun." Julian raised his eyebrows and then took it away from me, returning the pistol to the waistband of his pants. "Did that politician father of yours ever take you hunting?" He pulled his shirt down over his belt and waited for my answer.

"Maybe," I sassed, tilting my chin back with a cocky smirk. It had been ages, but Daddy had taught me how to use a gun. President or not, the man had a wall of mounted heads that fueled him to hunt.

"Why do your parents still live in DC?" he asked on our way back to the car. "Don't most Presidents return to their home state once the term ends?"

"Daddy is from the area," I answered, rubbing my hands together for warmth. "And I guess they like it there." I shrugged and kept my eyes down, a shudder traveling up my spine as the temperature began to drop.

"Are you cold?" Julian stopped in his tracks when I didn't answer. Then he took my hands and balled them into fists beneath his, blowing warm air over my fingers with his mouth.

I gazed into his eyes and let him care for me, never letting on how much I liked it.

"I'm sorry if I scared you," he said, paying attention to my hands. "I just want you to be prepared."

I pursed my lips and held still while the blood returned to my icy palms. "For what?"

Julian exhaled and glanced up at the sky, watching his breath materialize before him.

"For what, Julian?" I searched his face and tugged at his arm, bringing him back to me.

He blinked several times and then confessed, "If anything should happen to me—"

"Stop saying that!" I interrupted. "Nothing is going to happen to you."

"This isn't a dream world, Anna," he sternly declared. "Stop living in your fantasies."

"It's not a fantasy!" I cried. "I want to be with you."

As I leaned up on my tippy toes to give him a kiss, Julian turned his cheek to me.

Even though I should have felt hurt, his rejection only made me more determined in my efforts to keep him. "I want to run away with you," I confessed. It was a secret desire I had buried in my heart, waiting for the right time to tell him. "Please," I begged. "You're the only one who can keep me safe."

Julian snuck a peek at me from beneath his lashes, as though he were afraid to look. I leaned into his warmth and placed my hand over his heart, holding his gaze with a pretty pout. When he resisted me, I lowered my head and gave him his distance, turning to walk away.

But he cupped my warm cheek in his hand and brought my mouth to his. I furrowed my brow at the intimate touch, unsure of his reasons for pulling me so close, so fast. My hand settled on his shoulder as he tugged at my lower lip, drowning me in sensation as he stole every last breath away.

His kisses drifted along my jawline and down my throat as he got carried away. I shut my eyes and wrapped him in my arms, twisting and tangling my fingers through his hair. When I sighed his name, Julian paused and lifted his head to whisper in my ear. "Okay," he said.

"What?" I folded my hands at the nape of his neck and gazed up at him in wonder.

"You can run away with me." His hands slipped down to hug the curves of my waist. "If that's what you really want." Those glittering blue eyes darted over my face in search of certainty.

"Oh, Julian!" I leapt into his arms and shut my eyes, nuzzling his neck to absorb his smell.

He rubbed my back and held me to his strong body, but didn't say another word.

Reeling with excitement, I tilted my head back and planted a soft kiss on his lips. He smiled but it was forced—more for my satisfaction than his. But when I returned to hugging him, he let me.

Hardly any words were spoken for the rest of

the day. We walked around in the forest holding hands, and for the first time it felt like we were a real couple. In the late afternoon, Julian turned playful and gave me a piggyback ride beneath the trees while I soaked up every moment of our time together.

Once the sun set, we headed back to the car and got inside. I couldn't believe that Julian had agreed to my proposition, especially considering a man as fiercely stubborn as he was. But maybe some part of him did care for me, and that same part was neither willing nor ready to let go.

Now we would never have to say goodbye.

When the moon ascended in the evening sky, I climbed into the back seat and enticed Julian to join me. He dragged his long legs into the rear of the car and let me lay down on top of him. While the day had gone as planned, a feeling of dread roused up in the back of my throat.

I couldn't escape it, and I couldn't push it away.

Julian combed his fingers through my hair and touched my back. When I lifted my chin to look up at him, he brushed his nose against mine and claimed my mouth like he meant it. Buzzing from the kiss, I rested my head on his chest and closed my eyes.

I fell asleep in his arms. Not realizing that it would be the last time.

Chapter 20

I woke up alone in the back seat with a kink in my neck. The car was moving, but I hardly felt rooted to the spot without my seatbelt on. Bracing myself, I squeezed between the seats in the front and plopped down on the passenger's side. Julian drove in silence, failing to greet me now that I was awake.

Feeling groggy, I threaded my fingers through my hair and yawned. Last night had been a peaceful sleep, even if it felt like I had my arms locked tighter around Julian than he had been holding me. He gripped the steering wheel and gazed out the driver's side window when he wasn't looking straight ahead.

"So... where are we headed?" I was giddy and euphoric, excited for a new adventure. "I was thinking Canada or Mexico. If we skip the country, it will be a lot harder for them to find us."

Julian was unfazed by my words, his eyes on the road. There was a few days' worth of stubble on his face that I wanted to reached out and touch. But he seemed distant, so I didn't bother to try it.

"You really want to spend the rest of your life like this? On the road? Always on the run? No home. No safe place to go to at night." He chewed at his lower lip and rubbed his hand over his face. His cheeks were smoldering. "You really want to go the rest of your life without ever seeing your family again?"

"I want to be with you," I demanded, staring at him. "And besides, it's not like I won't ever see them again." Julian pursed his lips together, and I blanched. "Right?" I waited a beat, but he didn't answer. "Right, Julian?"

He clenched his jaw and refused to say anything. It was driving me crazy.

Then I looked out the window and saw a welcome sign that I did not want to see.

"Maryland?" I turned my head as we crossed the state line. "What are we doing in Maryland?"

Julian avoided my scrutinizing gaze, as his nostrils flared.

"What are we doing in Maryland?" I repeated, my skin flushing red with anger.

"Anna," he sighed. "You know that you can't come with me."

My heart sank as tears pricked the back of my eyes—the hot, burning kind.

"But you said—" I searched his profile and

278

those strong cheekbones as he smoldered.

But Julian didn't say anything.

"Yesterday, you said that I could go with you." I tried to be strong, but my voice was cracking.

"I know what I said."

"Why would you do that?" I demanded. "How could you...?" I dropped off, turning shaky.

Julian pressed his lips together and chewed at the inside of his cheek.

"You're a liar." My pain turned to anger, and I lost it.

My arms took on a mind of their own, the hands attached to them slapping and knocking his body with the intention to bruise. I tucked my thumbs over my fists and pounded into his chest with fury.

"You're a liar! You lied to me!" My knuckles ached with every punch, but I didn't care. I couldn't stop. "How could you do that? You said I could go with you! You said you would take me with you! You said we could run away together! You said—"

"I said a lot of things," he admitted. "I said what you wanted to hear."

I shook my head at his words, not wanting to believe them.

"Why?" I moaned, feeling my only chance at happiness begin to slip away.

"You need to grow up, Anna. Life isn't a fairytale."

As he sliced a knife through my heart, I raised

my trembling hand and slapped him. It hurt me worse than it did him, the inside of my palms and fingers aching with the sting. But wrath had taken hold, because the man I loved had betrayed me.

"Stop it, Anna," he hissed, clasping both of my hands in one of his. He had been dodging my jabs and trying to maintain a grip on the steering wheel with one hand. "You're going to make me crash the car."

I withdrew my hands from his hold and folded them in my lap, hanging my head in shame.

"You know I have to do this," he said. "It's the only way to keep you safe."

My lower lip quivered at the sound of his voice.

The voice of reason. The voice of truth. The voice I would never hear again.

"I know," I whimpered, fighting back the tears.

Julian was right.

He always was.

As reality washed over me, I broke down and started to cry. They were loud, cathartic sobs. The kind of noises a kid would make. But Julian didn't say anything, maybe because there was nothing to say.

He just kept driving.

As images blurred by on the interstate, I wrapped my arms around my torso and hugged myself. It wasn't like anyone else was going to. Julian let me weep. I loved and hated him for that.

He should have pulled me into his warm

embrace and told me that everything was going to be all right, that he was only joking, that we would be together again. But he didn't.

Somehow, I was more upset now than I had been when he left me with Jordan. We had been given a second chance that night, which meant that any hope of reuniting again was gone. This time, when we said goodbye to each other, that would be it. It—whatever you wanted to call the tangled, twisted mess of a thing between us—would truly be over.

The closer we got to Washington, the sicker I felt. Shivers raced across the surface of my skin even though the inside of my palms was slick with sweat. He was right here, sitting in the car beside me. But at any moment, he would be gone. Out of my life. Forever. For good.

Julian slipped a pair of sunglasses on once we entered the District of Columbia, and I was less than thrilled to return to my former home. There was a billboard with my face on it and a 1-800 number at the bottom for those to call with any information. I looked at the oversized photo and frowned. It was taken from high school when I was a bubbly blonde, helplessly naïve to the real world.

I didn't recognize this Anna.

I didn't know her anymore.

There was an empty parking lot behind a grocery store. When Julian pulled in and parked the car, I couldn't believe that this was it. No preparation. No warning. No means of turning back the clock.

Julian took the keys out of the ignition and set his sunglasses down on the dash. For that I was thankful, because at least he was willing to look me in the eye. I unfastened my seatbelt and glanced his way, reaching for the silver bracelet around my wrist.

Once he realized what I was doing, Julian leaned across the console and grabbed my arm. "No."

I gazed into those glittering blue eyes, and they pierced me to the core. I remembered the first time I had ever seen his face in the club that night. I wanted him then, and I wanted him now. Always.

"Julian. It was your mother's," I reasoned, placing my thumb on the clasp.

"I know." He studied the bracelet and then stared up at me. "Will you keep it safe for me?"

Julian dragged his thumb along the inside of my wrist, and I shivered. "Yes."

When I closed my eyes, a single tear leaked out and Julian wiped it away. I took a deep, harrowing breath that made me go weak in the knees. I didn't know how I was going to be able to get out of the car.

"Can I contact you?" It was a final plea, my last hope. "So I'll know that you're safe."

Julian scanned my face with a long suffering sigh. "I'll send you a postcard."

I blinked the tears away and lowered my head as every breath drifted away. The oxygen was practically impossible to grab, even harder to hold on to. It felt like I was having a heart attack.

Julian lifted my chin with his finger and leaned in for a goodbye kiss.

"Don't," I begged, holding my face still. "Not if it's going to be the last one."

His fingertips skirted along my jawline and down my neck. But he ducked his head and nodded, letting go. When he pulled away and glanced out the window, I opened the car door and got out. As my shoes connected with the pavement, I closed the door and pressed my palm to the cool glass.

Julian looked up and watched me through the window. And I could have sworn there were tears in his eyes.

"Goodbye," I whispered, covering my mouth as I turned on my heel to walk away.

With every step, I felt his eyes on me as I tugged at the jacket strings and pulled the hood over my head. We must have been a mile from home, easy walking distance for a young woman traveling by foot. As much as I wished it were the case, it wasn't like Julian could just pull up to the front door and drop me off. We had to part this way. And that's when it hit me like a ton of bricks. There was no *we* anymore.

Once I reached the front of the parking lot, I came to understand why it was empty. The grocery store was closed, which I found rather odd. But I didn't waste any more time on it, because a massive hole had been ripped right through me. And it ached. It throbbed. It hurt like hell.

At the sound of footsteps, I felt my blood thrum hot and heavy in my ears. Someone was following me. When I turned to look back over my shoulder, a large man bolted towards me. I fell forward and screamed, too emotionally drained to fight, too weak to put up a good defense.

From the first gunshot, I lay down and covered my head. Three followed, and the man collapsed to the ground beside me, his arm landing across my hip. I backed away and crawled on my hands and knees.

There was a running car right in front of my face, whose driver could mercilessly plow me over in an instant. I was shaking, my clothing covered in the dead man's blood. But then the car moved away from me and turned around, reversing until the passenger's side door opened on my left.

"Get in." Julian reached across the seat and dragged me inside. His foot hit the gas before I shut the door, and there was hardly any time to celebrate our reunion. But there was no need. It would be short-lived. An over-extended opportunity to say goodbye.

I held on to the side of the door as Julian raced down a back alleyway and kept his eyes on the rearview mirror. In what felt like seconds, there was a black SUV tailing us, and my eyes widened in fear. The windows were tinted, and I hated to think how many assassins were ready and waiting.

"Take this." Julian handed me his gun and merged into ongoing traffic, nearly crashing into a line of vehicles in the process. He ignored the road signs and ran red lights, while I braced myself for the end. Before long, the amount of vehicles chasing us multiplied and fanned out on the street.

My eyes darted to the side mirror on my door, as the assassins started closing in. "Julian."

"Hold on." He steered the car left and weaved in and out of lanes. A chorus of honking horns and angry drivers ensued, but Julian ignored the noise and maintained his focus. My head snapped back when he stomped the brake and changed course, slamming the gas pedal to the floor.

I bit my tongue and watched that mirror beside me as the slew of cars crashed and piled into one another. Julian never looked back as we got further and further ahead, retreating to an alley that reminded me of our rainy night in Connecticut. He parked the car sideways in front of the passage, blocking the entrance for any other vehicle. Then he took the gun from my hand and opened his door, jumping out and making room as I raced after him, our shoes pounding against the cement.

Julian spotted a ladder and gave me a boost, snatching my foot up as he propelled me higher on the steps. I climbed my way to the rooftop despite the sound of screeching tires and gunfire. Julian pushed at my hip and stayed right behind me, while we hopped over the ledge and landed on the rooftop.

In the time it took me to stand, I realized that we were surrounded. I looked to my right and left, and they must have known we would come here. There were men on either rooftop, their weapons aimed and ready to fire. As they formed a line at the edge, I knew it was all over.

There was a bounty on both of our heads. And when Julian chose to spare me and then hide me from his fellow assassins, he had done nothing more than piss them off. We would go out together.

"Anna! Get down!" Julian pushed me to the ground and shielded my body with his.

Bullets flew by and I screamed, clamping my hands down over my ears.

There was a wall along the rooftop, and part of that wall jutted out. It was the perfect place to hide.

"Anna," Julian gasped, whispering in my ear. "I need you to run. I'll cover you. Okay?"

"Okay." My entire body was shaking, but Julian didn't seem afraid at all.

"Now, Anna! Run!" Julian rolled off me and I darted for that corner of the roof, our only hiding place.

He fired his gun a few steps behind me. And that was when I noticed something odd.

Fleeing for cover was no feat, a simple hop, skip, and jump to a poor excuse for shelter. No guns were aimed in my direction, no shots fired my away. Even though I was open and exposed, an easy target.

The assassins weren't after me. They were after Julian.

Just like that, my whole world concaved like a mess of broken rock over a canyon.

"JU-LI-AN!"

A bullet connected with his leg. And then his back.

He jerked from the brunt force of each hit as his body shifted just enough to expose his front.

One shot to the chest, and he staggered backwards, falling to the ground like a defeated giant.

I crawled on my hands and knees and grabbed his shoulders, dragging his body out of the line of fire. Once I reached that wall, the bullets stopped flying, but I could care less about what was going to happen to me. For the time being, we were hidden behind nothing more than the uneven architecture of a jutting wall. But I would take it.

"Julian, Julian, Julian," I cried, saying his name like a prayer. "No. Don't. Don't leave me! You can't."

His lips were stained red as he coughed up blood, slowly opening his eyes to look at me.

"Sweet Anna." He reached up to touch my face but lacked the strength. So I leaned down and pressed my cheek into the palm of his hand.

"Yes, Julian?" I whimpered. "What is it?"

"I'm sorry," he wheezed. "But it's finally caught up with me."

"What?" I threaded my fingers through his hair, caressing the skin above his brow.

"My life," he rasped, mumbling through his words. "All the bad things I've done."

For so long, I had believed him to be invincible. I thought he couldn't be killed.

"No, Julian." I touched the stubble on his cheek. His skin was turning cold. "You're a good man."

"No, I'm not." He tried to shake his head, but it hardly moved. "But it's okay."

My throat was clogged with tears as I fought for my last few moments with him.

"Just promise me something," he said, squeezing my arm.

"Yes, Julian." I leaned in closer and dried my eyes so I could really see him. "Anything."

He furrowed his handsome brow as I had watched him do a thousand times before.

"Don't wait for me," he whispered, his voice hardly audible. "I don't want you to spend your whole life chasing a ghost."

"Julian," I moaned, grappling with the sleeve of his shirt. As I crumbled to pieces, Julian touched my face, and his hand felt like ice.

"Promise me, Anna." He pierced a dart through my heart with that glittering blue gaze. "Promise me."

Even though it ripped me in two, I nodded my head in agreement. "I promise, Julian. I promise."

I buried my face in his shirt, in his scent, in his

blood. And I hugged him for the last time.

"You healed me," he coaxed, his ragged voice in my ear.

I sat on my knees and held him to my breast. "What?"

"That's why I let you live. That's why I couldn't pull the trigger," he explained. "You healed me."

"Oh, Julian." I rubbed my hand over his face, gently stroking his cheek. "Please don't go."

"Don't be afraid, my darling girl." He lifted his shaky palm and placed it over my heart. "I'll always be right here."

I put my hand over his and cherished every second I had left with him. Deep down, I was holding on to the hope that it would be like all the times before. Where we would separate only to come right back to each other again. Especially when he tried to leave me in the parking lot at the end.

But this wasn't like all those times before.

"Thank you," Julian cooed, curving my face into the palm of his hand.

"For what?" I hovered close enough to feel his breath on my lips, or what was left of it.

"It's what I've always wanted," he confessed. "To die in the arms of the woman I love."

As the meaning of his words washed over me, I bent my head and pressed my lips to his. But Julian was right—life wasn't a fairytale. And true love's kiss was no match for a bullet to the chest.

When I lifted my head, the blue began to fade from his eyes. But he looked at me and smiled.

Stroking his face with delicate care, I opened my mouth to say "I love—"

But someone grabbed my arms and hauled me away while countless men swarmed his body.

"NOOOOO!" I screamed, fighting and bucking against the culprit who had cut our time short.

All I wanted was to watch Julian draw his last breath, have his final moments of life with me.

But they took that from us. They cheated us. They stole me away before Julian even reached the end.

They put me in a car, and I didn't care where I was going next. Out of the country. Off to travel the world as a sex slave. Nothing mattered now, because nothing could hurt me.

Julian was gone.

As it turned dark outside, I watched fireworks light up the sky through the back window.

"It's New Year's Eve," the man beside me explained. "Didn't you know?"

"No." I shook my head, stilling at the sound of his friendly voice.

For so long, I had been in a daze, but now I was finally able to understand.

The assassins weren't the ones who killed Julian.

The police were.

Chapter 21

Anna!" Mama raced down the staircase and crashed into me at the front door. There was an army of press at my back, reporters with their microphones and cameras. Daddy slammed the door on all of them and wrapped his arms around the two of us as I sobbed into Mama's shirt. She smelled like flowers.

"Anna, we were so worried about you." Daddy rubbed my back as we all cried together.

But the reunion didn't last long. Daddy talked to the handful of secret service who still worked for him, as well as the police. The officers who had arrived were ready and willing to talk to me, even though they had already seen that I was alive. But I was neither willing nor ready to tell them what had happened.

When the foyer was bustling with noise, Mama took me upstairs to my bedroom. I passed through the door and looked around at the familiar territory. The last time I had stayed here was Thanksgiving. But even then, it no longer felt like home. I was away at college now, and things had changed.

Mama flicked the lamp on by my bed and turned the covers down. I felt cold and lifeless, shivering from the shock of everything, so I got on the mattress and climbed beneath them.

"How long was I gone?" I muttered, as my mother took a seat on the end of my bed.

"A little over three weeks." She petted my hair and turned my chin up, worried about me.

Three weeks. It felt like a lifetime.

"Honey, I'm so sorry about what happened to you." She rubbed my cheek, and I saw the fear in her eyes. "Your father and I have been worried sick, but we knew you were still out there. We promised that we would do everything we could to get you back, to bring you home safe."

I forced a smile and touched her arm. "Thanks, Mama."

"Now, I know that you've just gotten back." She sat up straight and placed her hands in her lap. "But you don't have to go back to school right away. If you need to take a semester off, or even two..."

I watched my mother and listened to every word, but my eyes were dead. She could see that the light had gone out in them. I wasn't the same girl I used to be.

"Well, your father and I just wanted you to know that." She smiled and tucked me in beneath the covers. "Do you want something to eat? You look so thin." Her eyes watered as she pressed the back of her hand to my forehead, something she had done when I was a child with the flu.

I nodded, even though I had no earthly idea how I was going to choke down food at a time like this.

"How about some soup?" she suggested. "Chicken noodle? Like Grandma Anna used to make?"

"Yeah." I nodded again, wondering if that would be the only means I would have of communication from now on.

"Okay, sweetie. I'll go fix it for you." She patted my arm and turned to walk away, leaving the door cracked and the light on.

I rolled onto my side and curled into a ball, too afraid to close my eyes. The second I did, all of it would come racing back to me. I was a mere inch away from having a breakdown—I could feel it.

It was taking all I had to put on a brave face for my parents. The last thing I wanted to do was make them think that I was damaged, that something was wrong with me. Hadn't they been through enough?

When I was worried I might drift off, I slipped out of bed and peeked through the blinds over my window. There were cars all in the streets, TV vans, nosy neighbors, police. I jerked at the string to make sure the blinds were shut tight and then wandered out of my bedroom at the sound of a newscaster.

On my way down the staircase, I was careful to duck back into the hall as my father and his crew of secret service passed by. When the coast was clear, I snuck into the downstairs living room where a full news report was blasting on the flat screen TV. No one else was in here, so I seized the moment and stood in front of the couch, waiting to hear what I already knew.

When a picture of Julian flashed onto the screen, I wrapped my hand around my throat. My ears were buzzing so loudly that I could hardly hear what the news reporter had to say. And then there was a video of Julian being shot. It was strange to see it from a voyeur's perspective, as each bullet pierced his flesh.

At the time, everything happened so fast, yet felt like slow motion. But in the video, he hit the ground in a second, with no chance of survival against the snipers. He was outnumbered.

"Anna!" Mama ran into the living room and found me on the floor crying.

My whole body was shivering, so I pulled my legs into my chest and rocked back and forth.

"You shouldn't be in here watching that." She turned the TV off, which only reiterated the fact that Julian was gone for good. "That's not healthy for you. Come on, Anna. Let's get you back upstairs."

I leaned into her warmth and let her drape my arm across her shoulder.

"You may need to rest in bed for a few days," she said on the stairs. "And that's okay."

I kept my head down and wandered into the bedroom, colliding with the mattress.

"Do you feel like taking a shower, Anna?" Mama played with my hair. "It might make you feel better."

As her words resonated, I crossed my arms over my chest and nodded. "Okay."

"I'll get you some clean towels," she offered, scurrying out of the room and back.

I trudged into the adjoining bathroom and wondered why she no longer kept fresh towels in here. Then again, since I had gone off to college, I guess no one used it anymore. Not as much as I once did.

When Mama finally left, I shut the door to the bathroom and locked it. Then I walked over to the mirror and stared at my reflection for a very long time. Once I got undressed, the silver bracelet hung against my wrist, and I knew that I wouldn't be able to take it off. I didn't want to.

It was all I had left of him.

As I washed my hair in the shower, dirty water began to circle the drain. I shut my eyes as flashes of Julian cutting my long blond locks and dying them black came to mind. I felt his fingers in my hair and his breath ghosting across the nape of my neck. I turned around to see if he was there.

But I was alone.

Hurrying out of the shower, I wrapped a towel around myself and circled my hand over the foggy glass. Then I dodged the mirror I had just cleared and traipsed into my bedroom to put some clothes on. As I rubbed the towel over my wet locks, my thoughts dissipated to air in my mind.

I was blocking them all out. I didn't want to think. I didn't want to feel. I didn't want to know.

"Feel better?" Mama entered the room with a tray of soup and crackers.

After hanging up my towel, I climbed back into bed, and she placed dinner in my lap. I really wanted her to stay, but hated appearing so weak. Luckily, she read my mind and sprawled out on the mattress, making herself comfortable.

"I'm sorry you had to see that on the TV downstairs," she began, watching me stir chunks of chicken and noodle around in the broth. "I know you've been through a lot. I'm here if you need to talk, sweetie."

With a deep breath, I reached for her hand and squeezed it. "I know you are, Mama. I missed you."

"I missed you, too." She propped herself up on her elbow, pleased just to be in my company.

For a moment, I put myself in her shoes. I was her only daughter. If anything happened to me, that meant no children, no grandchildren, no more branches on the family tree.

"I'm so glad that awful man is gone," she announced, sighing with relief. "They got him, Anna. And you never have to see him again." She watched my eyes, but they were downcast. "It's finally over."

All of a sudden, emotion flooded through me like a tidal wave. My shoulders started to quake as I clamped my hand over my mouth to muffle the sobs. There was a lump in my throat the size of a boulder. Just like the hole in my heart. And my soul. And everywhere else.

"Anna, honey." Mama picked up the dinner tray and placed it on my nightstand. "Come here."

I leapt into her arms as she hugged me tight, patting my back like she did when I was a child.

"Everything is going to be all right," she assured me. "You don't have to go through this alone."

When I sat back against the headboard and dried my eyes, Mama touched the silver heart charm on my bracelet. I kept my hand elevated as she inspected it. Maybe she thought it was as pretty as I did.

"Where did you get that?" A crinkle formed between her brows. "I've never seen you wear it before."

"Julian gave it to me," I replied matter-of-factly.

Mama retracted her hand from the jewelry and tilted her head back. "Julian?"

"Yeah." I toyed with the bracelet around my wrist and smiled. "It was his mother's."

She held a finger to her lips and looked over me with worry. "You don't mean that man do—"

"Yes, I do." When her green eyes widened and she failed to blink, I continued. "It's not what everyone thinks," I insisted. "He was good to me, Mama. He kept me safe. I love him."

Mama turned slack when I hugged her, touching my back as I cried. But I felt the stiffness in her posture. She was thinking what everyone else must have imagined. That he had raped and tortured me, like one of those horrendous teenage kidnapping stories you hear about on the nightly news.

But this was different. Julian hadn't been my captor. He had been my protector.

And we had fallen in love.

"He loved me, too," I confessed, pieces of hair sticking to my tear-stained face.

Mama brushed the fallen locks out of the way and tucked a few behind my ear.

"I love him, Mama," I wept. "It hurts so bad."

She drew me into her embrace and held me close for a very long time after that. Despite the pain it caused me, I couldn't let his memory go. The thoughts of Julian I had in my head were all I had left.

"Listen, honey." She leaned back and framed my hair around my face. "There are two men downstairs from the FBI who would like to question you about everything that went on. But I told them that you needed some time, and we wouldn't bring you in until you were ready."

"Thanks, Mama." I wiped at my tears and dried my eyes as she handed me a box of tissues.

"I need to go check on your father," Mama murmured. "Will you be all right by yourself?"

"I think so," I whimpered, shutting my eyes when she pressed a kiss to my forehead.

"All right." She stood up from the bed. "I'll be right back."

Like the time before, I watched her go and then sank beneath the sheets. There was a steaming bowl of hot soup waiting for me on the nightstand, but I wouldn't touch it. I wasn't hungry.

When Mama took longer than expected, I ambled into the hallway and overheard her talking to Daddy downstairs. It sounded like all of the officers had left, and it was just the two of them alone together. They spoke in hushed voices, and I didn't like what either of them had to say.

"What are you telling me, Winifred?" Daddy hissed.

"I'm saying that I think he did something to her," Mama answered. "She said that she's in love with him."

Silence fell over the house, and then I heard glass shatter. Daddy must have broken something.

"He raped her," Daddy mumbled, his voice shaky and off pitch. "He must have raped her."

I pushed away from the banister when he started to cry and hurried into my room. As I snuggled beneath the covers, it occurred to me that no one else would ever view the situation through my eyes. To the general public, and my father for that matter, Julian had kidnapped, beaten, and raped me.

We didn't live in a world where stories of older men who didn't violate young girls were true. Considering the circumstances, a man of Julian's caliber would have done nothing but take advantage of me during our time hidden away in the forest. But that was just the thing. I was the only one to witness his kindness and good behavior. It was no more than my word. Who would believe me?

* * *

On my third day back, Mama took the liberty of driving me to a therapist. Since I was expected to meet with the two FBI agents later this afternoon, Mama thought it would be better if I were evaluated by a professional beforehand. I felt like a little girl all over again, Mama dragging me off to see Dr. Berry.

In her early sixties, Tabitha Berry was a staple in my childhood. It had been years since the last time I came for a session with her. But at least Mama had chosen a shrink that I was familiar with.

When I walked into her office, the cozy living area looked just as I had remembered it. Leather furniture. Soft carpet. Bay windows that let in just the right amount of light. There was a water fountain with small gray stones on a coffee table in the room. It was the perfect place for spilling your guts.

"Anna," Tabitha chimed, greeting us at the door. "How lovely to see you."

I turned back and looked into my mother's eyes. "I think I'd like to do this alone."

Dr. Berry gazed at Mama with a small smile.

"Okay," Mama complied. "I'll be waiting for you right out here."

"Okay," I echoed, kissing her cheek to let her know that her presence was still welcome. Even if it meant that I was more comfortable with her on the other side of the wall.

Once Mama headed into the waiting room, Dr. Berry motioned for me to sit down, and she shut the door. I wandered over to the sofa from my youth and plopped down in the middle of it. Then I set my purse on the cushion beside me and crossed my legs like a proper lady would. Even though it was winter, I felt the need to wear a dress today. It was some primal display of femininity that had been buried within me, repressed during my time away.

"So Anna..." Dr. Berry took a seat and adjusted her glasses. Her silver hair was short and straight, cut just above the shoulders, perfectly parallel to her thin flat bangs. In many respects, she looked the same.

"I know it's been a long time," I interrupted.

"But it is good to see you. I wouldn't go to anyone else."

"I see." Dr. Berry leaned back in her chair and shot me a pleasant smile, probably to help me relax. "Well, Anna. Why don't you begin?"

"With what?" So much had happened. It was hard to pin point just one thing.

"You've been here before. You know the drill," she chirped. "Tell me what's on your mind."

I folded my hands in my lap and looked down, toying with the bracelet around my wrist.

"That's a lovely bracelet, Anna." Dr. Berry leaned towards me. "May I see it?"

Blushing at her keen eye, I scooted forward and pushed my sleeve back so the bracelet was clear to see. Dr. Berry examined the individual links of silver and then fingered the small heart charm. When her eyes met mine, I saw the same look everyone had been giving me this week. Pity.

"Who gave it to you?" Dr. Berry dug her elbow into the arm of her chair.

Avoiding her gaze, I looked out the window in appreciation of the sunlight.

"Was it a family member?" she wondered, patient as ever, even though it seemed like prying.

"No." I pinned my eyebrows together with the shake of my head. "Not a family member."

Dr. Berry folded her fingers and curved her pink lips into a smile.

"Someone I love," I confessed, feeling that

painful knot in my throat. "Someone I lost."

Dr. Berry nodded, listening.

"At night, I try to sleep." I fluttered my lashes as tears sprang loose. "But then I see him in my dreams."

My lower lip quivered, but I set my sights on my therapist. This was a safe space. And I trusted her.

"I know he's gone," I sobbed. "And I know he's not coming back." My hands went around my arms in an involuntary gesture. "But I feel him everywhere. It's like he's all around me. Like he never left."

Dr. Berry held a box of tissues out for me as I took a few and thanked her.

"Loss is a pain that never completely goes away. But with time, it can grow dull. It can fade."

"But that's just the thing." I hunched forward, eager to spill. "I don't want it to."

Dr. Berry sighed and set the tissue box aside, gnawing at her lower lip.

"I know what you're thinking." I dabbed at my tears and wiped my nose. "It's what everyone thinks."

"And what is that?" She placed her hand on her knee, tossing the question back at me.

"That he did something to me, messed with my head." I stared at the floor and sniffled.

"Did he?" She shifted her posture to the side, those glassy eyes fully focused on me.

"Not in the way everyone thinks," I answered.

It was the honest truth, even if no one believed it.

"Well, I've seen the reports on TV. I've read the newspaper articles. I've watched the press conference with your father and the police." She paused until I looked directly at her. "But I never heard your side of the story. So why don't you tell me what happened? Tell me what you really think."

No one had ever put it to me that way before. Since my return, any chance I had of talking about Julian in a favorable light had been hushed up. Not one person wanted to hear about all the great things he had done. Instead, everyone was honed in on all the many ways he could have hurt me.

I glanced up at the ceiling and then shut my eyes, praying for the strength to do this.

"Take your time," she soothed. "You're my only appointment for the rest of the day."

When I was ready, my eyes opened and I saw her for what she truly was. A friend.

"Julian was a bad man," I admitted. "And he may have spent his life doing terrible things."

Dr. Berry pushed her glasses back over the bridge of her nose. "Go on."

"But he was good to me," I crooned, my voice cracking at the end. "I know how odd it sounds, and I know that nobody wants to believe that. But it's the truth. Julian was good to me."

Dr. Berry took her glasses off and angled her body towards me. I knew this stance. I remembered it from therapy sessions as a child.

She was about to tell me something that I did not want to hear.

"Anna, I'm not sure if you are aware of it. But there is a psychological condition known as Stockholm syndrome. It is a sort of reaction to being held captive or confined. The victim often develops strong feelings in the form of an emotional attachment, sometimes romantic, towards the captor."

"I study at Princeton University, and you think I don't know what Stockholm syndrome is?" I snapped.

Dr. Berry flushed red and put her glasses back on, perhaps not knowing how to react.

"I'm sorry," I swiftly apologized. I had never behaved that way in her presence before.

"You have endured quite a lot of trauma, Anna. It's all right to lash out, let it go."

I nodded and felt like crying all over again. "He's not the monster everyone thinks he is."

"I believe you, Anna," she chided, surely hoping that I would get more off my chest.

"Do you?" I wasn't sure what was more difficult to comprehend. Her being the first to actually believe me. Or me believing her when she said that she took my words as truth instead of delusion.

"Yes." She reached out and patted my arm. "I do. Now why don't you tell me about him? Tell me about the nature of your relationship. Was it romantic?"

"Not at first," I confessed. "But that was because I wanted to go home. I was mad at him for taking me there. In the middle of nowhere. And he wouldn't let me leave."

Dr. Berry raised an eyebrow, calling her earlier point into question.

"It was to protect me," I explained. "To keep me safe. I just didn't understand it then."

She nodded and waited, letting me take my time before going on.

"I remember the first time I saw him. I called him *the beautiful stranger* in my head."

"You were attracted to him," she elucidated. "You were attracted to Julian."

"Yes." I blushed at the memory, recalling what I had wanted him to do to me that night.

"I gather that the two of you were intimate during the time you spent together."

"Yes." I mashed my lips together and avoided her eyes, lost in the past. "But it was..."

Dr. Berry cleared her throat once I drifted off, bringing me back to reality.

"Julian was gentle and sweet," I divulged. "Especially the first time."

I sank my teeth into my lower lip, but knew I had to confess to someone.

"He made love to me."

Dr. Berry maintained eye contact and rested her chin in her hand. I felt comfortable talking to her about all of this, because she was a woman. It would have been too much for Mama. So I never told her.

"Sometimes the way things look can skew the judgement of the way they actually are."

At the resonance of her words, I cocked my head to the side. She had just summed it up perfectly.

"Wouldn't you agree?" she asked.

"Yes."

"You are perfectly normal, Anna. Anyone else in your shoes would respond the same way," she assured me, patting my arm. "You are still suffering a loss. Even if you are the only one."

"Thank you for listening to me," I murmured. "I mean really listening."

Nowadays, it felt like I had no one to talk to.

"Of course. You come by and see me any time, Anna. That's what I'm here for."

"Thank you." I forced a smile and dammed back the tears. I would rather cry at night, when no one could see. It was what I had been doing since I first came home. While everyone else was asleep.

"I'm going to prescribe you some anti-anxiety medication, Anna. It will help you sleep at night."

I cringed at the thought of having to swallow a pill to sleep for the rest of my life.

"Only take it when you need it," she advised.

I nodded and she handed me the slip of paper, our session coming to an end.

Mama would go to the drug store later to fill the prescription.

But I would never swallow the first pill.

Chapter 22

So... how did it go?" Mama led me to the car, her voice laced with concern.

"Fine," I muttered. "I'm glad I got to talk to her. She was really nice."

On the inside, I was concaving. But my mother didn't need to know that.

"Do you think I could meet with those FBI agents tomorrow?"

Mama stopped in the parking lot and turned back to me, lifting her sunglasses.

"I don't really feel like it now." I stared at my shoes and turned my lips down.

"Sure, honey." She opened my door, and I got inside. "I'll call them when we get home."

And so we went back to the house where I slithered into my bedroom to hide. Despite the brave face I had been putting on, it was a mask. One that I had been wearing daily ever since I arrived.

I took a long, hot shower and cried. I hated breaking down in front of my parents, because I felt like they weren't strong enough for that yet. Mama and Daddy could hardly handle what they thought Julian had done to me. How would they be able to cope with the fact that I missed him so much it hurt?

When I dried off in front of the mirror, I spotted the first signs of my natural hair. Julian had purchased cheap temporary dye at a convenience store, the kind that rinses out after so many washes. The black was fading fast, and I hated to watch it dissipate. Just another reminder that what we had was gone.

Mama made mac and cheese for dinner, knowing it was my go-to comfort food. With Daddy working late, it was just the two of us, but I was no fun. When she realized that my hunger had yet to return, Mama came upstairs to stay with me while I lay in bed and watched TV in my pajamas.

I knew what she was doing, sitting beside me on the mattress with a bowl of gooey noodles cradled in her hand. But that dish only reminded me of a particular night I had spent with Julian. When he first took me into that house in the wilderness. When I fought him every second of the way. If I had known now how quickly it was all going to end, I would have done so many things differently.

I wish I had savored those moments.

"Do you want me to sleep in here with you tonight?" Mama wondered.

Even though it would have been nice—not dozing off alone—I wasn't sleeping much anyway. If anything, I would only disturb Mama and keep her up all night. How she liked to worry.

"No. I'll be all right." In truth, I needed the time alone so I could cry, so I could suffer in silence.

"Okay," she said, slightly disappointed. "I'll be down the hall if you need anything."

"Okay, Mama." I listened for her footsteps until she had disappeared.

I wanted to die.

Even though I already felt dead.

Because that's what he was.

My days were made up of one big charade. And no one knew that I was playing them all.

I acted like I was fine.

I acted like I was.

I acted.

But I had never been more unhinged.

At night, my worst fears came to life. Visions traipsed through the darkest parts of my psyche. Even when I was tired enough to fall asleep, I hated dozing off because it would only mean reliving everything.

I wanted Julian. I wanted him to hold me and tell me that everything was going to be all right.

But it's hard for someone to console you over

loss when they're the one who is gone.

"Anna." Julian appeared beside me on the mattress, his warm body fitting mine like a glove.

"What are you doing here?" I asked, holding my hand to my chest. "You scared me."

"I missed you." He cupped my cheek in his palm and hovered above me. "You're so young."

I giggled as he trailed kisses down my throat and slipped his fingers beneath my top. The stubble of his beard tickled my skin, but I reveled in the sensation. When he slanted his mouth over mine, I grappled with the fabric of his shirt until he tugged it off and over his head, tossing it to the wayside.

Julian kissed his way across my ribcage and hugged the curves of my waist. But nothing ever felt right. When I tensed up beneath him, Julian placed his arms along either side of my face and stopped.

"What's wrong?" He rubbed his nose against mine and then nuzzled my neck.

"You're not here," I muttered, running my fingertips over his shoulder blades.

"Of course I am." Julian sealed his mouth over mine and then tickled my jawline.

"Yes, but you're not really here." I looked into his eyes and started to cry.

Julian lifted my chin in the palm of his hand as blood pooled at his mouth. I lurched forward on the bed, but nothing could stop the bleeding. Or the person causing him to bleed.

The bullets entered his body, but never made contact with mine.

That was the part I could never wrap my head around.

The fact that he could save me. But I couldn't save him.

"Anna," he gasped, coughing and gagging. "Promise me, Anna! Promise me!"

"I promise, Julian," I wept, holding the back of his head as he began to slip away.

Jerking awake, I snapped out of the dream and opened my eyes. After I turned the light on, my hands ripped the sheets back in search of the man who had been warming my bed. But he was gone.

It was the same dream every night with little variation in between.

A mixture of the good times and the bad. The beginning and the end.

I buried my head in the pillow and cried, hoping that no one would hear me.

Maybe I should have told Dr. Berry about the nightmares. But she had already prescribed me anti-anxiety meds. The last thing I wanted her to do was have me declared insane and thrown in one of those mental hospitals like Jack Nicholson in *One Flew Over the Cuckoo's Nest.*

"Anna."

I looked up but no one was there. Great. Now I was hearing voices.

"Anna." Mama opened my door and let herself in.

I breathed a sigh of relief and relaxed for a moment. "Hey, Mama."

"Are you having trouble sleeping?" She padded into the room in her house coat and slippers.

"I just had a nightmare, Mama. That's all. Go back to sleep."

"Honey, I really think you should take those pills Dr. Berry prescribed for you."

Mulling over the suggestion, I shrugged my shoulders and consented, "Okay."

Mama left momentarily and returned with the pills and a glass of water.

I twisted the cap off the bottle and dropped two capsules into the palm of my hand.

"Maybe if you get some sleep, you'll start feeling better." Mama brushed the hair out of my face as I placed the blue pills on my tongue and took a swig of water. She waited until I swallowed before she spoke again. "Are you sure you don't want me to stay in here with you? I don't mind."

"Yeah, Mama. I'm sure. Let me get some rest. I have to meet with those FBI guys tomorrow."

"That's right." She left a kiss on my forehead and left the door to my room cracked. "Holler if you need me," she murmured, letting that old Louisiana drawl come out for a change. I liked it.

Once she was gone, I hopped out of bed and waltzed into the bathroom, spitting the pills out in the sink. Then I rinsed my mouth and took a good hard look at myself in the mirror. With no one the wiser, I popped the cap off the anti-anxiety meds and flushed the whole bottle down the toilet.

* * *

I woke up feeling sick. My heart was pounding. My palms were sweating.

I was expected to meet with two FBI agents today to discuss all that had happened.

It felt like an invasion of my privacy, more so than the appointment with Dr. Berry. In that case, I was receiving therapy for my own mental state and well-being. But an interview with the FBI was all about retrieving facts and digging information out of me to better their case. It was all about them.

Mama dropped me off at the police station where two agents named Rodriguez and Hendricks would be conducting the interview. I wondered why no one had thought to place me in a room with female officers. After all, the therapy session with Dr. Berry had gone well since she was a woman. If the FBI truly believed that Julian had done all those terrible things to me, why force me to confess my sins to the opposite sex? Wasn't that common sense—that I might have an aversion to men after being kidnapped by one?

"Miss James." Agent Rodriguez sat at the table in the windowless room.

There was no escaping it now. No place to run and hide. He was waiting for me.

"Please. Come in." He motioned his hand and

stood up like we were in the 18th Century, waiting for the fragile, quiet mouse of a woman to take her seat. "This is Special Agent Hendricks. He'll be supervising the questioning alongside me."

I sat down in the cold, empty chair and looked at the cup of coffee they had waiting for me.

I didn't want it.

"Well, Miss James." Hendricks spoke with glib candor. "Certainly this experience has changed you."

I glared up at him and let my hair hang down my forehead.

"If you could, I would like to know exactly what transpired between you and, Julian, was it?" His blue eyes darkened with intrigue, curious as a cat. "That was his name. Your captor?"

I had already been to a psychiatrist. There was no need to have the same argument with a new face. So I stared at the table and muttered, "Yes. That was his name."

Hendricks scratched the back of his neck, his greasy black hair in need of a good washing. I hated him and Rodriguez too. I hated my parents. I hated all of them for putting me through this.

"How did you come to meet Julian?" Rodriguez asked, his skin a perfect blend of butter and coffee.

I folded my hands together and stared at my cracking nails. When they weren't splitting at the ends, I was biting them off. At least they couldn't see the markings on my wrists.

"I went to a nightclub with Bridgette—"

"Your roommate at the time?" Hendricks verified.

"Yes." I gazed into his paisley blue eyes without smiling. "She was my friend."

"All right, Anna. Go on," Rodriguez encouraged, clicking and unclicking his pen. When I glowered at the obnoxious disturbance, he set the writing utensil aside. "Take your time."

"I was tired of studying all the time," I muttered, twisting the ends of my fingers together. "I just needed a break, I guess. I wanted to have fun. And Bridgette suggested we go to the nightclub."

"And the nightclub is where you first encountered Julian?" Rodriguez inquired.

"Yes." I leaned back in my chair and held on to the sides. "He asked me to dance."

"And what happened after that?" Hendricks wondered, his eyes as steadily fixed on me as his partner's.

"While we were dancing, I saw the bartender taking Bridgette away. They had been talking earlier, and she was always a big flirt. But something seemed off. So we followed them."

Rodriguez nodded while Hendricks pursed his lips. They were both attractive men, and I suddenly wondered if matters had transpired that way on purpose. Julian had been attractive, too.

"The next thing I knew, I had a bag over my head and Bridgette was screaming."

Rodriguez nursed his cup of coffee, but those green eyes stayed on me.

"Julian had a gun. And he was going to kill me." I studied the flecks in the table and then flitted my eyes up to them. "But he didn't."

"Why not, do you think?" Rodriguez posed.

"He didn't have it in him, I guess," I mused. "For some reason, he just couldn't."

"But why would Julian want to kill you in the first place?" Hendricks asked. "What was the motive?"

"There is a bounty on my head," I answered. "What? You two don't know about it?"

"Anna." Rodriguez reached out to touch my hand, but I pulled it away.

"Julian was an assassin hired to kill me," I declared. "Because I was the President's daughter."

"There is no evidence of a bounty on your head," Rodriguez said.

"I am on a hit list. I am a target. If it weren't for Julian, I would be dead."

Hendricks looked over at Rodriguez and whispered something in his ear.

"What?" I felt shunned, like they had placed me under a microscope, a lab rat in a cage.

Rodriguez stopped whispering first and straightened his posture with a smile. "Anna."

"Yes," I snapped back, cutting him off.

"Why don't you tell us where Agent Jenkins took you?"

I cocked my head to the side and leaned back in the chair, taking my hands off the table.

"Julian was a Special Agent," Hendricks explained. "He was undercover working for us."

Rodriguez slid a photograph across the table with the name *George Julian Jenkins* on file.

"Is this the man who took you?" Hendricks asked, his voice as smooth as olive oil.

I fiddled with the picture and traced the surface with my thumb. Those glittering blue eyes stared up at me with a brilliance that never left. It was Julian all right. *My* Julian.

"Yes," I whispered, bringing my hand to my mouth in shock.

Before I could ask the question, Hendricks filled me in on the man I had been on the run with.

"George Julian Jenkins was a veteran of the US Army. Both of his parents and his uncle served but were all killed in combat. Julian was recruited after his service ended and trained as a sniper."

"But war did something strange to him, Miss James," Rodriguez butted in, turning formal all of a sudden. "Most survivors experience PTSD at some point, but Julian couldn't handle what he had seen."

"Julian was assigned to start working security detail at the oval office. But he had an altercation with one of the guards, so instead he was moved into a new position with the secret service. You see, there never seems to be enough protection for past presidents, as well as their families. So Julian was assigned to start watching you."

My brow furrowed at the flood of new information, but Rodriguez continued.

"You were sixteen at the time, still in high school, still living in the area."

Hendricks caught my eye and muttered, "He became obsessed with you."

"So he was removed from that job by the time you started college at Princeton," Rodriguez added.

"I don't understand." I shook my head with a heavy breath. "Julian said he had only been watching me for the past eight weeks. Eight weeks before that night at the club, I mean."

Rodriguez pulled a manila envelope out of his briefcase and set it down on the table. "By the time you were at Princeton, Julian was working undercover for us. There is a secret organization of assassins who kill individuals on a hit list, but then sell off the young girls as sex slaves to make a double profit."

"Yes, I know." My eyes darted from Rodriguez to Hendricks. "Julian told me all about it."

"He did?" Hendricks cocked his black brow in confusion.

"Yes," I demanded. "He said that he didn't want me to be like one of those girls."

Rodriguez sighed and scratched the top of his head. "We believe that Julian was still watching you while you were at Princeton. We believe he had been doing it even after he was removed from the position."

"It was his obsession that drove him to steal you away, to kidnap you," Hendricks declared.

"What about the assassins? The sex trafficking?" I clucked, staring at them both.

"You were in no real danger," Hendricks insisted.

"Then why did they find my best friend at the bottom of a lake?" I countered.

Rodriguez hunched forward. "Agent Eastwood should have been more careful."

My mouth dropped as clarity washed over me. "You're telling me that Bridgette—"

"Protection sent by your father," Rodriguez answered. "You were going off to college alone, and he wanted you to be safe."

"What are you talking about? I still had security on campus. Everywhere I looked. Bridgette and I had to sneak out that night to even get away from them and—" I dropped off, realizing the truth. The only reason we had been able to leave that night was because Bridgette was one of them.

"I understand that this is a lot to take in," Hendricks empathized. "Would you like to stop for the day?"

"Not yet," I replied, digging my heels in. "So why did he take me? If he was working for you?"

"Julian was told to bring you back to us. But he cut off all communication and disappeared with you."

"Yes, but he was only doing that to keep me safe," I urged. "Maybe he thought by getting the police involved that it would be too easy for the assassins to track me down and find me."

"Anna. No one is after you," Rodriguez said. "These are delusions he put in your head."

"No." I jerked my head from side to side. "They were after me. I've seen it. One night a man nearly strangled me to death. And he would have if Julian hadn't—"

"Listen, Anna," Hendricks boomed. "We know you've been through a lot. And we don't know what all Agent Jenkins did to you while you were held captive."

"He didn't hold me captive!" I stood up and slammed my hand down on the table. Even though it hurt. "He was protecting me. He was keeping me safe. Look at what happened to Bridgette! You really believe those men wouldn't have done the same thing to me, if not worse?"

"They killed Bridgette because she was an agent," Hendricks stated. "Nothing more."

"Julian did everything he could to keep me safe. Why are you making him out to be the bad guy?"

Hendricks rose to his feet, and I saw the vein throbbing across his slick forehead. "Because he took you away!" he yelled. "He broke protocol! He did something he wasn't supposed to!"

As my blood pumped with fury, I stretched

across the table and growled. "But I'm alive. Aren't I?"

Rodriguez played with his pen and then reached for his partner's arm. "Sit down," he said. "None of us in here know what happened except for Miss James. But maybe we should cool off for now."

Steaming, I pressed my fingertips into my forearms and turned around. Surely, someone was watching us through the pane, listening to everything I had to say. But I didn't care anymore.

"I know how all of it looks," I spoke under my breath. "But I loved Julian. And he loved me, too."

Rodriguez cleared his throat, and when I turned back, Hendricks had his jaw clenched.

"The funeral for Agent Jenkins is taking place tomorrow," Rodriguez revealed. "I understand if you would like to be there. And despite what has happened, he will have a proper military burial."

"Thank you," I whimpered, nearly breaking down in tears. "I would like to be there."

"Good." Rodriguez nodded as Hendricks backed out of his chair and left the room.

"Are we done here?" I asked, anxious to go home and crawl back into bed.

"Yes. We'll call you if we need any further information for the report."

Sniffling, I turned on my heel to hurry out of the place until he called me back.

"Anna?"

"Yes." I stopped in my tracks and turned around to face him again.

"We went through Julian's things, and there is something you might like to have."

My interest piqued, I approached the desk and felt an overwhelming surge of hope.

"Here." Rodriguez handed me a small square photograph.

It was a picture of me back in high school, when I still looked happy and free.

Unaware of the hell life planned to toss my way.

"We gave that to him a few years ago. When you were his first assignment."

I cradled the picture in the palm of my hand as warmth flooded my spirit.

"It was the only picture he kept in his wallet."

At those words, I looked up at Rodriguez and paused. In the depths of his green eyes, I could see it. I think he knew it, too. That everything I had said was true. Julian loved me, and I loved him, too.

"Let us know if you need anything, Anna. We're here for you."

"Thank you."

He bit his lower lip and watched me go.

I stepped into the hallway and clung to that picture in my hand like it was the air I needed to breathe.

Chapter 23

At dinner that night, I didn't know where to begin. The three of us had yet to have a family meal since my return. And after Daddy's outburst in the foyer, I had no idea how to tell him what I truly felt.

"How did everything go with those FBI agents today, Anna?" Daddy asked.

Mama prepared spaghetti and meatballs, which only served as a reminder of the romantic night Julian and I had shared. Looking back now, it was the closest thing we ever had to a date.

"Fine." I twirled the tines of my fork through the noodles. "I told them everything."

"Good." Daddy took a sip of red wine and then smiled at my mother.

"I made another appointment for you with Dr. Berry tomorrow," Mama said. "I hope that's all right."

My heart sank at the strength of her audacity. "Could you push it back a day?" I suggested.

"Well, I guess if you want me to. Are you not feeling well after today?"

"No." I stared at the food on my plate, since I had hardly touched it. I wondered if they noticed. "It's just that there is somewhere I have to be tomorrow. I would rather focus on that."

"Oh?" Daddy's eyebrows lifted to the ceiling. "Where is that?"

"Agent Rodriguez said the funeral is tomorrow," I explained. "I want to go."

"The funeral," Daddy repeated, slapping his tongue against the roof of his mouth.

"Julian's funeral." I looked at Mama, but her eyes were on Daddy.

"No." Daddy slammed his fist against the table cloth. "No, Anna! After everything that man did to you! If you think I am going to let you go to that freak's funeral—"

"Let me?" I butted in. "It's not your decision. I'm nineteen and about to turn twenty."

"You are living under my roof, Anna. So it will be my rules," he snarled.

"Walter, stop yelling at her!" Mama shouted, defending me.

"What do you expect me to think?" Daddy stood up and threw his napkin down. "That man kidnapped our little girl and did God knows what to her out in the woods for weeks! And you think I should let her attend his funeral? It's a good thing he is dead, because if he wasn't—"

"Enough!" I shouted. "I've been hearing a lot lately about how everyone else feels and what everyone else wants. What about what I want? I'm the one going through all of this! Not you or you!" I pointed at my mother and father, the latter of which seemed shocked by my boldness.

"You are not going to that funeral, Anna," Daddy firmly declared. "And that is final."

"But I have to," I whined, feeling like my knees were about to buckle.

"Why?" Daddy snapped back. "What do you mean you have to?"

"Because I'm pregnant!"

Mama gasped and covered her mouth as my father turned to stone.

"What did you just say?" he asked.

"I'm pregnant," I repeated, bracing myself for another outburst.

Fuming, my father took the bottle of red wine and threw it across the floor. Glass shattered as crimson liquid stained the curtains and carpet. He was so fueled with rage that he was shaking.

"This is sick!" Daddy proclaimed. "What kind of man in his thirties kidnaps a teenage girl and turns her into his sex slave?"

"Julian was twenty-nine!" I defended.

But he ignored me and kept on.

"Our daughter, Winifred! Our little girl! And he touched her!"

"I wanted him to!" I screamed, so on the verge

of tears that I couldn't control it.

Daddy stalked towards me and eyed my stomach. "I don't know what he did to you. He must have brainwashed you, messed with your mind. But we can get rid of it."

"Get rid of it?" I took a step back and draped a protective arm across my belly.

"Yes! You think I'm going to let something like this ruin the rest of your life?"

My lower lip trembled, and I felt weak. "Mama," I cried, turning to her for solace.

"You gave him enough, Anna," she reasoned. "You don't have to give up your whole life."

Julian gave his life for me. Why wouldn't I give mine for him? For our child?

"I want to keep it," I said, confessing my innermost desires. "I want my baby."

"No, Anna," Daddy protested. "He has already done enough damage. Enough! I'm not going to let him keep hurting you. Think about it, Anna. That man is dead, and he's still causing you pain."

"He's not some man!" I shouted. "He was the love of my life!"

Daddy drained his wine glass and then wiped his hand across the back of his mouth. "You talk to her," he said to my mother. "She's too far gone. I don't know what he did to her. But I want my daughter back."

As soon as he marched out of the room, Mama looked up at me with tears in her eyes.

"Mama," I cried, running into her arms as she

held me tight. Sometimes, it felt like she was my only friend. The only one who would listen. The only one who could understand.

"Oh, Anna, honey." She brushed my hair out of my face and wiped the tears from my eyes. Then she kept me in her warm embrace for minutes, patting my back in comfort.

"I just wish Daddy could understand." I leaned back and sat down beside her.

"I know, sweetie." She patted me on the shoulder and then squeezed my arm.

"It's my baby too, you know." I put my hand on my stomach. "It's our love child." I looked up at her and smiled at the sentiment, because the thought of having Julian's child sounded so romantic.

"I understand how you feel," Mama crooned. "But you know that you can't keep the baby."

"What?" I choked on the word, feeling my throat closing up.

"You're nineteen, Anna. You have your whole life ahead of you." She rubbed my head in reassurance, combing her fingers through my hair. "What about Princeton and finishing up college? Your future? Your life?"

"This *is* my life!" I barked, distancing myself from her. "And it's my decision!"

As I hurried up the staircase and slammed my bedroom door, tears streamed down my face. Not the kind that I was used to. Not the kind Julian. The kind of tears reserved for our unborn child.

I walked into the bathroom and locked the door behind me. Then I got down on my knees and prayed.

"Thank you," I cried. "It's the only thing that makes sense, the only thing that makes me want to live." I curled my fingers around the invisible bump that had yet to form. "Please help me keep this baby."

My head snapped up at the sound of objects breaking downstairs, more glass shattering.

My choking sobs ensued, but I bowed my head and kept on.

"And please, God," I begged, tasting the salt in my tears. "Please let it be a boy."

* * *

I was up all night talking to Julian. Maybe he wasn't there. Maybe he couldn't hear me.

Maybe I had gone a little crazy. But no one was taking my child away from me.

On the morning of the funeral, I rolled out of bed and took a cold shower. The black dye in my hair was gone now, my natural blond locks the only color that remained. As I slipped into a black dress, that lump started rising up in my throat again. The one that felt like a rock. The one that never went away.

When I got downstairs, Mama and Daddy were already waiting for me, nursing a pot of coffee.

"Well, I'm ready," I announced, trying my hardest to suck in the sadness and pain.

"Ready for what?" Daddy started, donning his house coat and slippers.

I clenched my jaw and wanted to scream. "The funeral," I demanded. "I told you I was going."

"And I told you that you're not!" Daddy stood up and peered down at me, exuding dominance.

Helplessly drowning, I reached out for something to hold on to and turned to my mother.

"Mama." I got down on my knees in front of her and grabbed her hands. "Please."

"We are just doing what's best for you, Anna." She cupped my cheek in her hand. "I really think it would be best if you saw Dr. Berry today. You seemed much better after the last time you talked to her."

Falling to pieces, I leaned against the wall and buried my face in my hands.

"Anna, honey," Mama coaxed, kneeling down beside me. "Don't cry."

I peeked through the slits in my fingers and eyed her carefully. "How can you do this to me? Either of you?" I set my sights on Daddy and glared, shifting my weepy green gaze between the two of them. "Don't you understand that this is my last chance to see him? Julian is gone! He's gone and—"

"Do not say that man's name in front of me ever again!" Daddy shouted. "Do you understand me?"

Shaking in my boots, I dabbed at my tears and cried. But no one cared. Not even Mama.

As I wrapped my arms around myself, Mama rose from the floor to stand beside Daddy. It was like they were on the same team, the same side. And I, their only daughter, had somehow become the enemy.

Everyone turned still when the doorbell rang.

"Who the hell is that?" Daddy grumbled, running his fingers through his hair as he left to answer it.

Mama looked over me with pity and parted her lips to speak, but I didn't want to hear anything she had to say.

My ears perked up at the sound of familiar hushed voices in the adjoining room. So I gathered myself and looked in the mirror to wipe away the mess my mascara had made. Then I walked to the front door and stopped when I saw Agent Rodriguez coming towards me.

"Oh." I stepped up beside my father and gazed into his green eyes.

"Hello, Miss James." Rodriguez shook my hand with a gentle touch.

"Hi," I muttered in a still, small voice. "What are you doing here?"

"Well, I had a few more questions for you, Anna. And I was in the area, on my way to the funeral. I was wondering if you would like a ride? I'll bring you back once the ceremony is done."

"Anna will not be attending the funeral today,"

Daddy interjected.

"Oh." Rodriguez took a step back in his suit. "I'm sorry, I—"

"That will be all now. Thank you." Daddy pushed Rodriguez over the threshold. "You can come back and ask your questions later." Then he slammed the door right in his face.

"Hey! What did you do that for? You didn't even let me say anything! I wanted to go with him!"

"Your mother has set up an appointment with Dr. Berry," he growled. "And you're going to that appointment, Anna. You're going right now!"

Daddy grabbed my arm and shoved me up the staircase, hauling me into my bedroom. When he slammed the door, I hurried to my feet and locked it. Then I rushed over to the window and peered through the blinds. Rodriguez got in his car and pulled away, while I cursed my father on the inside.

For the next hour, I stayed inside my room and refused to move. I knew the appointment with Dr. Berry was a lie, just some bogus attempt at locking me up so I couldn't attend the funeral. But then I heard tires coming up the drive and looked out my window. Agent Rodriguez was back.

I slipped out of my bedroom and down the stairs, eavesdropping in the foyer.

"I just have a few extra questions for her, sir. Especially after your phone call last night."

"All right," Daddy succumbed. "She is very upset today. I'll get her to come downstairs."

When he called my name, I rolled my eyes. But since I was already halfway down the steps, I put my best foot forward and met them in the living room.

"Oh, Anna, there you are!" Daddy steered me towards Rodriguez and then bolted out of the foyer.

I led Rodriguez through the house and into the living room, where he sat down in my father's chair. Trying to forget about what had happened the last time I was in here, I dropped my butt to the couch and threaded my fingers through my hair. After a day like this, what more could go wrong?

"Your father tells me that you're pregnant," Rodriguez chimed. He sounded surprisingly optimistic about the whole thing, treating it as nothing more than unexpected news.

"Yes," I mouthed, licking my lips before sealing them shut. I crossed my ankles and held my palms together in my lap. Rodriguez bowed his head and dug his elbows into his knees. He was an attractive man with boyish good looks—striking green eyes and pouty lips. While I assumed him to be in his mid-thirties, he could have easily passed for twenty seven or eight. I wondered if anyone had ever told him to audition for one of those night time cop shows in LA. Surely, he would have been cast during pilot season.

"While you were away with Agent Jenkins, did the two of you have unprotected sex?" he asked.

Usually, I would have blushed scarlet red, but I didn't. I wasn't ashamed of what we had done.

"Yes," I casually replied.

He cocked a dark brow at me. "More than once?"

"Yes." I stared into his eyes and thought of Julian.

"So there's no confusion as to who—"

"The baby is his," I interrupted. "There is no one else. There has never been anyone else."

Rodriguez pursed his lips with a nod.

"Even though he's gone, it's like I have this little piece of him." I placed my palm over my stomach, and he watched. My eyes drifted to the floor as I got carried away with an endearing smile. "I really hope it's a boy."

Rodriguez furrowed his brow and shrugged. "Why?"

My smile widened. "So I can call him Julian."

Rodriguez listened and then popped his head up when my father entered the room. Mama followed closely behind as they drifted into the kitchen, arguing about something in their matching house coats and bedroom slippers. It was like they hadn't even seen us sitting here.

"Anna." Rodriguez lowered his voice and leaned in closer. "I need to take you somewhere."

Tensing up at his choice of words, I searched his face and wrapped my arms around myself.

"Just trust me," he begged. "You need this."

Gnawing at my lower lip, I turned my head to

the side and saw my parents in the distant room. They believed I was being interrogated by an FBI agent. Would they even notice if I was gone?

I looked back at Rodriguez and said, "Okay."

* * *

The rain was pouring down in sheets by the time we reached our destination. Rodriguez hopped out of the SUV and came around to the other side with an umbrella. But I flew past him and ran across the cemetery until I reached the closed coffin.

I was too late.

"No!" I wailed, falling to my knees before the hard wood.

The funeral director rushed about with another worker as they took down a framed portrait of Julian that had been on display. I stretched my arm out to reach it, but the moment was gone. I should have been here to show my respects today, but I had missed it all.

"Anna!" Rodriguez found me on the ground and touched my back.

Sinking into his arms, I put my head on his shoulder and cried. "I'm too late."

He comforted me, taking the blame. "I'm sorry."

I felt like throwing up, as my knees began to quake.

"Shh..." Rodriguez held me close and kissed my hair, rubbing his hand across my shoulder blades.

Once I recovered enough to put more than two words together, I leaned back. "Can you give me a minute alone with him?"

"Yeah, sure." Rodriguez offered to help me up and then handed over the umbrella.

"Take it," I mumbled. "I like the rain."

Rodriguez shifted his face like he hadn't heard me and then eventually said, "Okay."

When he was gone, I pressed my palms into the lid of the coffin and began. "Hi," I whispered. "I'm sorry I'm late." I glanced down at my black dress, the one I had intended to wear to his funeral today. "I wanted to be here. But they wouldn't let me come."

Thunder rumbled in the distance, and it seemed like the rain was moving on.

"I'm pregnant, Julian," I revealed. "And I'm so happy. We made a baby. Can you believe it?"

When there was no reply, I put my cheek to the cool wood and sighed.

"I miss you," I whimpered. "I wish you were here."

With a deep breath, I stood up straight and gazed at the coffin.

"Mama and Daddy want to have it taken care of." I touched my hand to my stomach. "But I'm not going to let that happen." I took a breath and sniffled. "They don't want me to give my whole life up for our child. But how can they say that when you gave yours up for me?"

I choked on those words, running my hands over my face. Mascara must have been smeared across my cheeks, but I didn't care. The silver charm on his mother's bracelet dangled against my wrist.

"I have a plan," I confessed. "One that even you would be proud of."

I looked back at Rodriguez where he was waiting by the car. He was watching my every move. But with the distance between us, I knew he couldn't hear me.

So I returned to Julian and told him every word.

* * *

Rodriguez pulled into the drive and parked his SUV. As I fiddled with my hands in my lap, raindrops pelted against the window pane. I unfastened my seatbelt and went to open the door.

"Wait." Rodriguez leaned into the back seat and handed me a folded up American flag.

"We usually give this to the wife or family—"

"But Julian didn't have one," I finished.

His green eyes brightened. "You're the next best thing."

My lips curved up in a weak smile. I took the flag and held it to my chest, running my fingers over the fabric. "You know I can't take this in there."

"What?" Rodriguez questioned, confused.

"If Daddy saw me with this," I gave the flag

back. "He would burn it."

His nostrils flared with loud air, as Rodriguez gave a sure nod.

"Will you hold on to it for me?" I softly asked. "Keep it somewhere safe?"

Rodriguez looked me over. "Okay."

"Thank you." I opened the car door and stepped out.

"Hey Anna?" he yelled over the rain.

I paused in the driveway and looked back at him.

"Take care of yourself."

I shot him a sweet grin and shut the door.

His eyes remained on me, even once I stepped inside the house. Peering out the window, I held my hands behind my back and watched him drive away.

"Where have you been?" Daddy snapped.

The hairs stood up on the back of my neck as I turned around. "I went to see him," I confessed. "I went to see Julian."

"Well good," he snarled. "He's dead now. He can't hurt you. Especially once the doctor takes that thing out."

"Thing?" I echoed. "You mean your grandchild?"

Mama appeared in the foyer. "Honey, it won't be as painful. Not early on. Not like what you've seen on TV. You won't even have to have surgery.

"I'm not doing that," I demanded. "It's my baby!" I spun around with a growl. "Mine! And it will be my decision!"

Daddy jabbed his finger at me with the clench of his jaw. "Now, you listen to me, and you listen good. I don't know what that filthy man did to you, but you will not disgrace this family with an illegitimate child! You are getting rid of it!"

"No, I'm not!"

I swung my hand out to push him back and he caught my wrist, snapping the clasp on the silver bracelet. Link by link, the shimmering chain fell apart and scattered across the floor. The beautiful heart charm landed last, dribbling over the wood before it finally stopped.

The light drained from my soul as I crawled across the ground, breaking down on the spot. His mother's bracelet was ruined. I had promised Julian that I would keep it safe. And now it was gone.

"How could you do that?" I turned on my father and charged, slamming him up against the wall.

"Anna!" Mama jerked me away from him while I gasped for breath, falling apart.

"Is it true?" I screamed, getting in his face despite Mama's feeble attempts to keep us apart.

"What?" Daddy said, loosening his collar.

"Is it true?" I yelled. "You leaked government secrets! Innocent people died! All so no one would find out about the affair!"

My parents froze in their tracks, and it was a sight to behold.

"Yes, I know all about it," I seethed. "You and the press secretary."

Daddy sat down on the stairs and held his head in his hands. But Mama stood tall, afraid of nothing. "Yes," she revealed, incriminating him. "It's true."

"Winifred!"

"She's your daughter," she fought back. "She deserves to know the truth."

"You've been keeping his secrets?" I hissed.

"Yes!" she admitted.

My shoulders sagged as I frowned. "But why?"

"He's your father, my husband. And his secrets are my secrets." She took a step closer, and I moved back. "Just like that baby of yours will be a secret as well. No one will ever know about this."

I widened my eyes at her, enraged.

"And we're getting it taken care of first thing tomorrow morning."

I used my arms to cover my belly and eased away from her. I didn't know this woman. She wasn't my mother. She wasn't my friend.

"Anna, honey, I know you're scared. But it will all be over soon. And you won't ever have to think about that awful man and what he did to you again."

"No," I refused, barreling up the stairs. "No!"

I ran into my room and locked the door behind me, dragging out my suitcase to pack.

Chapter 24

Mama collected my empty bowl of soup on the tray as she tucked me in for the night. "Are you feeling better now, honey?"

"Yes." I relaxed my head against my pillow. "I think I was just tired is all."

"I understand. I'll come wake you up in the morning, all right?" Once I nodded, she patted my cheek and left a kiss on my forehead.

"You're right," I said as she headed for the door. "It will be better tomorrow. After everything is all over."

"You are a very brave girl, Anna," she chirped. "But you won't have to do this alone. I'll be there every step of the way."

"Okay, Mama."

She smiled and walked out the door. "Get some sleep," she chimed, gently shutting it behind her.

The minute she was gone, I listened for her footsteps padding down the hall. Then I ripped the covers back and leapt out of the bed, twisting the lock on the door. I pulled my backpack out from under my bed, since it was less conspicuous than a rolling suitcase.

Worried that I would miss my window of opportunity, I laced up my sneakers and pulled on a pair of black skinny jeans. Then I put on my grandpa's old baseball cap and jerked a loose sweatshirt over my top. Twisting my hair back in a bun, I tugged the hood down over my head and tightened the strings.

I looked in the mirror before I left and applied a few coats of mascara, a dab of balm to my lips and cheeks. Then I walked over to the window and waited, listening for any sign of activity. Only the booming TV that would drown out any noise I made and keep them distracted for hours.

When I was sure of myself, I slid the window open and slung one leg over, easing myself onto the roof. Security was light tonight—a final day off to celebrate the New Year. So I squatted down and shut the window, holding my breath from two stories up.

As my pulse thrummed violently in my ears, I was too chicken to test out the columns. So I closed my eyes and jumped. The rose bushes may have pierced my skin with thorns, but they did break my fall.

Shifting my gaze from side to side, I stood up

and darted across the lawn. Somehow I managed to trigger the alarm, and lights and sounds went off everywhere. In a panic, I took off with everything I had in me and sprinted down the sidewalk.

After about a block, I climbed into a tree and hid before journeying onward. It was almost too easy. And when I surfed down the branches with the heels of my shoes, I was greeted by a cold hand to the mouth.

Biting and scratching, I dragged my nails over the arms around me and cried. I could feel his warm breath in my ear. The breath of the next man hired to kill me.

"Stop it, Anna," the voice hissed. "It's me."

I spun around and gazed into the green cat-like eyes of Agent Rodriguez.

"What are you doing here?" I rasped, catching my breath.

"What are you doing, Anna? Running away?"

I hung my head and clung to the straps on my backpack.

"In your condition?" he added. "Don't do this to yourself. Please."

"They want me to have an abortion," I confessed, looking off into the distance, in the direction of their house. "This is the only way I can keep the baby."

Rodriguez scratched his head and sighed. "I guess there is no point in trying to stop you," he realized.

I leaned in closer and stated, "You couldn't if

you tried."

Rodriguez searched the empty street and then touched my shoulder. "Where are you going?" he asked. "Can I at least give you a ride?"

I heard sirens in the distance and flinched. "Yeah. Take me to the bus station."

Rodriguez grabbed my arm and led me to his car, helping me inside.

Even though I hardly knew him, he was the only one who had any real empathy for my situation. In the questioning, even Agent Hendricks seemed angry with me, almost like it was my fault—everything that had happened.

"I'll buy your ticket," he volunteered. "Where are you going?"

I sank into the seat and watched the faces of people passing by at the station. What if one of them recognized me?

"San Francisco," I divulged, reaching in my pocket to hand him the money.

"No. Let me." He got out of the car and pulled out his wallet. "It's the least I can do."

I waited in the car as he bought me a one way ticket to the other side of the country, nervously biting my nails. When he returned, I sat up and counted my breaths.

"Here." Rodriguez handed me the ticket. "The bus leaves in ten minutes."

I stared at the ticket and then took it.

"Do you have any money?" Rodriguez thumbed through his bill fold.

"A little," I muttered.

"Here." He handed me all of his cash and then stuffed his wallet back into his pocket.

"This is too much," I declared, fanning out the twenties. "Really. I'll be fine."

"Take it," he said. "You'll need more than that to get where you're going."

"Thank you." I tucked the bills away in my bra.

"Why San Francisco?" he wondered.

"You know a place farther away?"

Rodriguez cocked his head to the side and studied me. "I may send someone out there one day to look for you, to let me know that you're safe. Is that okay?"

I thought about it for a few seconds and then nodded. Turning to get out, I put my fingers around the handle until he blocked me.

"This is my number." He showed me his business card, and I took it. "If you ever need anything, don't hesitate to ask."

"Okay. Thank you Agent Rodriguez."

He stuck his hand out and said, "Andy."

Tears filled my eyes as I gave him a hug. "Thank you, Andy." The only person who understood, and I would probably never see him again.

When I pulled back, he lifted my chin up. "You're a beautiful young girl, Anna. I hate that you're having to run away like this."

"It's the only way I can have a life of my own. With my son."

He flashed a crooked smile. "So sure it's a boy already?"

I pressed my lips together and looked at him for the last time.

"I could get in a lot of trouble for this," he reminded me. "But go, and don't tell anyone I helped you."

As he delicately stroked my arm, I leaned in and kissed him on the cheek. "Goodbye."

"Goodbye, Anna." He watched me as I got out of the car. "Oh, wait." He reached into the back seat and held the American flag out for me to take, the one from the funeral today.

I rubbed my fingers over the cloth and then folded it into my bag, happy to have something to remind me of Julian now that the bracelet was gone.

"Take care of yourself," Rodriguez said. "And that little boy."

After one last look, I shut the door and darted out into the night. By the time I found a seat on the bus, I looked out the window and Rodriguez was gone. Accepting the path laid out before me, I stayed in the back from day to night, watching the sun rise and set from where I sat.

It took three days to get from Washington to San Francisco. And on that third night, I found myself loitering around in the rain, desperate for a place to stay. I was hungry and cold, wondering if I would join the homeless on these dusty streets.

But then I knocked on a certain woman's

door, and my luck began to change. Her name was Polly, and she was in her late sixties. She was a widow to an immigrant shopkeeper, and their only son died long ago of a heart attack.

Anyone would think that the two of us had nothing in common. But the opposite was true. We were both alone.

"I know you," she squeaked, peering through the screen door. "I voted for your father."

I lowered my hood and took the baseball cap off. She had already blown my cover.

"I heard about what happened to you," she continued. "I saw it on the news."

Assuming that the jig was up, I stuffed the hat into my backpack and turned to leave before she called someone and the police showed up.

"Do you need a place to stay?"

"Yes, actually," I piped up, finally giving her the chance to hear my voice.

"Well, come on in." She pushed the screen door back, and the smell of chocolate chip cookies assaulted my nose. "I've got plenty of room."

So I trusted her act of kindness and stepped inside. There was a quiet tabby cat perched on the sofa with orange eyes. Her apartment was cozy, warm, nice.

Polly made me a cup of tea, as we sat at her dinner table and watched the rain. She never asked me why I was here, even though it was obvious that I was running away. Instead, she told me about her life, and never pried into mine.

She must have talked for hours while I listened, nursing that same cup of tea. And as I grew fond of her laughter, it occurred to me how long it must have been since she had relished lengthy conversation with another person. She was animated and quirky, yet awfully humble and kind.

In that moment, sitting there in her kitchen with wet hair and a cup of tea, something finally felt right. I knew Julian would like it here, my precious little boy. It would become our little "City by the Bay." Deep down, I knew that all of the decisions I had made that led me here were right.

I thanked Polly and took the pull-out couch when she offered it. After she scuttled off to bed, that tabby cat crawled into my lap so I could pet her head. As she flexed her paws and purred, I rubbed my belly with a giddy smile.

Everything was going to be all right. Of that I was sure.

That cat curled into a ball on my stomach, as if she could sense the life growing inside me. I rubbed the fur behind her ears and looked deep into those topaz eyes. They were like crystal balls, letting me know that my future was clear.

Snuggling beneath the covers, I held that tabby cat close and shut my eyes.

And so a new chapter in my life began.

Chapter 25

Eight Years Later.

It was a warm, sunny day in San Francisco. After a restless night, I trudged into the kitchen and made a pot of coffee. Without that first cup, it was nearly impossible to wake up.

"Julian!" I called. "Time for breakfast."

"Coming, Mama!"

We usually ate cereal for breakfast. But Julian had made straight A's on his last report card, and it was one of the few ways I could reward him.

"Julian James!" I scolded, tapping my foot.

The little thing raced down the hall and into the kitchen with his school clothes on. He hopped up onto the bar stool, as I slid scrambled eggs, bacon, and toast onto his plate. Then he grabbed his fork and ate with ravenous delight.

I filled a glass with orange juice and set it down

in front of him. "Hey, quit kicking those feet."

"Yes, Mama." He chomped on a piece of bacon and looked up at me with those glittering blue eyes.

It tore me to pieces and put me back together every time.

"How about you and I go out to dinner tonight?" I suggested. "Just the two of us?"

"Why?" he wondered, a furrow between his brows.

"Because you've been doing so good in school." I ruffled my fingers through his dark locks and then took a comb to his hair. "You can even have ice cream for dessert."

"Any flavor I want?"

"Any flavor you want," I assured him, pinching that adorable cheek.

After he was finished with breakfast, Julian ran off to brush his teeth. I helped him with his shoes and then slid his books in his backpack. He reached for the door until I pulled him back.

"Forgetting something?" I asked, tickling his sides.

Julian giggled and gave me a kiss.

"I love you, Julian."

"I love you, Mama." He went outside and then turned back and waved before getting on the bus.

I walked onto the sidewalk and kept my eyes on my little boy headed to school. "Have a good day!"

He took his seat on the bus and waved, while I

waved back. When the street cleared, a shiver crept up my spine, so I spun around real fast. It had been like this for months. I couldn't get over the uncanny feeling that someone was watching me.

* * *

At work, I tried to shake the worry off, but it just wouldn't go away. Polly stopped by around noon, since it was her day to volunteer. I worked at the library by day and waited tables at a local restaurant most nights.

The double income paid the bills, but also allowed me the flexibility that the corporate world wouldn't. Since I dropped out of Princeton when I found out I was pregnant with Julian, there had been no attempt to further my education. Most companies that were hiring and willing to dole out the big bucks weren't about to invest in a college drop-out like me.

"I see that good looking man come in here every week," Polly chattered, while we shelved books in the back. "Why won't you go out with him?"

"Because I don't want to," I whined. "It's too soon."

"Anna, it's been almost ten years," Polly reminded me. "One day you're going to be my age and nearly dead."

"Polly," I laughed, sliding a copy of *The Gift of the Magi* onto the middle shelf. It had been so long ago, but it tugged at my heartstrings even now.

"Fine stock like that won't stay single for long."

"Well, I don't see you out there looking for a man," I fired back, making sure the books were lined up properly. The entire row of fiction was alphabetized except for one, so I moved to fix it.

"Honey, that's because I'm old," she jabbered. "You're still young. If I had your figure, I sure wouldn't waste it."

Rolling my eyes, I put my hands on my hips and replied, "I already have a man in my life."

"I know you love that little boy," Polly began, resting her hand on my shoulder. "But it's your life, too. Don't you deserve to be happy?"

I thought about that for a long moment and pinched the bridge of my nose when she walked away. Maybe she was right. But there was only one love of my life. Julian's father. Just because he was gone didn't mean that I no longer cared.

Back at the front desk, I attended to those checking books out. When a young mother said she was looking for *The Gift of the Magi*, my face lit up. "I want to read it to my son," she said.

"That's my favorite story," I shared. "I know where it is. I'll be right back."

Scampering off, I drifted into the aisle where I had just been stocking shelves with Polly. My eyes darted to the middle shelf, as I scanned the titles for the one I was looking for. *The Gift of the Magi* was gone.

I held my finger to my chin and stood there for

a good thirty seconds, perplexed. When I asked Polly, she couldn't remember. So then it was my memory against my sight.

"I'm sorry, ma'am," I told the young mother. "It looks like someone already checked it out."

I racked my brain and searched everywhere, but I could never seem to find it.

* * *

When I took Julian out to dinner, it was nice to be the one getting served a meal for a change. It was my night off, and my boss was kind enough to take care of dinner for us. "It's on the house," he said, sweet as sugar.

I leaned into the booth and ruffled my fingers through Julian's hair. He looked so much like his father that it scared me. And when he grew up to be a man, I knew that he would be the spitting image of his Daddy.

"Can I have ice cream now?" Julian asked, giving me a toothy grin.

I tapped my finger against his nose. "Of course you can."

When the waiter brought him chocolate ice cream with sprinkles, I sat back and enjoyed his excitement. Julian wouldn't be this age forever. I had to soak up every moment while I could.

Once Julian took the last bite, his mouth was a mess. I picked up a napkin and wiped the chocolate away. "Go to the bathroom and wash your hands."

"Yes, Mama." Julian slid out of the booth and headed for the men's restroom.

Always tired, I held my hand to my mouth and yawned. Something caught the corner of my eye. A painting on the wall of a single canoe drifting down the river between two rows of trees.

There was something familiar about it. Something that struck a chord. But I couldn't quite put my finger on it.

"Mama," Julian called.

I looked up at the sound of my name and realized that he was back from washing his hands. "Are you ready to go?"

He nodded and took my hand, dragging me along. I suppose he was hyped up from all the sugar and caffeine, but I rarely let him have treats. Especially on a school night.

But this was my boy. And he was doing so well in school. I had to let him be a kid every once in a while.

"Can I go see Miss Polly?" Julian asked the moment we walked through the door.

Her apartment was the one just above ours, where I had lived for a brief period before getting a place of my own. She was like a grandmother to me and Julian. And I guess we were family to her, too.

"Just for a little bit," I warned. "Don't let her give you any chocolate or cookies. You've already had ice cream tonight."

"Yes, Mama." Julian slipped out of his jacket

and hurried upstairs. I suppose it was good that he had more than just me.

Since Julian was born, my own mother and father were no help. One minute they wanted to pay for private tuition. The next, they wanted to have me declared an unfit mother and take him away from me.

I took him to Washington once every few years, but they never came to visit. In some ways, I guess they still held it against me—the fact that I ran. But not because I left.

Because of the way I made them look.

Thunder boomed in the distance as I turned on the kitchen light. I checked to see if all the doors were locked and then returned for something to drink. As I filled a glass from the tap, a shiver crawled up my spine.

I drained the liquid and then looked out the window. There was a man standing across the street in all black. And he was looking at me.

I dropped the glass in the sink and staggered back. Then I turned the kitchen light off and peered out the window again. But he was gone.

Feeling my breath catch at the back of my throat, I rushed out of the apartment and hurried upstairs. Julian was at the piano with Polly. She had taught him a few tunes when he was five. But when I barged in that night, my seven-year-old son was playing "Piano Man."

"Stop that!" I shouted. "No more piano tonight."

Julian looked stunned. But he was a good kid, and I was his mother. So he did what I said.

"I'm sorry, Julian," I immediately said, feeling terrible. "Mama has a headache."

He sat on the piano bench with Polly, while they both stared at me.

"Tell Miss Polly good night," I instructed. "You can see her tomorrow."

Julian gave Polly a hug and slid down off the piano bench. "Sorry, Mama." He reached out and hugged my legs. "I'm sorry you don't feel good."

"It's not your fault, baby." I ruffled my fingers through his hair. "Why don't you go downstairs and brush your teeth and put your pajamas on?"

"Yes, Mama." Julian followed my orders and left the room, while Polly looked a little angry with me.

"What?" I asked.

"That boy was playing so beautifully," she declared. "Why did you make him stop?"

"It's just that song," I revealed. "I couldn't stand to hear it tonight."

"Why? You don't like Billy Joel?"

"No, that's not it." I trudged over to the window and looked through the glass.

"You see something, dear?"

Lightning struck in the distance as the thunder rumbled closer.

"Someone once told me that there was a bounty on my head," I murmured. "Do you believe that's true?"

"No," Polly insisted. "Of course not."

"I'm an Ex-President's daughter. Wouldn't that make me a target?" I mused.

"Anna, there is a storm coming, and you've had a long day. Why don't you and Julian stay with me tonight?"

"No." I threaded my fingers through my hair, contemplating whether or not to tell her about the man I had seen. "We'll be fine."

"You're probably just tired," she assumed. "Maybe you should take the day off tomorrow."

"Maybe." I told Polly good night and headed back downstairs. Julian was already in bed waiting for me, teeth brushed and pajamas on. He wanted me to read him a bedtime story.

"All right. Scoot over," I said with a grin.

Julian lifted the covers and made room for me. We lived in a modest apartment, and Julian had a small bedroom. But he had yet to complain about his twin size bed. Not even once.

"What story do you want me to read?"

"This one." Julian grabbed a thin book from his night stand and placed it in my lap. It was *The Gift of the Magi*.

"Julian, where did you get this?"

"At school," he said.

"Yes, but where? Who gave it to you?"

"The man at school."

I blinked a few times. "What man?"

"The man on the playground today."

My eyes watered out of pure fear. I wanted to

scream and cry. I was terrified.

"Julian, Mama needs to lie down. Okay? I'll read you a story tomorrow night. You need to go to bed. You have school in the morning."

"Okay, Mama." He took the book and set it on his night stand. I closed my eyes and kissed his head, turning out the light. "Good night, Mama."

"Good night, Julian."

"I love you, Mama," he breathed.

"I love you too, baby."

I pulled his door to and walked down the hall and into the kitchen. My head was swirling with fear and panic. I didn't know what to do.

On the verge of a breakdown, I turned to the only thing that ever dulled the pain. Even if it was only for a little while. Alcohol.

I poured myself a glass of wine and gulped it down like there was no tomorrow. Then I poured another.

When it started to flood outside, I shut the blinds so I wouldn't have to worry about that man. For a second, I wondered if I should call Agent Rodriguez. I hadn't heard from him in years. But he had sworn that I was never on a hit list, that there was no bounty on my head.

But what if he was wrong?

What if the assassins were back? But this time, they were coming after my son?

After numbing myself out, I checked the gun under my bed. It was still loaded. I had never used it and prayed that I never had to.

Just as I began to doze off, lightning flashed, and a figure emerged in the doorway.

"Mama?" Julian called.

"Yeah, baby?" I sat up and noted the distress on his face. "What is it? Did you have a bad dream?"

He ran into my arms and crawled beneath the covers with me.

"What is it?" I wondered, petting his hair.

He lowered his voice and whispered, "There is a man in my room."

I froze for a moment and squeezed him tight, unsure of what to do. Then I lay down beneath the covers with him in my arms. While I contemplated his fate, tears streamed down my face.

But there was no time for sadness. So I scooped Julian up and hid him in the closet. Then I grabbed the gun and took one heavy step after the next.

I searched the whole apartment but never found anything. When I returned to Julian in the closet, he was crying. So I grabbed our things and headed upstairs where Polly welcomed us with open arms.

Chapter 26

I felt like a zombie the next day, but Julian insisted on going to school. He didn't want to miss his math class. So I drove him there myself and then returned to our apartment for the day.

Since there was no sign of a break-in, I never called the cops last night. For all I knew, Julian could have been having a nightmare. It wasn't like those weren't already natural occurrences for him. And I had been drinking last night, so that didn't help.

Polly insisted that I needed the day off, so I listened to her for a change and took it. Around noon, I saw the bottle of red wine on the counter from last night and picked it up. Before I could decide whether I wanted some or not, my reflection shifted against the window pane.

"I thought I told you not to wait for me."

I dropped the wine bottle and glass shattered

across the kitchen floor. I felt the alcohol on my feet and couldn't be sure if part of it was blood. My shoulders shook, and I felt weak in the knees.

"Anna."

I hopped around the edge of the counter to keep from stepping on the glass and tripped instead. When I looked back, my mouth fell open and I screamed. But then the sound left my lungs, and I broke down crying.

"Oh, God," I moaned. "I'm going crazy. I must have lost my mind!"

Julian was right here. In the flesh. Just like I had always hoped for. But it couldn't be real. He was a ghost.

"Anna." He knelt down in front of me. "Anna, listen to me."

I turned hysterical, sobbing so uncontrollably that I nearly went blind.

"You're a ghost." I struggled to my feet and moved away from his spirit. "You have to be a ghost!"

"Well, I'm not," he declared.

"No!" I shouted, pointing my finger at him. "No. No. No. No. No."

"Anna. Stop." He followed me around the couch three times, but I wouldn't give in.

"You're dead!" I announced. "You're dead. You're dead. You're dead. I saw it. I watched you die!"

Julian grabbed my arms with his hands. And it felt so real. I wanted it to be real.

"Nooooo..." I wailed in tortured agony.

"Think, Anna. You saw me get shot, but did you actually watch me die?"

I racked my brain for the memory, but there wasn't one.

"No," he answered for me. "Someone dragged you away. When they dragged you away from me, I was still alive."

"Yes," I realized, feeling dizzy. "You were still alive."

"What about at my funeral? Did you ever see my body in the casket?" he questioned.

I shook my head and looked up at him. "No. The casket was already closed by the time—"

"See?" He squeezed my shoulders and smiled.

I took a step back and pushed him off me. My body shuddered when I noticed the gray in his hair and the lines around his eyes. If he had survived, then Julian would be pushing forty by now.

"What's going on? Why did you lie to me? Why are you here now?"

"Agent Rodriguez told me where to find you."

"Andy?" I paced the floor in front of him. "He helped me get away from my parents."

"I know," Julian replied.

"Now just what the hell is going on?" I stomped my foot and glowered.

Really, I was just afraid. Afraid that it wasn't real. Afraid that it would all go away. Afraid that it was a parlor trick. Afraid that if he abandoned me a second time, I wouldn't be able to cope.

"Rodriguez lied to you," he murmured, stalking closer. "There was a bounty on your head. But he didn't want to tell you that, because he didn't want you living in fear."

With every step he took forward, I took two steps back. "I don't under—"

"I've spent the last eight years getting your name off that list, Anna. They're all gone now. No one will hurt you anymore."

I buried my face in my hands and cried, sinking down to the floor.

"My name is off the list now, too. It's finally safe for you to be around me again. You and our son."

"Was that you?" I whimpered, gazing into his glistening blue eyes. "Did you give him that book? Go in his room? Were you the one watching me last night? That man in the street?"

Julian lovingly stroked his fingers through my hair and then cupped my cheek in his hand. "I could never stop watching you."

I choked on heart-wrenching sobs.

"Or our little boy." He wiped my tears away with the pad of his thumb. "I'm sorry if I scared you. But I just needed to know that you were safe. Both of you."

I gazed into his honest blue eyes, but it felt too good to be true. "I must be crazy," I reasoned, "talking to a dead man. They'll put me in a strait jacket. They'll take Julian away from me for sure."

Julian rocked back on his heels and pulled off his shirt. Then he showed me the scars where bullets had once been. He traced my finger over that raised scar across his ribcage, even though it hurt.

"I know you must hate me," he whispered. "And I'm so sorry for leaving you alone. But it was the only way I could keep you safe. If me and you had been together, they would have killed us both. And Little Julian would have—"

I pulled his face to mine and sealed my mouth over his. When I leaned back, his eyes were closed. He was in a perfect state of bliss.

"Sorry," I crooned. "I just wanted to see if you still taste the same."

He caged me in with his arms against the wall. "Do I?"

"I don't know ye—"

Julian tugged at my chin and crushed his lips to mine. My arms dangled over his naked back as he pressed his fingertips into my skin and consumed me body and soul. When our tongues tangled and danced, he lifted me off the ground in his arms, and I curled my legs around his hips.

It had been eight years since a man had touched me.

I had never been so desperate for his love.

Reaching out, I pushed the bedroom door open, and Julian closed it behind us. I sank my teeth into his ear and tugged at his hair as he crashed onto the mattress while holding me in his arms. We wrestled with our clothes until they were all off, and Julian lay beneath me.

He sat up and draped the sheet around my naked body, cuddling me closer to him. As I leaned down and covered his mouth with mine, his hands worked over my back. I felt the stubble of his beard against my skin and discovered that Julian did not taste the same.

He tasted better.

We spent hours together in that bed, exploring each other like it was the first time. His hands sent shivers from head to toe. And since it had been so long, it was hard for me to touch him without eliciting a groan.

In the end, we were tangled in the sheets and exhausted. My legs felt like jellyfish, but it had been centuries since I burned for a man's touch. I never realized how badly I had needed this, how badly I had needed him, until now.

"Mmm." I sighed as he ran his fingers through my hair.

"I've missed you, baby." He pressed a sweet kiss to the nape of my neck. "God, I've missed this so much."

I peered up at him in curiosity.

"That's the first time you've ever called me baby," I noted with a sensual smirk.

"Well, it won't be the last." He kissed my nose and then my neck, trailing his fingers down my arms.

"Julian?" I hated to ask the question but knew

I had to. "Were you with anyone else? While we were apart?"

I hesitated and bit my tongue. Maybe it wasn't the right thing to say.

"No," he dryly stated.

"Why not?" I wondered.

"Well, if someone wasn't trying to kill me, then I was after them." He gently caressed my arm. "Every moment that was left, I came here to see you, watch our little boy grow up." He paused and then braided his fingers through mine. "You have no idea how many times I've wanted to bust down that door to be with you." He choked on his words at the end. "Raise our little boy together. You shouldn't have had to raise him by yourself."

"Shh..." I rolled over and put a finger to his lips. When I covered his cheek with my hand, he lifted my palm and kissed it.

"God, I've missed you." He hovered above me and touched his lips to my collarbone. "You don't know how badly I've wanted you, how badly I've needed you."

"I've needed you too, Julian." My lower lip trembled as water pooled in my eyes. "You were right about my father. You were right about everything."

Julian pulled me into his arms, coaxing and affectionate. "You still look like you did the day I first saw you," he whispered in my ear.

"Liar. I've had a baby, Julian."

"It doesn't matter. You're still young and

beautiful to me."

Grinning like a fool, I ran my fingers through his thick hair and eyed the gray along his temples and above his ears.

"You like it?" he asked. "Now you're with an old man."

"You're not an old man, Julian." I left kisses along his jawline. "I think it's sexy," I cooed.

Julian chuckled, a deep rumbling sort of laughter.

I shut my eyes and confessed, "I've missed the sound of that."

Julian dragged his knuckles across my cheek. "I got a job at the police station," he informed. "It's just desk work, you know, pushing papers. But that way I can be here with you and Little Julian."

It all felt too good to be true. Surreal. I was scared that it was a dream.

"They won't ask you to go undercover again?" I wondered, placing my hand on his chest.

"No, darling." He put one hand on my hip and used the other to frame my face. "My days as an agent are done."

I leaned my head back and looked up at him. "Won't you miss it?"

I knew military life had left him scarred. Julian wasn't the kind of assassin I had thought. He had been trained alongside men of honor to defend and protect. But killing was killing. And I knew it ate away at him. All the lives he had been forced to take.

Julian saw himself as tainted and bad.

I thought he was an American hero.

"I'd miss you more." He propped his head up on his elbow and watched me, those glittering blue eyes searching every inch of my face.

I relaxed beneath him and placed my hand on his arm. When he looked at me like that, I could barely breathe. He brought his lips to mine and then caressed my skin with his fingertips.

"Do you know what time it is?" I asked. "I haven't even had lunch yet."

Julian lay back and leaned over the bed to fish his watch out of his pants. "Almost three thirty," he relayed.

Needing him closer, I wrapped my arms around him and planted kisses on his back until he turned back to me. Julian draped his arm over my shoulders, and I snuggled closer to him. Then I ran my fingers through the patch of hair on his chest and put my head on his heart.

"Are you hungry?" I murmured, looking up at him from beneath my lashes.

"Always." His fingertips sank into my lower back as he molded his mouth to mine.

"Mama!" The front door slammed shut, as I sat up in bed. "Mama! Where are you?"

"That's Julian," I hissed. "He must be home from school."

As we scrambled to get dressed, the bedroom door opened and Little Julian stared at us with a pair of wide eyes. Even though I was tying the sash on my robe, Julian was still beneath the sheets with his naked torso exposed. Scared by the situation, Little Julian turned on his heel and ran.

"Julian! Wait!" I hurried after my little boy and found him in his bedroom.

Sensing a need for privacy, I stepped inside and shut the door behind us. Julian sat with his hands in his lap, kicking his legs off the edge of the bed. He looked upset.

"Julian, I'm sorry," I started.

"Who is that man?" he wanted to know. "When is he going to leave?"

I pursed my lips together and sighed. "He is someone very special to me."

"I thought I was special," he huffed.

"You are." I sat down beside him on the bed, thinking of a way to make him understand. "Julian, I named you after him."

He furrowed his dark brow in curiosity.

Fighting back tears, I touched his warm cheek with my hand. "That man in there." I searched his worried blue eyes, wishing he were old enough to see it himself. "That man in there is your father."

Julian lowered his lashes, taking it all in.

"He loves you, Julian," I said. "And he would like to see you." I took his hand in mine. "Do you think you could come out here and meet him?"

He stared into my eyes and sighed, "Okay, Mama."

Reeling, I pulled him into my embrace and

squeezed tight. "You are such a good boy." I ruffled my fingers through his dark locks. "I promise I'll explain everything to you when you are older. And it will all make sense. You'll understand."

Like always, Julian believed me. "Okay."

"He is so excited to meet you," I chimed, lifting him off the bed and setting his feet on the floor.

"He is?" Julian tugged at my hand as we headed out into the hall.

His father was already in the kitchen, waiting on us.

Once we reached the tile floor, I let go of his hand and said, "Julian, this is your Daddy."

The little boy was cautious at first, approaching the strong, tall man with careful footwork. The eldest Julian squatted down and stuck his hand out for the youngest to shake. Little Julian regarded him quietly, sizing his so called father up.

But then Little Julian took a brave step forward and wrapped his arms around the man who was a stranger to him. Tears blurred my vision as Julian held our son in his embrace and patted his small back. The little boy leaned up to kiss him on the cheek and then scampered back off to his room.

When I glanced over at Julian, he was still on his knees, crying. Not wanting him to feel sorrow or pain, I got down on the floor and pulled him into my arms. He put his head on my chest and sobbed quietly, while I ran my fingers through his hair. Julian squeezed my ribs so tight that it was almost uncomfortable. But I knew he needed this, so I let him.

"Shh..." I rubbed my hand over the side of his face. "It's all right. Just give him a chance. Let him get to know you."

Julian lifted his head and gazed into my eyes. "You're too good for me," he whispered.

"Shush." I grasped his chin in my hand. "I don't care about that. All that matters is that you are here with me now."

Julian rose up on his knees and tightened his arms around me. When he rested his head on my shoulder, I circled my palm over his back and cried into the fabric of his shirt. He smelled so good, and I had gone so long without his scent.

"I love you, Anna," he said, quivering. "I've always loved you. I'm so sorry. I should have told you every day."

I held on to him and never wanted to let go. "I love you, too."

After an emotional reunion, I encouraged Julian to wash up and then go lie down. While he was in the shower, I found our son in his room doing homework. It was the start of the weekend, and Little Julian was busying himself over math.

"Is Daddy going to stay for dinner?" he asked.

Lingering in the doorway, I brushed my hands across my arms. "Do you want him to?"

Julian looked up at me and nodded. "Yes."

My heart warmed with delight. For years, I had

accepted the fact that my one true love was lost forever. Now that he was back, I was so scared of it all being a dream. Like a mirage in the desert.

While I cooked dinner, both of my Julians set the table. I studied them from the stove, noting the similarities in their posture, the way they walked and talked. You couldn't help but notice that they were father and son.

Little Julian took a seat beside his father, as I spooned a generous amount of lasagna onto each of their plates. I knew how odd this must have been for him, for our little boy. Here this strange man pops up out of nowhere, and he happens to be your father. I had no idea what was going through his head. But I could imagine.

At dinner, Little Julian asked his father all sorts of questions. It was more of an inquisition than an interrogation. But still, the boy wanted to know all about him.

"Mama, I think I need help with my homework," Little Julian announced.

I was up to my elbows in dishwashing liquid when I turned back to him. "Let Mama finish the dishes, and then I'll come help you."

"No," he shook his head. "I want Daddy to do it."

Freezing in place, I looked back at Julian over my shoulder as he rose from the table. He was delighted, but shocked. And maybe even a little scared.

"All right," I consented. "Go ask him."

Little Julian skipped across the kitchen into the living room. "Daddy, can you help me with my homework?"

It was Friday night, and my son wanted to do homework. Math homework. While I hadn't known Julian as a boy, I had a feeling that ours was just like him.

"Sure," Julian chimed, happy to help.

Little Julian darted to his room like a bolt of lightning, and a single tear skirted down my cheek. Julian watched me across the way and smiled. Then he turned and went into our son's room to help him with his homework.

* * *

As I got ready for bed that night, Julian raved about how brilliant our son was. "And he's so smart, Anna. He wants to study all the time like you."

"Math was never my favorite subject." I smoothed lotion over my legs and arms and then slid beneath the covers. "He gets that from you."

I leaned over and turned out the light. Then I settled onto the mattress and closed my eyes. The thin night gown I was wearing left my shoulders and chest exposed. Julian ran his fingertips down the side of my arm, as I tilted my bare neck towards him.

"I want you," he declared, a desperate need to the sound of his voice.

My eyes shot open in the dark. "Oh thank

God."

His hands were all over me, as I held on to the back of his neck and brought him closer. Julian grappled with the hem of my night gown and pulled it over my head. He took his own clothes off and then rained kisses down my body.

"We have to be quiet," I gasped, struggling for air.

Julian tugged at my lower lip and then worked his mouth over mine. I curled my arms around his back and lifted my head to meet every kiss. His fingertips traipsed over my ribs and stomach, while I hooked my legs around his hips.

He kissed his way across my collarbone, and I thought I might perish. As good as it felt to be in his arms again, I was terrified that it all might slip away. He made me bite my lip, and I tore my nails across his back.

In the end, we had to cover each other's mouths so Little Julian wouldn't hear. As I caught my breath, Julian kissed the inside of my palm and then peeled my hand away from his mouth. I lay there on the flat of my back, gazing up at him, and Julian lowered his head to leave a soft kiss on my lips.

When he fell onto the bed beside me, I curled into his warm body and wiped the sweat from his brow. Julian planted his hand on my back and squeezed me tight. We spent the next hour hugging and kissing, relishing the comfort of being in each other's arms again.

I dozed off with a huge smile on my face. But when I woke up a few hours later, he was gone.

Paralyzed with fear, I dug my hands through the sheets, but they were cold and empty. Then I flicked the light on to find that his clothes were missing from the floor. Anyone else would have assumed that he had simply left. But I knew my fate was much worse than that.

I checked the date, and Julian was still dead.

It was all a dream.

Filled with anger, I dropped down to my knees and screamed. Then I ripped through the kitchen and broke every bottle I could find. What a cruel joke for my mind to play on me.

But then my shoulders began to quake, and I opened my eyes.

"No, baby. I'm right here." Julian pulled me into his arms on the bed.

"I thought you were gone," I cried. "I thought you were dead."

"I'm not going anywhere." He cradled my head in his hands. "I'm right here."

"I'm so scared that this isn't real," I mumbled. "I'm so scared that they are going to take you away from me again."

"It's all over," he whispered. "I promise you it's all over."

Sobbing, I sat up on the bed and looked into his eyes. They were there. They were real.

"I need you," I cried, glancing up at him desperately.

We came together like stars collide, and Julian made love to me a second time. Afterwards, he feathered his fingers through my hair and rubbed my back.

"I was so scared," I croaked. "When I thought it was all a dream. When I thought you were—"

"Shh..." Julian skirted his fingertips down my spine. "I'm back, Anna. For good. You'll be dying to get rid of me in a week."

I dried my eyes and laughed. "That's not true," I whispered.

"You say that now." He dragged his nails across my back, and I shivered. "But I'm not going to be able to keep my hands off of you."

"Good." I turned my cheek into the pillow and smiled.

Julian lay down beside me. "I've waited a long time to be with you, Anna."

My eyelids grew heavy as I murmured, "I've waited a long time to be with you, too."

I trusted that he was real, that he wasn't going anywhere, that he wasn't a dream.

And then I drifted into a peaceful sleep.

Chapter 27

It was hard to take it all in. The fact that Julian wasn't dead. The fact that we had a child together. The fact that all the pieces of my life were finally falling into place.

But I guess we had already paid our dues. We had paid the price to be together. Eight long years apart. The waiting was over now. And even though we were each nearly a decade older—me close to thirty, and Julian almost forty—we were still alive. We had been given a second chance together. It was time to start taking it.

* * *

The first week back, Julian adjusted to his new job at the police station, even though it was mostly desk work. I knew he must miss the thrill of his previous life, but at least Julian would still be in the field he loved. And for my sake, and the sake of our son, Julian wouldn't be in the line of fire.

I quit my second job and busied myself at the library full time. Anyone would think that I hadn't been able to settle into a relatively normal life here, being the daughter of an Ex-President and all. But humans acclimate to each other very fast. And quite frankly, I was old news.

Every Saturday we took Little Julian to the park and had a family picnic. He ran around and chased the birds, his dark locks blowing in the wind. While I watched him, Julian circled his arms around my waist and pulled my back into his chest so I was sitting between his legs.

As he touched his cheek to mine, I placed my arms over his and smiled. "I've missed so much," he said, planting a kiss on my temple. "By the time he gets to know me, I'll be an old man."

We looked out at Little Julian as he laughed in the sun.

"That's not true." I turned around in his arms and put my hand over his heart. "He loves you now. And he'll love you more as time goes by."

Julian curled his lips into a crooked smile and leaned down to kiss my mouth. I ran my fingers through his hair and then traced the prickly hairs of his beard. There were highlights of gray here and there, but I didn't care. I just wanted my Julian.

And he was here.

* * *

Later that night, Julian put our little boy to bed, because he had expressly asked that his *Daddy* be the one to tuck him in. My heart warmed every time he said that word. Life isn't perfect, but I thought ours was shaping up to be pretty nice.

Julian came into the bedroom and closed the door, while I slipped beneath the covers. There was a big fat grin on his face, and I knew why. After watching us from afar for so long, on the outside looking in, he was finally able to be with the people on the other side of the glass.

"Hey Daddy," I purred, patting the spot beside me on the bed.

But Julian walked across the room without saying a word. Before long he was pacing the floor. I had never been more confused.

"What's wrong?" I asked, turning to face him as I sat on the edge of the bed.

Julian bit his lip and blinked several times. "What would you say if I asked you to marry me?" he got out in one breath.

I opened my mouth to say something, but I was speechless.

"Oh, Anna." He took my hands and got down on his knees before me. "I've waited forever for you." He cupped my cheek in his palm, staring into my eyes. "And we're here now. And we've got Little Julian."

My throat closed up, and I started to cry.

"Marry me," he begged.

Blinking back my tears, I pressed my lips together and sobbed. "Yes."

Julian sat up on his knees and brought his chest to mine, hugging me close. I wept onto his shoulder and squeezed him tight. Pulsing with excitement, Julian lifted me out of the bed and spun me around in his arms.

When he set me down on my feet, I pushed his back up against the wall and clawed at his shirt until it was off. "I guess I should ask you to marry me more often."

"Shut up," I growled, jerking him onto the bed.

Julian soaked up every moment of it as I made love to him in the night. I guess the upside of our unfortunate separation was that we could never seem to have enough of each other. We had a lot of catching up to do.

Three weeks later, we were married by the water at sunset. Polly and Little Julian were the only two guests in attendance. And once the officiant gave us the cue, Julian drew me into his arms, and our mouths stuck together like glue.

For the honeymoon, we went to a nice hotel and stayed locked in our room for days. I loved Julian so much. And I was so happy that it made me want to cry—the fact that we were together again.

When we came back down to earth, I fiddled with my gold wedding band on the car ride home, twisting the ring around my finger. We found Little Julian at the piano upstairs, while I greeted

Polly. My husband walked over and joined my son at the set of pretty black and white keys. They played together, and then Julian taught our son a new song.

Polly put her hand on my back and spotted the tears in my eyes. "Are you okay?"

"Yeah," I sniffled in reply. "I finally am."

Epilogue

Towards the end of summer, Julian stopped by the library one day. I took my lunch break early and left with my heart in his hands. Julian drove me to the other side of town and made me promise to close my eyes.

"All right." I put my hand over my eyes, even though they were already closed.

"No peeking," he sternly declared.

"Okay," I giggled. "What is it with the big surprise?"

Julian parked the car and got out, scrambling around to open my door. He helped me onto the road that felt like dirt and then set his hands on my waist. "Okay. Now open your eyes."

I did as he said and looked up at a beautiful white two story house with a wrap-around porch. The home must have been straddling about ten acres of land with a scenic view of the bay down below. Birds chirped as they flew by, while the wind whipped through the trees.

It was paradise.

"Well, what do you think?" he asked.

"It's gorgeous," I murmured. "What is this place?"

"An old carpenter lived here who recently passed away. I read about it in the paper. It's all for sale. The house. The land. Everything."

I looked out at the cool blue water and felt the sun on my face. It felt so good to be out in the fresh air.

"What would you say if I bought it?"

"Julian," I shook my head. "We can't afford this. It's—"

"Listen to me, Anna." He clasped my hands and then braided my fingers through his. "I'm not some young man anymore. I've been saving for a lifetime. The inheritance I got from my parents and my uncle? I invested it. I never touched any of it back then."

"What are you saying?" I searched his face, those vibrant blue eyes had a sparkle about them today.

He stepped into me and dragged his teeth against his lower lip. "I'm saying, why don't we live here?"

I took a deep breath and let it all sink in. It felt too good to be true.

"It's close enough that Julian can still go to the same school," he said. "We're not that far away from work. It's the perfect place to have a family."

I hung my head with a furrowed brow.

Julian lifted my chin with his finger. "I know it's not Princeton, but there is a local college nearby. You could go back to school if you want. Or stay at the library. Julian is getting older now. We could make another one." He placed his palm to my stomach with tender affection.

So many choices, the world at my feet.

"Anna, what I'm trying to tell you is that you can do whatever you want." He gingerly took my face in his hands and brushed his thumb against my lower lip. "I'm going to take care of you, of us." He pressed his forehead to mine and whispered, "Our little family."

Tears streamed down from my eyes, and it felt like I could hardly stand.

"Hey," he gently crooned. "You okay?"

"Yes." I nodded, clinging to the collar of his shirt. "Yes."

"Yes to what?" he raised his brow.

"Everything. All of it. The house. The library. Going back to school. Making more babies with you."

"If it's too much all at once—"

"No." I put my hands on his face and stroked his beard.

"I just want you to be happy," he said.

I leaned in until our lips nearly touched and spoke against his mouth. "You make me happy."

Julian kissed me, and I'm sure he tasted the

salt in my tears. "You make me happy, too."

So he bought the house, and I finished school in one year, even though I had two and half left. It seemed like Julian had just turned ten. But time moved on by, and before I knew it, Julian had a little sister named Polly after our family friend.

She looked like me with her blond hair and green eyes. And it was about time. Julian looked just like his Daddy. Finally, I had a mini-me of my own.

In the summer, we had a family barbeque and the kids played in the yard by the water. Julian turned the radio on and danced with me, while the kids watched us in sheer fascination. When he dipped me low, Little Julian and Polly clapped their hands together and laughed.

The thing about small children is that they wear out fast. Polly fell asleep before I could even get her to bed. And Little Julian nearly crashed into the wall on his way up the stairs. His Daddy picked him up and carried him the rest of the way.

It was past eight o' clock when the sun went sinking down. I took a seat in one of the chairs we kept outside and looked out at the water. I couldn't believe this was my life.

"Hey." Julian crept up behind me and swept the hair off my neck, leaving a kiss there instead.

When he sat down in the chair beside me, it didn't take long for me to crawl into his lap. I put my head on his chest as he rubbed my back. Together, we watched the final tinges of sunlight disappear until there was hardly anything left but black.

"Let's go for a swim," he beckoned.

"What?" I wiggled out of his lap as he approached the water. "Julian, no."

"Come on." Julian took his shirt off and then unzipped his pants. "No one is going to see."

"Julian," I whined, stomping my foot.

He kicked his shoes off and waded out into the water. Then he swam around enough to get his hair wet. As I stood at the edge, he ducked below the surface, only to pop up and grab me.

"Ah!" I squealed as he ripped my shoes off and then pulled me into the water.

I was laughing by the time I was drenched and then I dunked his head beneath the surface. Julian emerged and lifted me in his arms. My hands settled on his shoulders as I leaned down to reach his lips. His hands slid beneath my dress, and soon I wasn't wearing it anymore.

Julian and I swam to a secluded shelter hidden by the cover of trees. Ravenous, I tangled my fingers through his hair and brought his mouth to mine. He grabbed the backs of my knees, and I sat up at the touch of his hands. Before long, my ankles were crossed at the small of his back.

"If you get me pregnant again," I warned, losing my breath.

"Don't tempt me," he groaned, sliding his hands up my thighs.

"I love you," I whimpered. His eyes connected

with mine, and I felt everything charging through those electric irises.

His perfect lips parted to meet mine, and he said it back.

Tell Me Your Favorite Part!

If you enjoyed Mercy, I invite you to head over to Amazon and let me know your favorite part. Reviews are so important to an author's career, because they help new readers like you discover the book. Even if you didn't enjoy Mercy, I'd still love it if you could take three minutes to let me know what you think of the book.

Leaving a review is super easy:

1) Go to Mercy Book Page on Amazon

2) Scroll Down and click "Write a Customer Review"

3) Sign in to Amazon if prompted

4) Select a star rating

5) Write a few short words (or long words, I won't judge)

6) Click the 'submit' button

I thank you in advance!

Acknowledgements

I cannot start the long list of all those I am indebted to without first mentioning my close family and friends. Thank you to my mother and father for always believing in my dreams and encouraging me to pursue them every step of the way. As well as my grandparents, aunts, uncles, and cousins who always show their support. To my childhood friends who listen to me ramble at long lunches and dinners—you know who you are :)

Thank you to every blogger who has ever featured my work on your site. There are too many of you to count but most notably Susan Meachen, Rose & Margie at Can't Stop Reading Blog and SJ's Book Blog. If you have ever left a review, posted a spotlight, let me participate in a takeover, interview, feature, or guest post, I cannot thank you enough.

Special thanks to H. C. Bentley for the podcast interview. That was so much fun and I am so glad that I have had the opportunity to get to know you. Jessica Hernandez, my amazing book trailer maker, thank you so much for bringing *Mercy* to life!

To Micalea Smeltzer—thank you so much for letting me write a blurb on the back of *Dark Hearts*. Jace and Nova are amazing, and I can't thank you enough for letting me be a part of their love story.

I would like to thank all of my readers and fans out there. I know how busy you are, and you could spend your spare time doing anything else. But you have chosen to take a chance on me and read one of my books. I can never thank you enough for that. I greatly appreciate the reviews, the messages, the emails, all of your kind comments. I love getting to know each and every one of you and am truly grateful for your support. You are the reason why I am able to live my dream. So let me know what books you would like me to write next. They are all for you :)

About the Author

Lindsay Marie Miller was born and raised in Tallahassee, Florida, where she graduated from high school as Valedictorian. At sixteen, she started writing her first novel, *Emerald Green*, after being inspired by Stephenie Meyer's International Bestselling *Twilight Saga*. During her time in college, Lindsay wrote 5 more novels and over 100 songs. After graduating Summa Cum Laude from Florida State University, she put her B.A. in English Literature to good use and published her debut novel, *Emerald Green*. An author of over 10 Romance Titles, Lindsay currently resides in her hometown of Tallahassee where she is always working on her next novel.

To learn more, please visit:

www.lindsaymariemillerauthor.com

Sign up for Lindsay's newsletter:

lindsaymariemillerauthor.com/claim-your-free-book/

Join Lindsay on Facebook at:

facebook.com/LindsayMarieMillerAuthor

Follow Lindsay on Twitter at:

twitter.com/Lindsay_MMiller

www.ingramcontent.com/pod-product-compliance
Lightning Source LLC
Chambersburg PA
CBHW050902250626
47155CB00001B/73